PRAISE FOR THE *PORTLAND HAFU* SERIES

"*Dream Eater* brings much-needed freshness to the urban fantasy genre with its inspired use of Japanese culture and mythology and its fully-realized setting of Portland, Oregon. I'm eager to follow Koi on more adventures!" —Beth Cato,
author of *Breath of Earth*

"A timely book that happens to be a rollicking read. *Dream Eater* has it all: mythological and social diversity, strong characters, and a tender romance. I can't wait for the next one."
—Keith Yatsuhashi, author of
Kojiki and *Kokoro*

"I came for the Japanese mythology, and I was not disappointed. Readers who want variety in their urban fantasy beyond the werewolf and vampire staples are advised to pick up *Dream Eater*."
— Laura VanArendonk Baugh, author of
The Songweaver's Vow

"Lincoln infuses Japanese folklore into the Pacific Northwest, creating a fascinating world where a young dream-eating heroine, Koi, must learn to use her frightening talents to save her family in a tale of ever-increasing peril. By the end you'll be anxious for the next book!"
—J. Kathleen Cheney author of
The Golden City and *Dreaming Death*

"The characters really drew me in—Koi and Ken are intriguing on their own, but even better together. Overall, the book is as quirky and edgy as Portland itself."
—M.K. Hobson, author of
The Native Star

BLACK PEARL DREAMING

PORTLAND HAFU, BOOK 2

K. BIRD LINCOLN

World Weaver Press

Published by World Weaver Press, LLC.
Albuquerque, New Mexico
www.WorldWeaverPress.com

Edited by Rhonda Parrish
Cover designed by Sarena Ulibarri.
Cover images used under license from Shutterstock.com.

*

First Edition, October 2018
ISBN-10: 1-732254613
ISBN-13: 978-1732254619

Also available as an ebook.

DEDICATION

This one's for Rhonda. All the Kwaskwi scenes are for you, my friend. Thanks for being his first, biggest fan :)

BLACK PEARL DREAMING

CHAPTER ONE

"Benadryl acts like speed on some special people instead of making them drowsy," Kwaskwi observed from his seat across the aisle. He smiled widely, revealing a plethora of large, white teeth in orderly rows. Stupid smile. Stupid slick, black pony tail making him look like that Anishinabe actor, Adam Beach. Stupid jay. Why didn't he just fly over the Pacific Ocean by himself? But no, he had insisted on sticking with Dad and me. And Ken.

I glanced over at Ken, deeply asleep in the window seat. Irritatingly tidy and unrumpled. His thick, Asian-black hair was smoothed into a loose pompadour with a smelly brilliantine I saw for the first time this morning back in Portland. Ken had shelled out two Benadryl tablets after take-off and promised Dad would sleep before abandoning me completely for his own nap.

That left only me to deal with the third man in my trio of men-not-to-be-stuck-with on a trans-pacific flight: Dad. He looked tired—his gray hair smashed into gnarly swirls—but also sweaty and agitated.

"Dad," I said. Then repeated in Japanese, "*Otoo-san*." Dad

wouldn't even meet my eyes. I murmured to him in a low, hopefully soothing voice, telling him over and over in Japanese who he was, who I was, where we were. His hands were clenched into fists, foot tapping so hard I could feel the vibration through the metal floor— one of the most powerful Kind in the U.S. and Japan was having a meltdown.

Apparently he didn't like flying. That would explain a lot of my childhood. Like why we rarely went to Hawaii to visit Mom's relatives, and had never gone to Japan before.

It would have been nice to know about this fly-o-phobia before we got on the plane.

I tipped my Dutch Brothers French Toast latte to my lips, but it had been drained to dregs hours ago. Plane coffee wouldn't cut it. Six hours to go to Narita. How would I survive?

I tried again, this time in Dad's Northern home-town Aomori dialect. "It's okay, nothing's going to happen to you."

If only I could hold his hand.

But we were Baku, Dream Eaters. A touch was enough to exchange dream fragments, and Dad was tottering on the edge of sanity since he'd used his Baku abilities to help me fight a dragon of the hidden, magical Kind in Portland's Ankeny square.

My whole life only Dad had been safe to touch. Even when I thought it was Alzheimer's causing his dementia, I could risk his bare skin contact without getting overwhelmed by a dream fragment. But not now. Because of the dragon, Ullikemi, Dad had just revealed it wasn't Alzheimer's at all, but a dream fog resulting from self-imposed exile in Portland. He'd run away from Japan so he could completely stop eating dreams. Lucidity came in brief, awful flashes. Since Ankeny Square, they'd been almost non-existent. There was no way to tell if his usual defenses were up. If I gave him a fragment now accidentally, it might tip him over the edge. Or worse, if he was caught in some kind of dragon dream-eating blowback and he gave a fragment to me, my Baku inexperience meant I might join him in fogland.

Thus the plane trip. Ken, an emissary from the Council in Tokyo, had convinced me through his help with the whole dragon situation that the Tokyo Council Dad had run away from was actually Dad's only hope. And my CPA classes at Portland Community College had ended for the semester.

Kwaskwi had crashed our party under various flimsy pretexts. He was huffy at not being officially notified of Dad's presence in Portland, for one. And my endangering of his giant eagle Kind friend, Thunderbird, during my fight with Ullikemi was a sore point too, along with a dozen other complaints he made up on the spot in his usual roguish, insufferable way. I suspected the real reason he was coming to Japan was to keep an eye on me. I'd acknowledged a debt bond to Kwaskwi during the dragon fight, and apparently I was too valuable to let slip away.

I tucked the red Delta blanket around Dad—it was chillier than I'd foreseen at this altitude—and hoped a momentary lull in the tapping meant he'd calmed down.

My phone vibrated. My sister, Marlin, had sent me a Snapchat. I swiped right. It was a selfie of her bossy face, doodled so that her eyebrows were comically arched and granny glasses perched on the end of her nose, staring accusingly into the camera.

I smiled. She was worried about Dad. I hadn't contacted her since before passing security.

"Good thing Akihito isn't wearing a turban," said Kwaskwi, now chewing on a toothpick. Actually, the entire five seater middle row was populated entirely by middle-aged Asian men chewing on toothpicks, but Kwaskwi still made it into some kind of annoying comment on my inability to keep Dad calm.

My right hand reached for the Tcho Mokaccino bar I'd stashed in my cardigan pocket. *No.* Mental slap. I had no idea how hard it would be to find good chocolate in Tokyo and Mokaccino was for serious emergencies only.

It occurred to me I didn't really understand Kwaskwi's turban reference. "What?"

"Your father's got all the terrorist warning signs. Nervous agitation, sweats, flying while non-white," Kwaskwi said around the toothpick. He turned to the in-seat entertainment system and started flipping through romantic K-dramas.

Dammit, he was right. We were attracting attention. I'd have to touch Dad. See if a fragment was causing this.

Back when I still thought I was just a freak, I used to meditate on the clean, simple strokes of elementary level kanji like "sun" and "moon" to suppress invasive dream fragments I'd accidentally acquired from clumsy everyday touches. The mental discipline of drawing kanji in my mind kept the fragments from taking over my waking hours. That had worked right up until Ken and Kwaskwi sauntered into my life. Kind fragments were different. Kanji were about as useful as limp noodles in staving off the dream fragments of the Kind.

Still, I pictured traditional ink brush painting's pure, clean swathes of inky black on thick rice paper anyway, to prepare. I took a deep breath. Okay, here we go. *Once more into the breach.*

I rested my palm lightly on Dad's wrist.

The airplane went tilt-a-whirl. For a stomach-wrenching moment all I could do was sit, hands clenched tightly, muscles and tendons spasming out of control. Then with a whoosh, it felt like my belly opened up and a thousand butterflies escaped onto the plane. Everything stilled, pins and needles pricking across my skin. The seatbacks, tray tables, thick-paned windows, even the bent comma form of sleeping Ken began to bleed at the edges, growing fuzzier and fuzzier, the color spreading in slow, dropped-molasses pools until everything was a formless, cerulean blue.

A sky. And I was flying through it not in an Airbus A320, but with the joyful strength of my own, gloriously gold-feathered wings, drinking in the heat and energy of the sun like solar panels.

Oh. Nausea sifted into the emptiness in my belly. This was Thunderbird's dream. Dad was still experiencing Thunderbird's dreams, so I got the joy of feeling them, too.

This was a tattered echo of the true, powerful dreaming a waking Thunderbird had forced on Dad and me in a misguided attempt to hold us in thrall. There was a hint of kernel-self in this dream. An echo of Thunderbird the ancient one dreamed over and over each night, but no real connection to him anymore.

Good. No danger if I ate the dream as I'd learned to do back in Portland. With a deep inhale, I drew in the blue of the sky, the Thunderbird-flavored echo, down, down into my belly. To where the kernel-self of me, Koi, resided as a dim, candle flame.

Eater of dreams.

The flame flickered into life, burning with a tingling heat that balanced on the knife-edge of pain and pleasure. Muscles spasmed up and down my back and I arched away from my seat like a taut bowstring. The dream fell away. My bones settled heavily into the narrow seat, the slick chill of the vinyl unpleasant against the sensitive skin underneath my knees and wrists.

"You are truly a glutton for punishment," said Kwaskwi. I glanced at his laughing, opaque eyes, and then back at Dad. He looked less pale. Breath inflated his chest in an even rhythm. Eating some of Thunderbird's dream lessened the pressure on him. I patted his hand and—

The airplane jerked out from under me and the world spun 360 degrees.

I plunged into an eddy of silt-flavored fresh water, granite pebbles gliding beneath my wide belly, slipping past thick stems of young lotus, leaves spread like hearts overhead. Temporary safety warred with excitement. Salt-water home left behind to travel upstream, upstream to the promise of—

"That's enough."

A sudden pain pierced my hand. "Ouch!"

My eyes fluttered open to see Ken leaning over Dad, my hand caught between his lips, biting deep into the fleshy pocket between thumb and forefinger.

"What the hell?" That *hurt*.

Ken released my hand. Dad turned toward me in the cramped seat, raking a shaking hand through the bottle-brush thickness of his more-salt-than-pepper hair. He exhaled, a long, slow breath. A calming breath to control the chaos inside.

"Dad?"

His eyes, darkest brown like my own, were hard to read. "Koi-chan, what you do?" English. So not Herai Akihito, Baku, talking, but my own father. The sushi chef. The singer of silly Japanese counting songs. The husband who absented himself when Mom lay dying in the hospital.

"Thunderbird's fragment was still in you. I thought—" I swallowed something bitter. "—it was bringing on the dementia again."

"Never do again," said Dad. "You don't touch me."

Heat flushed my cheeks despite the altitude chill. I'd invaded his privacy. I couldn't run away and I couldn't drown unhappiness in lattes. Airplane travel was the worst.

"Excuse me," said Ken, indicating with a chin-jerk he wanted to get up. I stood stiffly, rubbing my arms to get rid of uncomfortable emotions. Clambering over Dad, Ken blocked the haunted, angry look in Dad's eyes.

Kwaskwi suddenly gave a braying laugh. Heads turned our direction.

"*The Crow*," he said, pointing a finger at his screen. "I love this movie. They get so much right."

I glared. He shrugged and went back to watching the screen—missing nothing of the little father-daughter Baku spat despite the movie.

The ambient heat of Ken's body standing very close to me in the narrow aisle suddenly became a very salient detail. Hesitantly, I turned to face him. This close, he looked down on me from the foot's difference in our heights. A scattering of scrubby beard outlined his wide mouth and his fleshy lower lip pouted out a bit.

"Airplanes are hard. Don't upset him," said Ken in a low voice. His warm breath brushed my ear—but the feeling didn't bring its usual ticklish heat. Anger prickled instead.

Who was he to butt his bossy nose in? Napping foxes didn't get to go all salty. Heat flushed down my neck and moisture started pooling on my upper lip and under my arms. Dad was my responsibility. Ken and his Kitsune bossypants had no jurisdiction here. He was *my* Dad.

Wait.

This wasn't normal Koi irritation. This was the dream-eating. Such a little fragment shouldn't result in the usual dream eating hangover, but here was the PMS-like irritation, and the hot flash, and soon there would be—

"Ow." And there it was. Icepick-to-the-temples headache. The full hangover experience.

A worried crease appeared between Ken's cleanly arched brows. "You look a little green." I pushed him aside with one hand in the middle of his infuriatingly close chest. No line to the restroom, thankfully, but I spent a minute fighting the stupid folding door before sinking into blessed aloneness inside the stall.

I dug out the Midol mini-pack from my pocket. It worked better than Tylenol or even Advil on these hangover headaches. Two dry swallows, a palm-full of water to the back of my neck, and a couple of deep breaths later, the ice picks turned to dull throbs of manageable pain.

Digging knuckles into my eye sockets also helped. What was that second fragment? A river? Whatever it was, it had nothing to do with Thunderbird. I'd been underwater and scared. Where did Dad pick that up?

A knock sounded.

"Koi," called Ken, softly. "Are you okay?"

Annoyance flared. He could have saved me the embarrassment and asked in Japanese so I wouldn't get stares when I emerged. The plane dipped, forcing me to catch myself on the wet sink.

You're on a plane to Tokyo, a perfectly reasonable part of my brain pointed out. With tons of Japanese passengers. No privacy here for Japanese or English. My stomach had a weird airiness, like the prickly, exposed feeling I'd gotten the few times Dad took Marlin and me to Obon Festival dances at the Portland Japanese School. We'd start speaking Japanese, our usual private language, and then have to stop mid-sentence.

"I'm okay," I said. "Just give me a minute."

After taking care of business, and wrestling my ratty hair into a marginally cleaner ponytail, I struggled the stupid door open. Ken hovered, that worried crease between his eyebrows deepening. We took each other's measure in an awkward pause. I fought back an urge to smooth my thumb over his worry crease. Ken broke first, brushing past me into the bathroom.

Ah. Maybe I'd mistaken concern for a different urgent need. Thinking a few kisses and some heavy petting in the bare weeks we'd known each other made me expert on Ken's facial tics probably wasn't that smart. It was just that a part of me, only recently acknowledged, yearned for the closeness, the feeling of someone watching out for me, that I'd been missing since Mom died.

Kwaskwi was still engrossed with his movie when I teetered down the aisle back to my seat, but he turned away from the screen long enough to pinion me with a serious look. Kwaskwi, serious? *Uh oh.*

"You can chuck all this Council crap anytime you want. Just say the word."

Say the word? And what, he'd take me back to Portland? And then me and Kwaskwi and his Kind buddies the Bear Brothers and the ice-breathing hag Dzunukwa could all go to Stumptown for celebratory mochas? *Ugh. No, thank you.* A large woman in a tie-dyed shirt huffed behind me.

"Excuse me."

I angled myself to let her pass as Kwaskwi flagged down a passing stewardess and requested green tea in flawless Japanese.

I blinked, headache forgotten. Kwaskwi spoke Japanese. Of course he did. Of course he hadn't revealed that until now. As I clicked the seatbelt shut, I mentally reviewed everything I'd said to Ken in Japanese, thinking it private.

"No Council chucking word from me," I answered in Japanese. Was that a curl of disappointment in the usual, wide smile?

"Have to keep trying," he said, returning earbuds ten times more expensive than my cell phone to his ears. Apparently First Peoples Kind didn't face the same kind of socio-economic disadvantages as the humans did. Kwaskwi hadn't even blinked at the last-minute trans-pacific fare.

Prosaic, much? My mind was doing the usual, going off on tangents so I didn't have to think about weightier-but-more-difficult things. Like Dad. His eyes were closed and his chest rose and fell in even breaths.

Better because I'd left him alone and my nearness agitated him? No, it had to have been the fragment I'd consumed. Like releasing a pressure valve. Either way, no way in hell was I going to let Ken wake up Dad by climbing over to his window seat coming back from the toilet. I gripped the backs of the seats and more or less hoisted myself over Dad's folded legs.

Ken had already completed the flight magazine's crossword puzzle. Crumbs from the snack biscotti covered his seat. Worst of all, my cheapo earbuds were tucked away in the seat back pocket completely out of reach unless I jostled Dad. For a good five minutes or so I fumed. Where was Ken? I imagined him chatting up one of the cute Japanese stewardesses and closed my eyes, until the crazies settled back into the box where I usually kept a lid on pathetic thoughts.

The seat was warm, and the vibration of the plane made me so, so tired.

Next instant, completely without fade-in or other helpful transition, I woke with a start to a pounding headache.

"Koi," said Ken, ensconced in the aisle seat. "We're about to land."

"What?"

"You slept four hours. We're landing in Narita. Can you wake up your father?"

That was definitely crusted drool on my cheek. Sleeping while sitting up was the worst. "No," I said. Then gave a weird little laugh at the taken-aback expression on Ken's face. "I mean, I don't want to touch him. Can you?"

Ken started to say something, and then visibly back-tracked. "Thunderbird's fragment?"

"I don't think so. He's dreaming something I've never seen before." I glanced at Kwaskwi, watching avidly over Ken's shoulder. He pointed at the corner of one eye and then at me. Ah, crusted drool wasn't my only post-nap surprise. Eye-cheese was also on the menu.

"Akihito," said Ken, gently shaking Dad's shoulder. With a jerk, Dad's eyes flipped open and every muscle in his body flexed, tendons standing out in stark relief in his wiry neck and forearms. His mouth opened in a silent scream. Ken hadn't even touched bare skin, and Dad looked like someone was force-feeding him nightmares. I reached for his sleeve, but Dad knocked my hand away.

"We have to calm him down," I said.

Ken rapidly whispered in Herai dialect.

"Good luck getting through customs and immigration," said Kwaskwi.

"Dad, what's wrong?"

"I can't do this," said Dad through gritted teeth. He was lucid. This wasn't the dementia. All the breath whooshed out of him, visibly deflating into a heap of bones covered in a Delta red blanket.

"We'll be off the plane soon," said Ken in English.

"It's not the plane," said Dad. "We're too close. I thought I could handle it, but I was fooling myself. Resisting made me weaker, not stronger."

"Close to what?"

"I didn't want this for you, Koi," said Dad. The vague unease I'd felt as we gotten closer and closer to Japan joined my overall ill feeling. The plane touched down with a jerk. All around us passengers rustled, stretched, and began rooting around for belongings.

"It's okay," I said. "We'll get you off the plane and then you'll be okay." Even as I spoke the words, it was clear they were meaningless sounds. Everything wasn't okay. We were very far from okay. And far from home. I'd thought letting Ken take us back to Japan to meet the Council was our only hope for Dad to fight this dementia and for me to figure out how to control this dream eating business. But a small part of me worried it was only going to make things worse.

"Do it, Kitsune. It's the only way I'll survive Tokyo," said Dad to Ken.

"Are you sure?" Ken asked.

"Do it!" The people in front of us paused in their sleepy conversation.

"What are you doing?"

Ken ignored my agitated whisper. He pulled out a slim syringe filled with a deep green liquid from a zipped, black toiletry bag.

I gasped. "How did you even get that past security? Don't even think about injecting that into—"

Ken plunged the syringe into the juncture of Dad's neck and shoulder.

"God damn it!"

Dad opened his eyes and cupped my cheek, thumb gently smoothing back a stray lock of hair. Dad was touching me. Voluntarily. I reeled from shock, or altitude drop or whatever. I almost missed his whisper in Japanese. "Listen to Kawano-sama, not Tojo. But don't let them trick you. Don't touch the Black Pearl."

CHAPTER TWO

"Black Pearl? Dad. What are you talking about?"

Dad's eyelids fluttered shut. The urgency dissipated. He relaxed. At peace. No wonder this touch hadn't given me a fragment, Ken's syringe knocked him out.

Great. My life was turning into a thriller movie complete with a cryptic warning.

"What was in that syringe?"

"It's for the best."

"Did your plan include getting him off the plane in this state?" There was no way I could lug Dad off a plane even with the guys' help.

"Yes."

What? That was all the explanation I got? Guess Mr. Kitsune was cranky 'cause I questioned his syringe decision.

Passengers filed past us, towing roller-suitcases. Kwaskwi exchanged some kind of intense, guy-challenge look with Ken, but exited out the far aisle with only a wink my direction. Once the back of the plane had cleared, a stewardess made her way toward us.

"Ready to deplane?"

Ken shook out his arms, cracking knuckles in his left hand. "I'm ready."

The stewardess backed up a few paces, reaching for an overhead bin just in front of the bathroom marked with a red cross. She pulled down a folded dolly and pushed it back to our row. Ken scooped up Dad and wrestled him to a sitting position on the dolly.

"You are not bungee cording my father to that dolly."

"She going to make trouble?" asked the stewardess in Japanese at the same time as Ken said in English, "Trust me."

My Dad. People needed to start listening to me.

I reached for the stewardess as she wrapped the bungee around Dad's chest. She flinched just as my fingers circled her uniformed wrist, and my pinkie brushed bare skin. "Hey, what do you think you are—"

Heat shimmered down my body from crown to toes, then back up my legs to my belly. A cramp bent me double. Gray static clouded my vision. I gasped for breath. Chest heaving, I straightened up with a feeling like I'd just spent the past few hours on a boat battered by waves, landlubber wobbles and all.

The static slowly cleared to the very edges of my eyes, leaving behind the old-hay smell of tatami mats and dim light of a room with closed windows. I knelt in seiza, robe folded neatly under my knees, in a room with gorgeously-painted door panels. A tiger with vivid green eyes, a pair of emerald-feathered pheasants, and a dragon, long and sinuous like a snake coiled in black-scaled rings, stared down from the walls.

Heavy layers of robe weighed down my shoulders. Sweat gathered on my upper lip. I used a bit of power to make the sheen seem to disappear. But that bit of power drew the attention of the Council Lord. Frowning down at me from his seat of honor on the platform, I could almost read his thoughts. Halfbreeds used power for such lowly purposes. A dark storm cloud of disapproval practically hovered over his head. I would be still, and not flaunt my power here. I didn't want the Lord to make trouble. I needed to appear docile.

Something stung my cheek. My stomach clenched, static spreading thickly again, and the weird sensation of falling backwards while standing still. The room, the robes, and the dragon's black coils all dissolved into tattered wisps of illusion and streamed away like smoke from a blown-out match. Ken's face, eyebrows knit together into a furry caterpillar of worry, filled my field of vision. Over his shoulder the stewardess rubbed her arm. "What was that?"

"A dream," I said, voice gravelly as if I'd been silent for a month. "Your dream." Just my luck the stewardess was Kind. I'd learned to handle regular dreams in the past week, a surreal experience no longer having to fear casual touch, but Kind dream fragments were super-charged.

"You're Baku, too," she said in an irritated tone.

Ken told her in Japanese that I was untrained, a neophyte, and half human as well. I was still reeling from the tatami room and the fearsome lord in her dream. Since when were fragments so vivid and first person? It felt so much like a memory. I mean, Kind dreams were always strong, but this was like Technicolor, Dolby surround sound. The vivid dreams I'd gotten from other Kind before were memory dreams. This was just like a memory dream. But how could samurai and painted castle walls be her memory?

"What are you?"

Ken gave me a pointed look. "We don't usually ask that, but she's like me."

I bit my tongue against the urge to point out she'd asked me first. A Kitsune. I should have guessed from that small bit of illusion she'd used in the dream fragment. Ken rubbed his hands together and smoothed them down Dad's shoulders and arms, ending with a little flounce. Suddenly, it wasn't Dad strapped to the dolly anymore, but two large oxygen tanks.

The stewardess smirked at my dumbfounded expression. *I have a feeling we're not about to become besties.*

We fell in line behind the dolly-pushing stewardess, filing past the smiling pilot and up through a chilly, overly air-conditioned walkway. A teeming mass of humanity swirled around us as soon as we exited. I shivered. *So. Many. People.*

The narrow corridor curving around the outside of the departure lobby barely contained all of us with our rolling luggage. Someone stepped on the back of my shoe. A lady, somehow magically unrumpled and hair picture-perfect, knocked my rollerbag over with her own Gucci monstrosity. I hurried to keep close to Ken as everyone else in the corridor tried to reach immigration first in the passenger melee. Down another two escalators, through another narrow hallway, and then I was cut off by a posse of blonde kids. By the time I caught up with Ken, the stewardess was waiting with the dolly and a pursed expression in front of a bank of elevators.

"*Ato de,*" said the stewardess. How much later did she mean she'd see us? The surging migration of other passengers broke around us, ignoring us three completely.

"Wait," I said. "What are you doing with…the oxygen tanks?"

Ken shook his head.

All of sudden, I realized the last passengers had crammed themselves onto a long down-escalator. We were alone. The skin on my neck and shoulders felt oddly tight and warm, as if the other passengers had pushed all the air conditioning in front of them. The elevator door just behind the stewardess dinged. Startled, we all turned. The doors slid open.

Three young, wiry guys with the same angular chin and muscled swimmer physique as Ken stepped out of the elevator. They were dressed all in black, including leather gloves, except for one wearing a red, button-down shirt. Ignoring the stewardess' startled protest, the tallest one grabbed the Dad-dolly and the other two planted themselves like a living wall in front of me and Ken. I lunged around Red Shirt, but he casually blocked me with a swift kick.

Ow. I grabbed my leg.

Ken tore off a guttural string of curses dripping with rolled r's like a yakuza boss in one of Dad's TVJapan movies but the living wall stood implacable. The elevator dinged again. The tall guy yanked the dolly with him into the elevator.

Dad! They were taking Dad, and I was standing here, useless and frozen. Ken dropped his roller bag to grapple with the third guy, while the stewardess scuttled backwards like a scared crab. Red Shirt held me off with one outstretched arm. If I could touch bare skin, draw his power along with a fragment like I had the ice hag Dzunukwa back in Portland, then maybe I could—

Red Shirt dodged my questing fingers. His buddy, caught in some kind of complicated headlock by Ken yelled in warning. "*Baku ni ki wo tsukete. Sawarareru yo!*"

"*Hai,*" muttered Red Shirt. He backed up a couple steps, elbows cocked in front.

That's right. Don't let the dangerous Baku touch your skin.

They were Kind. They knew I was Baku. As I stood there gaping, a small, dark blue shape came hurtling past my left shoulder and crashed into the back wall of the elevator.

The doors slid shut on the dolly and the startled face of the tall attacker.

CHAPTER THREE

Ken swung his guy by the arm, crashing him headfirst into Red Shirt. They both hit the floor and I jumped over them to punch the elevator call button. Two times. Three times. Frantically I punched the buttons so hard I swear the plastic cover cracked. Nothing.

Two minutes in this damn country and I'd already lost Dad. I turned and slumped against the wall with suddenly floppy knees. I closed my eyes against welling heat. When I opened them, Ken faced off against the only attacker still standing, Red Shirt.

"You won't hurt us," said Ken in Japanese. Red Shirt had gotten a stranglehold on the stewardess. "You're an extraction team."

"Care to wager her neck on that, Bringer?"

Ken bristled, then flicked a glance at me. Nervous about being called 'Bringer' in front of me? I had bigger fish to fry. They had Dad. Which way was the stupid elevator going? The digital numbers at the top of the doors counted down. Down was good. I could jump down stairs faster than running up them.

"Where's the stairs?" I said, propelling myself off the wall with a jolt of adrenaline.

"You're too late," said Red Shirt in accented, deliberate English. "The stairs!"

Ken shook his head. "Once they're out of our sight, they can use illusion to look like anybody. Our best chance of tracking Herai-san is this guy."

The attacker lying on the floor suddenly executed one of those acrobatic kick ups like a ninja or a hip-hop dancer. He shook out his arms, cracking his knuckles.

"No hard feelings, handmaiden," said Red Shirt, giving the stewardess a little shake. "We can't have you following us."

Mr. Hip Hop Ninja pulled a riot stick from the back of his pants. Ken crouched low, arms in a defensive karate-looking posture. I would have snorted at the cinematic surrealism of it all, but instead I smacked my forehead with an open palm.

The escalator! Maybe I could still catch Dad.

There was a muffled thud as Red Shirt tossed the stewardess against the wall. She gave a strangled yelp. That distracted Ken long enough for Hip Hop Ninja to nail him in the stomach with the riot stick.

"Back off. Let us go and no one will get hurt. Or at least not more hurt," said Red Shirt as he circled Ken, keeping him boxed in. He almost seemed rueful. *Bastard.*

I made for the escalator, but Hip Hop Ninja lunged in front of me, riot stick raised in a block. "We keep here you two more minutes," said Red Shirt behind me. His lame English felt like an insult.

Ken kicked out his legs, but Red Shirt nimbly spun away, sneaking in a punch to Ken's kidney on the rebound.

"Okay, okay," I said in English. No need to let them know how well I spoke Japanese. "Stop hitting him. What are you doing with my father?"

"Sorry, can't telling you in front of Council slave," said Red Shirt. This dude was unreal. His mangled grammar made me want to gnash my teeth. The elevator dinged again.

"If you hurt my dad, I swear, I will hunt you down and suck out your dreams until you are dry husks."

The elevator doors slid open, revealing a disheveled Kwaskwi grinning with those damn, white teeth and Dad slumped on his shoulder. Dark, wet streaks and an explosion of blue feathers coated the inside of the compartment.

"Simmer down. No need to scare the pants off these guys by going all Baby Baku-berserker on them. Akihito is safe."

I lunged into the elevator, wedging a foot against the closing door. Dad seemed unharmed, if still unconscious. Ken helped the stewardess stand up. Hip Hop Ninja advanced with his riot stick.

"Ah-ah," said Kwaskwi, waggling a finger at him. He cupped a palm under his mouth and blew. A stream of blue feathers swirled directly into the guy's face. He doubled over in a fit of gagging coughs.

"Leave now," said Ken, all growly alpha male.

"This won't help your case at all," the stewardess piped up in Japanese. Showing some spunk now that the tide had turned in our favor. "Once Murase finds out you tried to kidnap the Baku…"

But the two attackers turned tail and bounded down the escalator in great leaps as soon as she began speaking.

"You recognized them," said Ken. He bent over, breathing in gasps, hands resting on his knees. When he stood upright again, he handed me my abandoned roller case handle.

The stewardess closed her mouth into a grim line. She jerked her chin at me in a "not in front of the crazy American" way while she straightened the skirt of her uniform.

"Don't fall all over yourself thanking me for coming to your father's rescue," said Kwaskwi. He thrust Dad into my chest. I staggered under the weight while Kwaskwi sketched a slow, formal bow.

"Thank you," I said.

Kwaskwi blinked, and closed his mouth against whatever quip he had prepared. Apparently had hadn't expected straight up gratitude.

"Could you at least have brought the dolly back?" said the stewardess. She blew disdainfully at some stray, blue feathers encroaching on her spotless uniform jacket.

"Your buddies had other plans for it," said Kwaskwi. "Let's get this show on the road. I'm starving."

Ken came around my side and shifted half of Dad's weight on his shoulder. "We can't just walk through customs with an unconscious man."

"Can you make him invisible?" said Kwaskwi.

"Not if I have to carry him, too."

"Let me see if I can get another dolly," said the stewardess.

"What if the attackers come back?" I asked quietly. "We can't be sure they gave up."

"I ensured my guy gave up," said Kwaskwi, rubbing his hands together.

"We need to get Dad someplace safe."

"Japanese immigration is pretty strict," said Ken. "Especially since SARS and Zika."

Kwaskwi rolled his eyes to the ceiling. "Oh Grasshopper," he said. "Ye of little faith. Follow my lead."

"You can't possibly—" the stewardess started to say.

"Come on," I interrupted, tugging Dad and Ken to the top of the escalator stairs. *Enough of Princess Stewardess.* "Move now, doubt later." We wrestled our bags and Dad down the escalator to trail after Kwaskwi through empty, endless beige halls with signage in English, French, and Kanji.

We finally emerged into a large room cordoned off into multiple rope mazes. Half a dozen tired and rumpled people of various races dutifully lined up on one side, and on the other, two or three Asian folks waited for their chance with the crisply uniformed officers at desks behind bullet-proof glass. Princess Stewardess strode toward the crew lines, leaving us without a backward glance.

Dad's weight lifted from my shoulder. Ken frowned and pointed toward the tired people. "You go that way. Japanese citizens are this way."

Dad's eyelids fluttered open. His gaze was unfocused, but he stumbled along with Ken.

Huh. I hadn't thought about being separated here. Weird thinking of Dad as a Japanese citizen.

Kwaskwi ducked under the ropes, heading straight for the front of the line. He flashed his trademark grin. "Check this out."

Reaching into the battered, brown leather messenger bag he'd toted through the battle with the attackers and the endless beige halls, he cupped something in both hands. He carefully pulled it out, uncurling his fingers to reveal a large jay with gray feathers and white beak. The jay blinked, arching its neck.

A live bird. Kwaskwi brought a live bird on a transpacific flight and into Japanese customs. He leaned down and whispered something close to the jay's head. I glanced in Ken's direction, but he and Dad were quietly waiting behind the solitary remaining passenger in the Japanese citizen line. A uniformed, gray-haired man directing the foreigners in my line was giving them a harried look that did not bode well.

"Whatever you're going to do, now would be a good time."

Kwaskwi immediately dropped his hand, but the jay was already in motion, skimming just beneath the ceiling and fluorescent lighting to roost on top of the closest bullet proof barrier. The female customs agent gave a comic double-take.

The jay screeched, and then took off again directly into the face of the harried old guy. A slightly hysterical hiccough slipped from my lips.

This is serious. Pay attention.

When Kwaskwi grinned like a proud papa, I had to clap my palm over my mouth to keep in the giggles.

Now a whole posse of uniformed, gray-haired men converged on the harried guy. The jay perched on the harried guy's head, hopping in little circles as the posse yelled conflicting instructions, shooing the queued-up foreigners into a chaotic, milling mass.

Ken slipped in front of a female immigration officer's desk, slapped two red passports onto the counter, and somehow managed to make Dad look like he was standing under his own power. The officer was half out of her chair, clearly wanting to help the harried guy, but unable to leave her post. Ken said something, and the officer sat down with a thump, rapidly shaking her head.

"Kwaskwi," I hissed.

He had joined the circle yelling advice in various languages to the harried guy. Or maybe he was egging on the jay—hard to tell. It pecked at any hand that reached out. At my hiss, he glanced back. I rolled my eyes to Ken and Dad.

"Okay, you asked for it." He gave a high-pitched cough. The jay blew out its chest feathers and flapped its wings. A chorus of ohs sounded as the posse froze. A thick, viscous white goop began oozing down the harried guy's forehead directly onto his bottle-thick glasses. The room erupted into laughter. Officers scurried in all directions, desperate for towels, and Ken and Dad were waved past the barrier by the female officer.

"We did it!"

"That's two you owe me now," said Kwaskwi. He coughed again. The jay took off, skimming under the ceiling until it reached the next set of escalators leading down from the balcony to the baggage claim area below. It nose-dived between escalator-riders, leaving behind a stream of startled gasps in its wake.

If only Kwaskwi could have turned me into a jay. It took another quarter hour for the officers to rescue the harried guy, settle down, and queue up the milling foreigners again. Duly fingerprinted and photographed, I made it through the cursory customs inspection and emerged, blinking, into the dingy gray, smoke-tainted hall of Narita

Airport's arrival lobby.

Princess Stewardess and Ken stood near the double glass doors to the street, arguing. When Ken noticed us, he changed his expression to a smile and waved us down. I hesitated, wanting to drink in the sight of Kanji and Romanji signs, noodle-slurping businessmen in suits, girls sporting furred, thigh-high boots, and an obstacle course of designer roller cases.

I'm in Japan. This is Japan.

"Come on," Ken called, reaching for my roller case handle. Outside, humidity hit like a wet wool blanket. A black limousine idled by the curb. Ken herded us over and indicated we should head to the back. The door opened automatically.

CHAPTER FOUR

"Now this is what I'm talking about," said Kwaskwi.

"We're going straight to the Council," said Ken after Princess Stewardess waved goodbye and the rest of us settled on the two plushly upholstered bench-seats covered in what looked like lace tablecloths of a weird linen-plastic hybrid nature. My slipping in next to Dad forced the other two guys to sit together. Both of them man-spread to take up as much space as possible.

Dad shifted uneasily. His lips were dry and chapped, split into a pinkish fissure at one corner.

I turned to Ken. "Isn't there time to go to the hotel first?" Viewed from the window, a wide expanse of green cut into geometric shapes by mounded dirt and paths distracted me. Rice paddies. Modern looking houses featured old-fashioned curved ceramic tile roofs. I turned away from the tinted window. "At least get something to drink?"

Ken opened up a panel in the door to reveal a black glass refrigerated compartment. "Here."

I took the bottled water from his hand. It proclaimed 'I Lohas' next to a pastel mikan orange on the label.

"Sure you want to present us to the Council looking like something the cat dragged in?" said Kwaskwi. He crossed one leg over the other and lounged back like a playboy millionaire in a reality show. "Obviously I'm presentable, but these two? Yikes."

Infuriatingly, Kwaskwi was right. Both Dad and I had hair sticking up in strange directions and a definite eau-de-airplane.

A double shot macchiato and a hot shower with my favorite Dr. Bronner's peppermint soap was needed—something to push back the fuzzy gray blanket of fatigue encroaching on my brain.

"I need a latte," I sighed.

Ken made a clicking noise and gun-fingers, pointed directly at the panel on my side of the limo. "It's best just to go directly, not only because of danger to Herai-san, but there are also Council members made, ah, uneasy by Herai-san's return."

I'd wrestled the panel open. Plastic tumblers emblazoned with a suspiciously Mt. Ranier-like mountain and Starbucks-esque green letters appeared. Iced lattes in the limo. I would never ride in a normal taxi again. Just stick the accompanying pink straw through the foil top and…bliss. What else did this fabulous limo have hidden? "Afraid of Dad?"

"Yes," said Dad simply, his eyes fluttering half-open. That one syllable was worse than any explanation. I squeezed his sleeve-covered arm with one hand.

"Are you okay?"

He gave a barely perceptible nod.

"Where does the Council hang?" said Kwaskwi. "Tokyo Tower. No, wait, the Imperial Palace?"

Ken shook his head, affronted. "The Emperor lives at the Imperial Palace. The Council sits at Yasukuni Jinja."

Kwaskwi snorted. "Subtle."

"What does he mean?" I asked Ken.

"Yasukuni Shrine was established by Emperor Meiji for the souls of the war dead."

"Yeah, including Class-A war criminals," said Kwaskwi. An obvious aura of discomfort crept over Ken. Kwaskwi ignored him. "And the Prime Minister goes there to commemorate the dead each year. Causes all kinds of problems with Korea and China."

"Those who support Japan's modern incarnation as a country with no standing army think the yearly visit in poor taste," Ken said. The overly formal inflections felt like a defense mechanism. Kwaskwi was challenging him.

Kwaskwi scoffed. "Yeah, Manchukuo and Nanking survivors totally have their panties in a twist."

"All war dead are honored there," said Dad in a raspy voice, "not just criminals."

Kwaskwi sat up a bit, the lazy mirth abandoned as he zeroed in on Dad. None of us were used to Dad contributing much to the conversation, but this was his country. His history.

"Dad," I said. "You're lucid, right? You know we're on our way to Yasukuni Shrine to see the Council?"

"Yes," he said quietly in Japanese. "But you cannot rely on me. The pressure in my skull…it will be too much soon."

The limo slowed to a crawl. We'd left the rice paddies and entered the outskirts of the Tokyo mega-city. Billboard after billboard covered in Roman letters, Kanji, Hiragana and vivid images all jumbled together. Concrete buildings squished side by side with structures of more outrageous architecture—was that a church or a love hotel?—as if eager to swallow up the streams of pedestrians and bicycles headed every which way.

Ken cleared his throat. "I will present you to the Council."

"The hell you will," said Kwaskwi. "I can present myself."

The two men glared. "Certain formalities must be observed. This is the Council. You can't just barge in there and let loose a flock of blue jays."

"My jay saved your ass at Narita."

"The Council already sees you as a loose cannon. Arrogant. Brash. Not quite civilized. If you want—"

"I am arrogant and brash," said Kwaskwi, settling back again. Tension ratcheted down a notch. "It's part of my charm, right, Koi?"

Darn him for dragging me into this. This false sense of camaraderie was meant to maneuver me into a position of foreigner versus the Japanese.

"They will dismiss you if they think you don't respect the power and traditions of the Kind," Ken insisted.

"They already dismiss us. Walking in all meek, led like a horse on a rope by the Bringer won't change that." Kwaskwi looked directly at me. "Americans have never gotten anywhere by being quiet and docile."

Dad gave a little huff. The limo jolted into motion and general plane queasiness sloshed around my stomach along with the overly-sweet latte. I really didn't feel good. When were we going to reach the shrine? And would I have a second to at least run a brush through my hair, or possibly barf in a toilet, before having to meet the Council?

"Coming with a Bringer tells them you are nothing to fear," said Ken.

Dad's eyebrows formed a worried line across his forehead. "But they should fear us, fear me," he said. "They cannot continue on like this." He paused, gasping like all the air had suddenly been sucked from the inside of the limo. Or like a fragment was taking over again. "They cannot. They will—" His eyes rolled upwards until only white showed.

"Dad? Dad!" I dropped the latte into the cup holder and grasped him by both shoulders.

"They can't keep the Black Pearl," he said, eyes closing. "They know that's why I'm coming." Under my palms, muscles slackened, strength melting away until Dad was boneless, chin bent to his chest. *The mysterious Black Pearl again?*

"So much for lucidity," said Kwaskwi.

"It's okay," said Ken, putting a hand on my knee.

"How is this okay? He was okay back in Portland. He spoke, he sat up, and he could function. He's been a shadow of himself since we boarded the plane."

"But at least he provides entertainment with cryptic pronouncements," said Kwaskwi.

I glared at him. "You are *not* helping."

Ken whispered in rapid Herai dialect. "Don't be fooled by *charm*. The blue jay has a hidden agenda."

I bit my lip against a sudden upswell of bitterness in the back of my throat. "And you don't?"

Ken's eyes turned the darkest, Italian espresso brown. They bored into me diamond-hard, peeling away flimsy defenses I'd been trying to erect ever since we'd first met on a Portland street. All of a sudden I had a lot more to worry about than just awkwardness. "I believe you and Herai-san needed to come here," he said. "I'm trying to help."

"So far it's only Kwaskwi who's managed to help." As soon as the words hit the air, I wished I could reach out and catch them in a fist and squash them out of existence. *Not true.* Ken was trying to help. I had to believe that. Or grab Dad and catch the next airplane out of Narita. *I did believe that.*

But it was too late to stop Kwaskwi from grinning at the window as if he'd won some kind of victory. Or to smooth away the bloodless, pale line of Ken's usually plumper lower lip as his face took on a stony, shuttered look.

The limo jolted again into a stop-and-start pattern as we passed some kind of city center area. Dad was restless in his pseudo sleep, eyeballs swimming in all directions under closed eyelids. Battling car sickness, I soothed Dad while shying away from bare skin contact. Whatever fragment he dreamed wasn't one I wanted any part of, especially if it was more of that weird river dream.

It was evening Portland time. I checked my texts. There were ten messages from Marlin, progressively more and more snippy, demanding updates on Dad. As if I couldn't be trusted with him by myself.

Why are you being so crazy? I texted back one-thumbed.

The reply came back so quickly I jerked, startled, in my seat.

You aren't responding to texts! How am I supposed to know what's going on if you don't communicate? We talked about the importance of not shutting down.

I was on the plane. I'm sure you could have everything under control even in your sleep. Sorry I had to actually close my eyes for two seconds. I'm doing my best.

This time there was a pause. A pregnant, meaningful pause that probably meant Marlin was typing, deleting, and typing again. I sighed. It sucked being the sister who had to be handled with kid gloves.

When the text came, it wasn't the tirade I'd braced myself for. *That's the problem. You are doing your best.*

I sent back an emoji face with wide eyes and a dozen questions marks.

Her text came back very slowly. *It's weird not being needed. Suddenly I'm the one struggling to keep up.*

I rubbed my eyes. *Enjoy not having to babysit me or Dad. Expand your client base. Spend weekends guilt-free with your friends instead of being forced to binge-watch Marvel superhero shows with your hermit older sister.*

This time her reply came back with its usual snappiness. *But I like Jessica Jones. Luke Cage is hot.*

A suspiciously wet heat gathered in my eyes. I coughed, clearing phlegm and emotion from my throat. Ken gave me a concerned look.

You shielded me all through high school and college. Relying on you meant I wasn't lonely like I should have been.

That's seriously fucked up. She added an angry Asian emoji face.

Let me shield you from this, I typed.

"We're here," said Ken. I tucked my phone away. I wasn't going to get a better exit line.

The limo was pulling onto a gingko tree-lined lane, clusters of fan leaves shivering in a light breeze. We crunched over white gravel, stopping before a path framed in drooping purple wisteria blossoms and closed off by a velvet rope.

"Here we go," said Kwaskwi in that infuriatingly gleeful voice. *At least someone's looking forward to this.*

"Wait," said Ken. "They will come for us." Just as he spoke, two high school-aged youths, with sleek, orange-brown hair tied back in long ponytails that brushed the back of their knees, emerged from behind the wisteria. Plain, white *haori* jackets and red, divided *hakama* skirts gave their skin a joltingly pale creeptastic vibe, while somehow suiting the landscape. I realized one of them was actually a boy, shorter than the girl by at least a foot, and he was pushing a wheelchair.

Dyed hair? They would have fit in with Mom's Pierce family kaleidoscope of hapa-haole, no problem. Maybe the Council wasn't all conservative geezers.

"*O-Miko-san,*" said Ken. "A shrine maiden and her brother. They are servants of the Council. Kind."

"Yeah," I said. "Figured that out."

Kwaskwi was already out the door flashing his trademark grin at the shrine boy. "You Tokyo folks sure know how to treat guests," he said with a John Wayne twang he'd never sported before. He made to sit in the wheelchair.

The shrine boy was caught off guard, or possibly blinded by Kwaskwi's shining, white teeth. His face flushed for just an instant before turning into a marble almond-eyed expression of calm. He pulled the wheelchair back.

"I apologize, this is for Herai-san." He approached the side of the limo and opened it. "Let's make Herai-san more comfortable."

As if I had been torturing him in the limo? These two were already raising my hackles.

Tall Maiden reached for Dad's arm, purposefully grasping his sleeved forearm above the bare skin of his wrist. *Okay, so she's rude, but not an idiot.* I tapped her forearm. "What's your name?"

She bristled, eyes widening for a second as if I'd hurled a curse instead of asking the name of the person putting their hands on my father.

Ken cleared his throat. In English he said quietly, "We don't ask names." Ah yes. I'd forgotten the whole names-have-power thing. After blabbing Kwaskwi's and Thunderbird's name to Ullikemi back in Portland, the whole reason Kwaskwi was mixed up in this at all, you'd think I could remember Kind were touchy about names. I sighed.

"We will bring Herai-san to an anteroom. The Council will proceed with formal introductions." Tall Maiden used extremely formal Japanese. Her nose wrinkled. "You may wish to refresh yourself before the Council arrives."

Ken squeezed my knee painfully hard as I opened my mouth to respond. I whacked him with the back of my hand. With a bright, tight smile I said, "This meeting is such an honor. I humbly thank you for your kind offer." Tall Maiden didn't get my sarcasm. She nodded in approval and took over the wheelchair, hustling Dad along the gravel path.

Shrine Boy wrapped up his conversation with Kwaskwi and followed after, casting a glance back over his shoulder just before the three disappeared behind more lushly rioting wisteria. I jumped out of the limo, followed closely by Ken.

"Hey, wait for us."

"It's okay," said Ken. "Trust me. They will take him directly to Yukiko-sama and the Council."

"What the heck I gotta do to get with *him*?" Kwaskwi said. It took me a second to process who he meant. And then I mentally went over what I knew about Kwaskwi. Usually my gaydar worked better than this.

"You need to treat this more seriously," said Ken in English. "The Council won't appreciate your little jokes."

Ken had turned into quite the uptight guy since getting on the plane. I wondered if the Ken I had gotten to know in Portland was just a temporary persona he'd been using. He was a trickster Kitsune, after all.

"I ain't joking," said Kwaskwi. "That boy is a serious fox."

"More like serious wolf," Ken said. "He is Horkew Kamuy."

Kwaskwi ran a hand through his hair and straightened his battered, leather jacket. "First peoples, then. No kidding." He shot a startled glance at Ken. "The Council chose these two on purpose. Damn, they're slick."

I looked questioningly at Ken. He made an impatient gesture and set off down the path. "What? What does Horkew Kamuy mean?"

Ken stopped in the middle of the path, hands clenched into fists at his sides. "Neither of you seem to understand the power the Council may wield over you. You can't be flippant. They are here to judge you."

"I understand," I said. "I am taking this seriously. I just don't understand why both of you are freaking out over the shrine youth."

"They are Kind of the Ainu. The Council chose them to meet us especially because they knew Kwaskwi would be with us."

"Trying to get on my good side. Aw, shucks. They don't have anything to fear from little, old me," Kwaskwi said.

I would have lifted an eyebrow, Spock-wise, if I could. Kwaskwi had no trouble reading my disbelief anyway. He chuckled.

Ken huffed impatiently, then returned down the path and grasped my elbow, hustling me forward.

"You should stay close to Herai-san."

"Huh? You literally just told me he was safe here. Welcomed with open arms."

"There is no danger to Herai-san. Just…stay close."

The gravel path widened into a little yard surrounded by an army of pines clipped as carefully as poodles, standing at attention in dozens of straight rows. A paved road curved deeper into the trees and up a slight rise. The pointing leaves of a wooden signpost bristled in several directions.

Alas, the archaic characters were beyond me. The one leaf pointing along the path started with "*hon*," which I vaguely remembered could mean "central," but I had no clue about the Kanji it was paired with. All those Saturdays spent whining as Dad forced me to practice writing them over and over rose up like a mist of vague uneasiness.

When I was little, the sense of Dad's otherness was like an aura that only manifested when we ate together in restaurants, or when he came to school events.

I am in Japan. It felt oddly dreamlike and freeing not to be able to read the sign. Like going back to childhood. Or it could have been just a bonus side effect of the lack of caffeinated milk in my immediate vicinity.

Kwaskwi pointed up the path. "We going to the main shrine, the *Honden?*"

"You can read Kanji?" *So not fair!*

"It pays to learn the language of the Evil Overlords."

This earned another pursed-lip look from Ken. I had only a hazy idea of Kind politics, but did he mean this Council in Japan somehow ruled over Kind even in the States? My entitled American self was offended.

Up the path, the shrine youths' red *hakama* turned a corner, disappearing into the trees. All of a sudden an urgency to not let Dad out of my sight welled up within me. Whether it was due to Ken's warning, or just being in a foreign country, I didn't know, but I stepped lively past Ken and reached the turn just as the shrine youths pushed Dad up a ramp into a low, yellow building shingled with traditional, curved, dark tiles over roughly hewn wooden eaves. Nestled in a grove of trees bounded by a dirty, concrete block wall, it looked nothing like my imagined version of a shrine.

The shrine boy bent down and pushed the ramp away from the entrance, saw me, and beckoned in that 'go away' fluttering motion I'd only ever seen Dad do before. A large, white sign held the Kanji for "*cha*" and "*ie*". *Teahouse. The Council met in a teahouse? I guess the main shrine must be beyond the groves of trees.* I hurried over to the entrance, strangely low even for a historically shorter-statured people, and entered the teahouse.

A man shorter than my sister wearing shiny, faux-leather pants, and a dark button-down shirt open to a muscled, hairless chest hovered over Dad's chair. The slicked-back hair and sunglasses worn low on his nose gave him a Rockabilly air that screamed Harajuku dancer from an old Gwen Stefani video.

"What did you do to him?" he demanded.

"You must forgive me, I dared to administer a sedative on the plane," said Ken, coming to stand close behind me, slightly hunched over due to the low ceiling. The exchange was in Japanese, but I barely could follow the convoluted honorifics in Ken's sentence. This must be a Council dude, then. Was he Kitsune like Ken? Rockabilly really didn't hook into any kind of Japanese myth I'd ever heard.

Rockabilly sucked in a slow breath through closed teeth—a sound I associated with Dad at his most disapproving. "He is lost to madness, then?"

"He isn't mad. There are moments of lucidity. The airplane was hard for him." Rockabilly looked at me, as if appalled I'd spoken at all.

Hairs on the back of my neck suddenly stood at attention. I shivered. A tall, willowy woman stepped into the room. Her skin was a colorless white, like skim milk, and her hair a glossy sheen of ivory. Her eyes were so dark a brown that the pupils bled into the irises, creating twin slits of narrow black in a face with sharply slanted, cut cheekbones. She raised an arm, the sleeve of her asymmetrically cut white robe billowing in an impossibly graceful gesture, and shook her head. Rockabilly deflated a little, visibly backed down.

Ken bowed to her, holding the bow an absurdly long time.

She lowered the hand on Dad's shoulder. Then she turned to Ken with an artfully raised eyebrow I realized must be entirely painted on her otherwise lashless and hairless face.

"Herai-san's daughter," said Ken formally. "Pierce Koi has accompanied us home."

She made another graceful arc of hand and wrist, indicating Dad. Ken cleared his throat. "He should awaken in the next hour. There is one more traveling companion I should introduce."

I glanced around. The lady raised an eyebrow again, her lips pursed. Kwaskwi was nowhere to be seen.

"I will retrieve him." Ken bowed and retreated backwards out of the little entryway room. Without him at my back, I suddenly felt tired and nervous about being left alone with Rockabilly and Snow Lady. *Awkward.* I couldn't leave Dad here alone with them, could I? What the hell was taking Ken so long?

"Why is there a blue jay perched on Pon-suma?" said a male voice from the next room. Rockabilly slid open a paper shoji door behind him to reveal the main room of the teahouse where a bald man in ochre robes sat neatly on folded knees in *seiza*, hands folded into a perfect triangle on his lap, his gaze directed out the window.

Snow Lady and Rockabilly went in the other room, too. I followed. Apparently Kwaskwi had found the shrine youths again. They held brooms made of bundled rushes and were attempting to sweep up a light carpet of blue feathers from the pristine gravel, but as soon as the boy swept up a pile, the blue jay perched on his shoulder let fall another small flurry. Tall Maiden followed behind with a dustpan.

"Does the Siwash Tyee mock us with this behavior?"

Snow Lady gave a meaningful glance at me. The bald monk turned, slowly. He looked me up and down. "You are?"

"She is Herai's daughter," said Rockabilly.

"Baku?"

"So says Fujiwara Kennosuke."

"Ah, so." Apparently this wasn't important news to the monk. He addressed Rockabilly as if no one else was in the room. "Enough. Gather the Americans."

Rockabilly clicked his heels and gave a military bow, strode back through the antechamber to scuff his feet into traditional wooden clog geta. Through the window I saw him issue a series of commands. The shrine youths dropped their brooms. Pon-suma, evidently the boy, carefully lifted the blue jay from his shoulder with both hands and flung it with surprising strength ten feet in the air.

Screeching, the blue jay frantically flapped its wings for balance, pausing at the apex of its journey, and then folded them tight against its body so that it made a streamlined dive-bomb straight back at Pon-suma's upturned face.

The shrine boy stood his ground unblinking. At the very last instant, the jay veered to the right, skimming over Rockabilly's pompadour. The Council dude flinched.

Snow Lady gave a slow exhale. Somehow it conveyed a long-suffering disdain at the same time as it cooled the air in the room several degrees.

Ken, Kwaskwi, and Rockabilly filed into the anteroom in a cluster of cleared throats and steely glares, trailed by one blue feather that wafted slowly through the dusty air to settle on the spotless tatami floor, as garish as lipstick on a white collar.

"Your father is waking," Ken whispered in my ear. His warmth at my back was the only thing holding me in place. Every survivalist instinct within me jangled to get out of there.

Too many people. Too little space.

In the past week I'd learned enough from Dad and Ken to take care of minor, accidental brushes with most people. It was like coughing to dislodge something stuck in your throat, a brief flare and the dream fragment would be gone. But none of the people in this room would have minor dream fragments. Kind dreams were a whole different kettle of crazy fish.

"It's okay," Ken whispered in English. "Go stand with him. Ease his waking."

Kwaskwi flashed me his trademark toothy grin as we did an awkward shuffle past each other in the doorway.

Dad's eyes were open. "This is the Teahouse?" he asked quietly.

I pressed his clothed arm with both hands, kneeling beside the wheelchair, nodding, trying to give and receive strength at the same time.

Dad's hand trembled in the air as he reached for my head. It rested there, heavy. I braced myself, but no dream or fragment sparked between us. *Lucid, Dad was lucid.* Enough to know where we were. Enough to hold back his own fragments.

"Why did you warn me away from the Black Pearl? Are you afraid of the Council?" I whispered, wary that those gathered in the next room not hear our conversation.

"The desire is hardwired into all of us," said Dad quietly in Japanese. "To be with our own Kind. Japan may have emerged from World War II with a new constitution and no army, but Japan is an island country with an island mentality. It is no coincidence the Council meets at Yasukuni Shrine."

"Dad," I said. He was side-stepping my questions.

His hand moved to cup my cheek. His skin felt like brittle, dry parchment. "I never meant for you to have to…to be here. They will bring you to the Black Pearl. The Council will ask you to eat dreams."

"They will meet you now," said Ken, pulling me up by the elbow. Dad and I exchanged a look so crammed with emotions I could barely breathe. He stood up from the chair, moving with steady purpose instead of as the befuddled, weakened man I'd traveled with across the Pacific.

Ken lead us back into the main room. There, Rockabilly and Snow Lady flanked the monk, all three sitting in formal *seiza*, symmetrically spaced in front of the *tokonoma* alcove. Behind them rested an ink-and-brush painting of foxes, a lone Calla lily in a rustic, ceramic vase, and a glass bowl of water.

Aesthetic perfection like this made my teeth ache. I helped settle Dad into a cross-legged position flanking Kwaskwi.

Ken knelt and bowed so his forehead brushed the perfect triangle of his hands on the tatami. "May I present to the esteemed Council Herai Akihito, Pierce Koi, and a representative of the Western Alliance Kind, Tyee Kwaskwi."

The monk frowned. "Tyee Kwaskwi is known to us, of course, but you were charged with giving full names at this presentation, Bringer." Ken's face changed. His eyes went full black, the planes of cheek and jaw sharpening, elongating—what I thought of as Ken's true face, his Kitsune face.

Bringer, the monk had called him. The servant of the Council. He took a deep breath, bowing his head. "Koi AweoAweo Pierce. Tyee Kwaskwi Wematin."

Shock hit me like a snowball to the face. For a moment, Kwaskwi and I mirrored each other with perfect, comical expressions of disbelief. Ken had given them my name. My full, true name. Kwaskwi recovered first.

"Your humble servant," he said with a mocking tone that made it absolutely crystal-clear he was only momentarily thrown for a loop and not afraid at all.

"Why?" I asked quietly. But Ken turned back to the Council.

"Asylum for the *Hafu* Baku *girl*, and treaty negotiation for the Siwash Tyee is requested," he said.

What did you just do, Ken?

Cold shock was joined by an icy trickle down my spine. It was the realization that I could have been fooled all this time by Kitsune illusion. Was everything he'd said in Portland a lie? Even the kissing?

I bit my lower lip. No, I'd tasted Ken's dreams. They were honest, earthy fragments of running in primeval forest. It was his dream fragment in the final moment of my fight with Ullikemi that had helped me hold on to myself long enough to set that ancient dragon free of its Vishap Stone prison. He'd revealed a shining, warrior version woman in his fragment that turned out to be how he saw me.

Or was that an illusion, too? It had been in Ken's best interest to release Ullikemi so he could bring us to Tokyo. I was only a baby Baku after all. What if he had manipulated the dream in some way I could only guess at?

There was only one person in this room I could truly trust. "My father is ill. *The Bringer*," I emphasized the title hoping Ken noticed the little dig, "said that you could heal him."

The monk's direct regard felt like putting your face directly over a cup of Plaid Pantry coffee—sour heat and an impenetrable sludge of black. *God help me, would I ever drink a Stumptown latte again?*

"Herai-san has not explained, then, what his illness is?" The monk turned that powerful gaze on Dad. "It is because you fight your true self that you lose your way in the mists of your mind."

"This is a greater issue than the question of my true self!" said Dad, thumping an open hand on one thigh.

Snow Lady put out a flat palm and the air got several degrees colder. Everyone tensed, as if unsure if Snow Lady was going to soothe Dad or casually gut him. She rose in one, smooth glide and beckoned for Dad to follow. Dad had been startled by her gesture, but now a rueful smile crossed his face as he struggled to stand. I rose, too, but Ken put a hand on my shoulder, pushing me back down. I brushed away the hand. "Don't touch me."

A muscle ticked in his clenched jaw.

"Yukiko-san will attend to your father while assessing his condition," said the monk. Then, as if appeasing a small child, "She can give him a measure of peace."

"It okay," said Dad in English. "She old friend."

Kwaskwi answered my worried look. "Yukiko is known as fair and impartial."

I watched them leave the Teahouse with a sinking heart. I didn't trust these people, but Dad evidently thought it was in his best interest to go. If she could help him, it was worth the trip, all this fear, and even Rockabilly's current infuriating smirk. Why couldn't I help Dad? What was the point of being a baby Baku if I was so helpless?

"Now for the *Hafu*. I will give you a fragment. Show us your Baku power," said the monk. He pushed back a sleeve. "Come."

"You already have my name," I said. "Isn't that enough?"

Rockabilly's smirk got bigger. "She is not truly Baku, is she?"

"I do not lie," said Ken. "She ate Thunderbird's dreams, taking in his power. She set Ullikemi free and stopped his human servant, Mangasar Hayk."

"Herai Akihito is known to us." The monk looked to Rockabilly as if for confirmation. Rockabilly raised his chin, and almost seemed to *sniff*, as if something was faintly rotten in my direction. He gave a slow nod. "You are not. Show us what you are so we can deal with you."

"Put you in your place is more like it," Kwaskwi muttered. The monk turned the implacable stare his direction, but that trademark grin only got bigger, teeth gleaming white in the soft shadows.

I considered several ways to refuse the monk and decided honesty was probably the easiest all around. "I'm inexperienced. Kind fragments are overwhelming. Is there a regular, old human around I could touch instead?"

The monk and Rockabilly focused on Ken. Bright spots of red appeared on his cheeks. The tic in his jaw worked overtime.

"Take a fragment from the Bringer."

From Ken? The monk totally didn't get it. "I apologize. I am very tired, full Kind fragments are too intense for me to handle right now."

Rockabilly muffled a guffaw. Kwaskwi looked inordinately pleased. "Still haven't told her, have you, *Kitsune*?"

The monk gave a slow smile. "You do not know Fujiwara Kennosuke is *Hafu?*"

CHAPTER FIVE

Hafu. Ken was half-human like me.

He'd kept that a secret. Even when he explained how he was the Bringer, how other Kind could not kill, but he could, he stayed silent about this. What was he afraid of? Knowing he was *Hafu* should make me feel closer to him, but it felt like a wedge driving us apart and making me even more uneasy with the trust I'd so blindly given him back in Portland.

All of a sudden, an urge to touch him, to dream his fragment bubbled up from my stomach into the back of my throat. *If I touched him, ate his primeval, pure forest dream, I'd know for sure, right?* And it would mollify the monk.

Ken's head was still slightly bowed, gaze determinedly on the floor in front of the monk. I reached out and grasped the back of his neck under the slight curl of his longish hair. He gasped as if my hand were red-hot.

I relaxed, letting the weight of my hand settle fully on his neck. For a long moment where dust sifted through a sunbeam across Ken's shoulders, nothing happened. Then, all of a sudden, the bottom dropped out of the world. Dust motes ballooned up and shrunk in a weird rhythm, and when it settled again, I was no longer in dim sunlight, but under the guttering light of a torch. There were cobbles cold and hard under my knees and tears choking my mouth and nose.

A woman with long dark hair sat nearby, head bowed in grief. Slender and beautiful, in a quilted puffy happi coat and split hakama, there was an ageless quality to her.

Mother.

She cradled a man's head in her lap. His eyes were closed, and his chest did not rise. Pain like the ancient weight of mountains on the tender flesh of my heart, sharper pains up and down my forearms where long scratches still bled...

"Koi AweoAweo Pierce."

Blinking furiously in the brighter light of the Teahouse, I dragged myself away from the fragment. *Mother*. Ken had given me a fragment of his mother, not the forest and the moon and the running through underbrush he'd given me every single time I'd touched him before. What did this mean?

"And so?" said the monk.

My heart was pounding, a light buzzing ran up and down my spine, restless energy from the fragment. The vise across my temples tightened. My body wanted to consume this energy. Ken's pain and grief, a memory-dream, was a tantalizing morsel for the voracious kernel-flame of my Baku self.

"So?" I ground out through clenched teeth.

"Did you eat the dream?"

I stared at the thin, bloodless set of the monk's mouth, unable to make sense of his words. This wasn't just a regular fragment. Something about being here, being the Bringer in front of the Council had brought out this deep emotion, redolent with life force.

"It's okay," said Ken softly.

"That's not a fragment you can share without losing a part of your life force," I gulped down a wave of grief. "I mean, that wasn't what you wanted me to see."

"No," agreed Ken. "But still it's okay."

"Either you can handle fragments or not. Which is it?" The monk looked indignant.

Rockabilly sucked air through closed teeth. "Don't bother, Kawano-san. This one is no use. Herai Akihito will have to do."

Kwaskwi muttered again. "Well now, that really gets us fired up to cooperate, doesn't it?"

How did he get away with snark all the time? Maybe it was part of trickster magic.

"Don't be so quick to dismiss—" Ken said.

"We are done here, then," the monk interrupted.

Dismissed, just like that. Fresh off the plane, my full name offered like tribute to the Council, and I had been judged, found lacking, and discarded.

God damn it. I was going to get myself to the nearest Starbucks equivalent and treat myself to a giant hazelnut, dark chocolate mocha. And then take a bath.

"Where's Dad?" I said, standing up.

"Koi, wait," said Ken, following me out the door after a quick series of backing-away-bows to Rockabilly and the monk. He made a series of swipes on his phone.

Outside, deepening twilight gave a washed-out patina to the courtyard like an old-fashioned photograph. I thought of pictures of Japanese Kamikaze pilots I'd seen in history books—young, fresh-faced, ready to die. How many had memorial tablets here at the shrine? I kicked at some errant gravel.

Ken and Kwaskwi reached my side. Ken put out a hand to grasp my elbow. I jerked away.

"This is the not the Baku they are looking for," Kwaskwi said.

I rounded on him. "You. Go find my dad and bring him back here." I whirled back to Ken, poking him in the chest. "And you Mr.

Bringer—" Stabby stab went my finger on his chest. "—will take us to a coffee shop and then our hotel, and you will say *nothing*." Wincing, I dug thumbs into my temples. "Stupid headache."

Kwaskwi clicked his heels together with a mocking salute and sauntered away on the tree-lined path leading to the main compound. Ken tried to grab one of my hands, the movement aborted mid-air as he reconsidered. *That's right, jerk. As if I'd let you after that show in front of the Council.*

Ken's face began to soften, shifting, the planes of cheekbone rounding and eyes enlarging at the corners. His lower lip got fuller. Despite everything, I couldn't keep my eyes off that pouty lip, wanted to touch it, flick it like strumming a ukulele. "Your salesman face doesn't work on me, Kitsune."

Ken sighed, sticking his hands safely in his jacket pockets. "The Council would never allow a Baku loose in Tokyo that they had no measure of control over."

The words made sense but were no kind of balm for the hurts he'd dealt my heart. Giving up my name, keeping secrets from me, failing to defend me. But this lame attempt at damage control wasn't over. "They will help Akihito," he said in English. "They won't stop us from contacting other Kind who can help you figure out what you can be, even with your human half."

All I could focus on was that I'd let that pouty, lower lip kiss me. Apparently it didn't mean the same thing to Ken that it meant to me. Why didn't he tell me he was *Hafu*? And why share a fragment more intimate than his forest fantasy? I'd thought that dream fragment meant he was uncomplicated. *Ha.* "Because they did such a bang-up job with you? Already figured out what *you* can be with your human half, *Bringer*?"

A rueful glance, a blush, I wanted some kind of acknowledgement. Instead, anger tightened his jaw, the tic beating madly, his eyes going from milk chocolate to burnt espresso in an instant. Little fluttery things winged up and down my belly. The feeling like an electrical storm gathered, settling over me like an itchy blanket. "I have always known what I am," he said slowly.

My phone vibrated in my pocket along with the startling loud caws of a murder of crows. Ken glowered as I pulled it out.

"What? I put in the sim card Marlin bought me in the limo."

"Tell me that isn't Kwaskwi's ringtone."

"There were no blue jay sounds."

I answered the phone. Kwaskwi's voice was calm, bemused. "Akihito says he should stay here with the lady. He wants us to go to the hotel without him."

Ken was shaking his head. "You have Kwaskwi's number? I don't even have Kwaskwi's number."

I brushed him off. "You're the one who brought him into this in the first place." Ken had contacted Kwaskwi because we needed a safe place to stash Dad when Hayk and Ullikemi were out to use any member of my family they could get their hands on.

"Don't be jelly, Ken, you know I love you, too," said Kwaskwi's amused voice, tinny from the phone.

"Put Dad on."

"She's all yours," I heard Kwaskwi say in the background, and then Dad's voice. "There is a measure of peace for me in the presence of Yukiko-san."

Somehow Kwaskwi's snort was perfectly audible. He quipped sotto voce, "If you call 'peace' standing frozen like a Popsicle."

"We stick together, Dad, or we go home."

He'd argued strongly that Japan was the only place I'd be able to learn to control the Baku. It wasn't fair to blackmail him this way, but I no longer felt like fair was an option. Dad sighed. "I see. Well, then, I will meet you at the back gate in a moment."

He hung up. I stared at my phone; the screensaver was an old picture of Marlin, me, and Dad. My sister must have put it there. We were lined up behind the blue and red sushi counter at the restaurant, us girls looking gangly and awkward but Dad as close to happy as I ever saw him.

"He's meeting us at the back gate."

Ken nodded, falling back so I could lead the way into the trees, retracing our steps. His presence loomed at my back like a dark cloud.

Kwaskwi lounged against a post where we had left our limo. Dad stood stiffly next to him. There was no limo.

I stopped, putting my hands on my hips. "How are we getting to Starbucks?" I walked over to Dad putting a hand on his lower back. Even through his shirt, he felt oddly cold. Ken gave me a tentative half-smile. "There's a Doutor Coffee Shop at the main intersection. I've called a taxi."

"And here it comes," said Kwaskwi, jerking his chin at a black van, oddly narrower and shorter than its U.S. equivalent, pulling too fast into the driveway. Spraying gravel, it stopped dangerously close, cutting off the guys from me and Dad. The back door slid open, and a pair of gloved hands reached out and lifted Dad into the vehicle. Ken's panicked warning came too late, and then I, too, was jerked into the van face-first. The door closed with a slam, and the van took off, rocking me forcefully into the metal side.

A strange girl and a familiar, pale face with long, orange-brown hair no longer tied back in a pony-tail, but loose and flowing down his back, regarded me with cautious eyes. The shrine boy. What had the monk called him? "Pon-suma."

He blinked. "Your Japanese inflections sound like an old man."

It was my turn to blink.

"My fault, I'm afraid," said Dad, trying to settle upright despite the jerky motion of the van on the crazy backstreets. He shrugged. "I'm an old man and Koi hears my Japanese the most. You should tell us now why you are resorting to this dramatic method of getting our attention." Polite, but with a firmness that reminded us all Dad was a Baku, and not to be dismissed despite how he hunched and shivered.

"We are dissenters," said the strange girl. She appeared as young as

Pon-suma, but with short, dark hair moussed up into spikes. "We will not sit by and let a dried-up old Kappa and Tojo decide the fate of our Kind."

"I am well aware of The Eight's existence. Spare us the propaganda. Just tell us what you want."

"The Eight?" I asked.

Pon-suma refocused on me. "The Eight Span Mirror," he said, pointing at the girl. "She's Ben. We're *Hafu* like you."

I waved in a rolling motion trying to indicate he should continue the explanation, instead, he took it as an invitation to sidle closer to Dad.

"The Eight had no idea you were even still functional, let alone that you had a daughter, until I heard from Ken about who he was bringing home," said Ben.

Wait. Ken was part of this?

Dad didn't seem afraid, exactly. More irritated. And pale. And definitely shivering. It wasn't that cold in here. What had the Snow Lady done to him? I let loose the breath I'd been holding far too long. "You don't happen to stash lattes in the back of this van, do you?"

Ben looked at me like I was crazy, but Dad gave a little chuckle. *Nope, not scared. So he knew these people? Did he and Ken plan this somehow?*

I patted my cardigan pocket, reassured by the solid rectangle of my phone. They hadn't tried to take it away.

"Where are you taking us?" Dad asked. *So not his plan, then.*

"North, far from the Council. Where you will be safe."

Dad tensed up, his hands curling into claws, the whites of his eyes showing. "No!" he yelled, lunging at Ben. "Don't take me there. You can't take Koi there!"

Pon-suma whipped out a country doctor's little black bag and withdrew a syringe filled with a green, slightly glowing liquid. Like Ken's on the plane.

This was going sideways fast. Fear thickened my lungs.

"Herai-san, we won't hurt you or your daughter. If you get away from Tokyo, you'll see—" Dad broke through Ben's upflung arms, his hands going around her neck to choke away the words.

"Dad!"

I wrestled his thin shoulders, but somehow he held onto Ben with a wiry strength I didn't know existed in his thin frame. Ben began to shake, growing paler as sweat formed at her temples. Dad was forcing a living fragment from her, eating a dream to drain life force from her. I couldn't believe it, even as I felt the echo of a rushing heat where my bare fingers brushed Dad's neck.

"I dreamed the world wyrm's dreams, and it was only pain," Dad mumbled.

Pon-suma plunged the syringe into Dad's thigh. With a groan, Dad flung himself away from Ben, leaving angry red marks on her porcelain throat. He leaned against me, the muscles in his arms and legs slowly loosening, betraying him under that damn drug's influence. His eyelids lowered. "The Black Pearl. They're taking us to the Black Pearl."

CHAPTER SIX

"What the hell!"

Pon-suma positioned a *zabuton* cushion under Dad's head and laid him out at the back of the still madly careening van.

"Sorry," said Ben. "It seemed best. Herai Akihito is unstable. And dangerous."

"Fuck you."

Ben shook her head. "It doesn't have to be this way."

"Where the hell are you taking me?" I pulled up one hand, curling it into a claw like Dad's. "Do you have another one of those syringes? Either answer questions or shoot me up. I may be *Hafu*, but that doesn't mean I can't rip dreams from your living bodies and suck your soul dry!"

Damn, I'd have to remember that line the next time Kwaskwi was driving me crazy. If I ever saw Ken or Kwaskwi again. Ben and Pon-suma didn't seem eager to hurt us, but I'd learned dealing with Kind meant I couldn't completely trust my instincts.

"Herai-mura!" said Ben. She held up both hands, empty. "No more drugs. We're taking you to Herai-mura." And then, unnecessarily, "Your father's birthplace."

"Isn't that like five hundred miles north in Aomori Prefecture?"

Pon-suma nodded.

"Aw hell, no. I am not riding in this van all the way to Aomori! Let us out."

"Sorry," said Ben. "My brother will find us if we stop too close to Tokyo."

"Brother."

"Kennosuke is my eldest brother." Somehow this felt like another betrayal on Ken's part, even though it didn't seem like he was part of this particular kidnapping and he'd told me back in Portland about his four sisters.

"That's just fabulous." Ken and Ben. If I wasn't so tired I would have snorted. Dad wasn't scared of them, but he was scared of where they were taking us—his hometown. It was a lot to process but the Council gave me the creeps and at least Ben and Pon-suma were treating me like a real person instead of a tool. Anyway, it wasn't like I could overpower them in the back of this van and carry Dad back to Tokyo.

"You won't regret coming with us. I promise. The Council doesn't have all the answers. Give us a chance." Ben tilted her head, giving me a quizzical look.

"God, I need coffee."

"Well that," said Ben, "I can do."

But it was a false promise. The blue, insulated bag emblazoned with the Sanrio rabbit-puppy mascot Cinnamoroll she pulled out from a corner had only cans inside. She offered me one. Deepresso espresso drink. Oddly summative of how I was feeling at the moment. *Does she have a confused-croissant in there, too?*

The can did nothing to assuage my aching head, but did add a bonus layer of queasiness to my stomach. When the van finally got on to a highway Ben leaned against the front panel, folding her hands in her lap, and closed her eyes. I kept a wary eye on her and Pon-suma, who sat straight-backed next to Dad. After a long silence, Pon-suma opened a packet of crackers, methodically chewing each one. He handed me a packet, too. I stared down at it, my eyes blurring, vowing to stay alert. But my will was weak and the gentler driving and jet lag were catching up with me. My eyes closed between one bump and the next.

When I awoke, it was dark. Immediately I fumbled for my phone, but couldn't find it anywhere which meant I didn't know the time, and I couldn't contact Ken about my oddly lax kidnappers who were currently dozing away on the other side of the van cargo area. Marlin was going to freak when I didn't return any of her texts.

Though I wished I could shut out the world through sleep, I was utterly awake, and still exhausted. To make things worse, the van smelled like the bottom of a dude's gym locker, and I was starving. The tiny packet of crackers shaped like crabs and shrimp Pon-suma had given me with the Deepresso felt like a drop of water in the vast desert of my stomach.

I patted my cardigan pockets again, hoping against hope. Ah yes, at least something was going my way. The rectangular shape of my Tcho Mokaccino bar was still there. I ripped open the wrapper and shoved it into my mouth, relaxing into the deep, roasted bean creaminess melting on my tongue. Then I reached over to Dad's clothed wrist. He was still out, but I could make out a slight whistling snore and he wasn't restless or sweaty. That strange coldness was gone.

"Let's stop at the next rest area," Ben suddenly called out in a loud voice. The front of the van, or actually a thin panel at the front of the van, slid open, letting in the rhythmic wash of oncoming headlights. *Still on the highway, then, still heading toward Dad's backwater hamlet of a birthplace in the wilds of Aomori Prefecture.*

Oh, the driver. We hadn't been introduced last night. A long, lush fall of black hair straight out of a Tresemme shampoo commercial indicated a woman, most likely.

"Are we far enough away?" said the driver, showing her profile for an instant. Definitely a woman, much older than Ben.

Ben cleared her throat and checked her phone. "It's almost five a.m. If he hasn't caught up with us by now, he hasn't figured out where we're going yet."

He? Does he mean Rockabilly or Ken?

"Council knows," said Pon-suma. *Great.* Everyone but Dad was awake. I liked the sound of a rest stop; my eyeballs were floating.

"Maybe," said the driver. "But they'll still send Kennosuke."

"Tojo's a hammer, not a diplomat," Pon-suma agreed.

"And Kennosuke brought them the Baku in the first place." Ben smiled at me earnestly, as if she wanted to be friends. "Two Baku, actually. That was a lovely surprise."

Weirdest kidnapping, ever.

"Are you going to tell me why you went to all this trouble for a trip to Herai-mura?" I asked.

Ben and Pon-suma exchanged one of the most obvious *you deal with this* looks I'd ever seen. "Somebody tell me something," I said with a yawn. "I'm willing to listen," I said. "But I'm also willing to become a problem if you don't start explaining."

The driver turned her head to speak again. "We need her on our side," she said.

"What do you know of Herai-mura?" Ben asked.

"It's a hick town in the northern wilds of Kanto where my father and his weird surname originated from."

Ben breathed in. "You know Jesus's grave is there, right?"

I blinked. "Jesus?"

"Your father never explained any of this?"

"Dad kept me ignorant of a lot of things." I crossed my legs. I really, really needed a bathroom soon.

"Well, there are some very strange customs started long ago in the current town of Shingo, or Herai-mura. A strange chant that sounds like Hebrew. They traditionally carried babies around in reed baskets.

And there's a grave there where Jesus of Nazareth is buried."

"What about that whole crucifixion on Golgotha thing?"

"His brother," said Pon-suma, completely serious.

"Are you trying to distract me from this kidnapping with craziness?"

Ben made an impatient waving gesture in front of her petite nose. "The word Herai itself is believed to be a Japanese Katakana distortion of the word 'Hebrew.' The whole Jesus grave thing was started in 1935 by a professor and the mayor of the town. The professor 'discovered' an ancient scroll about how Eoshua came to Japan to study, and ended up staying."

I rolled my eyes, shrugging my shoulders up to my ears. My tired brain couldn't process this level of weirdness. And what did this have, like, *anything* to do with why they'd kidnapped me? I was going to get answers, but first I needed a bathroom.

"Morioka rest stop ahead," called the driver.

"Okay," said Ben.

"Dad," I said, gently rolling his shoulder. No response. What should I do? I had to get to a bathroom but I couldn't carry Dad with me.

Pon-suma took Dad's pulse again, gently wiping his forehead with a damp cloth. He gave me a slow nod, full of grave promise. "No harm will come to your father in the next ten minutes," he said.

"I will stay in the van with Herai Akihito," Ben cut in. "Midori-san, can you take her in?" She leveled a stare at me as intense as Ken's most feral Kitsune expression. "If you do anything to call attention to us, I will drive off with your father."

"Of course you will," I said, furiously trying to figure out a way to get a message to Ken or leave some kind of sign here at the rest stop. No phone, no money, and the threat of being separated from Dad forced my mind into useless circles.

"And do you mind getting me a Mugi-cha and Konbu onigiri?" she added, as if we were just friends out on a jaunt.

We pulled into a large parking lot at the top of a grassy hill bordered on one side by *yatai* food trailers selling yakisoba, teriyaki rice balls on a stick, squid grilled over charcoal, and round sweetbuns with a cookie crust called Melon Pan.

Katakana and Kanji characters emblazoned on flags rippled in the light breeze, advertising even more non-breakfasty delights. A low building huddled at the far end of the lot, where a young couple and an elderly man loitered near the stairs up to the building's entrance eating soft serve cones.

Not my idea of a tempting breakfast, but then, the seaweed rice balls Ben expected us to bring her didn't appeal to me, either.

As soon as Midori parked the van, Ben slid open the side door. I pushed past her out of the van and raced across the parking lot to the stairs. Quickly confirming the hunched over Kanji for *woman* on a tempered-glass door, I let myself into a stall in the obsessively clean bathroom. Thankfully, it was Western style. There was no way I'd wrestle myself into the correct squat for a Japanese *benjo* this early in the morning.

As I was washing my hands, Midori came in and checked her face in the mirror. She pursed her lips and applied a thin, paper slip to her nose and forehead, soaking up a thin layer of oil.

She caught me watching and offered me a paper.

I snorted after a cursory look at my reflection—yep, face still sleep-creased, hair flat and listless from recycled dry airplane air. "It'll take more than rice paper to fix me up. When am I getting access to a shower?"

Midori turned back to the mirror. Not a good sign. "I apologize," she said, finally. "But don't worry, dear. You have nothing to fear from Ben-chan or Pon-suma. Your father's life is very precious. We must hurry, though. The Bringer will track us down quickly."

"Then what's the point of this kidnapping?"

She opened her mouth, closed it, and then shoved her makeup pouch toward me on the sill above the sinks. "That requires quite a deep knowledge of our background, the Kind in Japan, and the Council. If you can be patient a bit longer, your questions will be answered. There is another who can better explain. Here. There are some moisture wipes and eau de parfume in there that will make you feel fresher."

But she wasn't getting off that easy. "What do you plan to do with us once we reach Herai-mura?"

A trio of girls in navy skirts, white blouses, and horrible plaid bows barged into the bathroom.

Midori's relief at this interruption was almost comical. She escaped me and the question by retreating into a stall. I looked into the pouch, biting my lip.

Ben, Pon-suma and Midori hadn't done anything threatening beyond drugging Dad when he was agitated and they'd given me a certain amount of freedom here at the rest stop, but I wasn't foolish enough to think I wasn't in some kind of danger. Dad was adamant about not going north. I just didn't know if that was the dementia talking or if he had good reason to stay away from his hometown.

There were three of them and one of me. I didn't count Dad, not in this state. I needed to contact Ken. If only I had Kwaskwi's ability to turn into a blue jay, or Ken's illusion, but all I had was a touching-phobia and some rice papers to take oil off my nose.

I dug out the little wallet of papers enclosed in a beautifully printed washi paper of white rabbits on pink. There was an eyebrow pencil and lipstick underneath. Midori's stall latch rattled. Quickly, I grabbed the eyebrow pencil and stuffed it into a pocket.

The school girls burst out laughing, trading slangy phrases so quickly I could barely understand.

"Ready to go?" Midori said, washing her hands. "I can buy you something. Do you eat Japanese food?"

"Ah, yes." *Think. Think.* There had to be way to leave a message for Ken without Midori realizing. I mentally scrolled through every Mission Impossible and Bourne Identity movie I could recall.

Nothing. "You go ahead," I said as innocently as I could manage.

"No, I'll wait for you."

Not letting me out her sight. There went my daring 'write on a paper towel with the eyebrow pencil and leave it in the parking lot' plan. Not that it was even viable. Who knew if Ken would even track us to this rest stop. And the towel would have blown away out in the parking lot, or been picked up by the legion of white-gloved old men employed for just that purpose.

Stupid idea. If I were Ken, where would I think to look for some possible clue I could leave him?

Coffee.

I led the way out of the bathroom. The rest stop was divided into two sections—a crowded cafeteria smelling of curry and shoes, furnished with tables in tidy rows and a few not-so-tidy travelers, and a larger section filled with island displays of boxed treats used as *omiyage*, or souvenir gifts. There were black sesame sable cookies, green tea roll cake, pancakes shaped like red snapper and stuffed with red sweet bean paste, and so many different kinds of rice cracker *senbei* I almost stopped to take a taste from the acrylic sample-boxes at the edge of each island.

But mine eyes had seen the glory of the small convenience store foods by the *omiyage* checkout counter—not one, but two entire display cases of various hot and cold canned coffee. I beelined for the hot case, Midori hustling after me. Just as I reached the last island of boxed cookies before the checkout, I tripped, sending an entire tower of pink sandwich castle cookies flying with an outstretched arm.

Gasps and exclamation filled the air. I stood up. "I'm so, so sorry."

"No, no," said the yellow-aproned counter girl rushing over. "It's totally and completely fine." We stood there for an awkward moment, sharing realization of how not-fine it was, and then Midori heaved a sigh and bent to pick up a box.

This caused even more agitation. The other counter girl joined the first. "No, no." She started grabbing boxes left and right.

I glanced at the hot coffee case with the eyebrow pencil gripped lightly between my fingertips. There were six different brands of canned hot lattes. I zeroed in on the Emerald Mountain label affixed to the shelf of the left most row. It sported a familiar, bordering-on-trademark-infringement green, chunky font and a mountain that instantly made me think of Mount Hood. In the white snow topping the mountain, I quickly drew an outline of a fish and in English letters wrote "Herai." Then I picked up two cans of latte.

"Ouch!" Very hot. I dropped them back in their row. Midori came over, and I turned to the cold case. She regarded me with suspicion. "Can I buy one of these?" I said, holding up an apricot soy latte from a Japanese maker. I held my breath, willing her not to look at the hot case, but all she did was grab the latte from my hands and make for the check out where the aproned girls had regrouped.

They exchanged sympathetic looks with each other while Midori paid for my latte. It took a heroic effort not to keep glancing back at the hot case. We emerged out into the warm morning sun, and I stopped at the top of the steps, caught by the gorgeous view of a white-topped mountain rising in the distance. I'd thought Mt. Fuji reminded me of Mt. Hood, but this was a different mountain, and it was almost a perfect twin.

Pon-suma was suddenly standing next to me, although I hadn't seen him exit the van. He barred me from the bottom of the stairs with an outstretched arm, as if expecting me to make a break for it. "You need to see the Black Pearl." A trickle of unease wound its way down my spine. The Black Pearl. Pon-suma was joining the cryptic announcement club. "You need to come to Herai Village. Trust me." He grabbed my left forearm with his bare fingers.

Oh, fudge nuggets. What'd he have to go and do that for?

The mountain, parking lot, and blue sky slid down like dripping paint on a canvas. Ice slid through my veins, freezing muscles and making blood sluggish while the taste of salt coated my lips and gray static like a snow flurry blinded my vision.

White. So much white, a familiar ache behind sightless retinas. Slowly, shadows formed on the unbroken expanse, and in the distance, darker shapes of what must be trees. I trudged across the snow under a cloudy sky. Harsh breathing reached my ears, and I looked over a shoulder to make sure my sister followed in the path I'd broken through the drifted white. Cold. Another step. Wind stung my exposed cheeks. Another step.

Now it was night, and the sky burned with the icy fire of a million trillion stars. The forest was silver, glimmering in the bright night. My sister trudged behind as we entered the forest, the silver branches and leaves reflecting so much starlight that even under the canopy I could see. A river joined us, winding deeper into the forest, and I followed. Soon the trees became gold. Ahead appeared a peaked-roof house on stilts. Geometric patterns adorned the roof beams. On one side there was a mural of a stormy sky and on the other side a sunny sky.

Excitement filled my veins. Eagerness for this home-coming made my footsteps faster as I climbed the step ladder. Inside a large room, an old woman hunched over a dying fire. Cradles suspended from the ceiling by ropes swayed in an invisible, rhythmic breeze all around her.

The world spun, realigning on an off-kilter axis. A tiny flame, born of something other than the gold trees, the house, the rocking cradles, flickered to life in my belly. I stopped. A name joined the taste of salt in my mouth: Koi.

This was Pon-suma's dream fragment, a heart fragment pulsing with his very life spirit. So honest, like Ken's forest-running fragment. Clean as the driven snow. There was a sense of danger in the creaking of the cradles, but also a vast patience in the gold forest.

Ken had called him a wolf in some strange language. This was something different than the werewolf legends I was familiar with. But I could consume this winter forest fragment; already my little flame hungered to burn more of the punishing cold. I could draw

Pon-suma's life-force into me through this fragment, gaining the temporary strength to physically overpower Ben and the driver.

But what then? I jerked away from Pon-suma, gasping like I'd run a mile, bowing my head so travel-tangled hair covered my face as I rested elbows on the stair's railing. My temples began to beat with a hard pulse, the start of a migraine vise.

Could I drive myself back to Tokyo? Pon-suma had kidnapped me, true, but he'd just willingly shared a dream fragment from the true heart of himself. I felt no ill-will in that dream, just a cosmic patience and an implacable sense of belonging to that snow-covered land that made my chest ache. Now he stood waiting for me to make a decision, hands curled loosely at his sides as if to reinforce he wouldn't touch me again, indicating he'd known exactly what he was doing by touching me in the first place.

The Council's Rockabilly and the monk had regarded me only with suspicion. They wouldn't have touched me bare-skinned to save a life. The feeling was mutual. Just because I trusted Ken, didn't mean I trusted his bosses.

Suddenly the little plot I'd contrived, marking a fish on a can coffee shelf label, seemed utterly ridiculous and a shameful heat flooded my neck and back. Mission Impossible, I was not. I was out of my depth here in Japan, but I'd been out of my depth back in Portland facing a homicidal maniac and a sea dragon spirit. It wasn't Ken who waltzed with the sea dragon. I was the one who set it free.

Why am I getting so angry? My hands were clenching and unclenching into fists and Pon-suma was watching me like I was a marshmallow too long in a microwave.

I had eaten a small portion of his dream fragment. The hair at his temples started to curl from sweat. Did he look pale?

Midori came out of the store, bent over and picked up my apricot soy latte from where I must have dropped it. "Here," she said.

What cruel torture. As if anything containing apricot flavor could assuage my deep, deep need for roasted espresso beans. I took it anyway and nodded. "We'll go with you to Herai Village for that explanation, but I'm not promising anything. And if you try to drug Dad again I will suck living energy from your soul. I don't like that you kidnapped us."

"Understandable," said Pon-suma at the same time Midori said, "At Herai village you will understand why we needed to get Herai Akihito quickly away from the Council."

Pon-suma strode across the parking lot, now bathed in bright sun. I tipped my face to the sky, drinking in the warmth, trying to feel something other than alone and angry and scared.

CHAPTER SEVEN

For the next couple hours in the van, Midori and Ben kept up intermittent conversation that was jarringly banal. Apparently there was a Youtuber called "Susuru" who filmed himself eating ramen every day at a different Tokyo restaurant. You would think people who kidnapped other people would use their time more productively. Like for ninja training, or world domination. Yikes. Meanwhile, Dad dozed on and off and Pon-suma stayed in the back, keeping an eye on Dad's condition.

After the fifth time he picked up Dad's wrist and used a phone to time his pulse, I decided my campaign of disdainful silence wasn't causing any guilt. "So are you a nurse or something?"

Pon-suma gave a little shrug. "Nursing assistant at a senior home."

I pictured a bunch of people like Ken, Rockabilly, and the Snow Lady sitting around in wheelchairs. "A Kind home?"

Now he frowned a bit, eyebrows knitting together. *Oh. Stupid question, I guess.* Pon-suma shook his head. "He is not lucid."

"Dad dozes a lot."

"The sedative should have worn off by now. Yukiko-sama did

63

this?"

"Yukiko? The Snow Lady Council member back at Yasukuni shrine? No. He's been this way for four years. The doctors diagnosed him with Alzheimer's. That was before I found out he was a Baku refusing to eat dreams."

"Refusing?" Pon-suma was not happy. He didn't wait for a reply. "Ben," he called out. "Problem."

Ben turned around, saw Pon-suma's expression and crawled into the back of the van. "We've just passed Ninohe-machi. Only forty minutes until we reach Herai-mura and lunch."

Pon-suma grabbed her forearm. Apparently he was an arm-grabbing kind of boy. "Herai-san refuses to eat dreams."

Ben turned to me with an expression identical to Ken's when I'd gone charging into a homicidal professor's office alone to rescue a kidnapped Marlin. Same angry caterpillar eyebrows and narrow, dark eyes. "How long has he been this way?"

"I'm not sure," I stammered. My mini-migraine stubbornly refused to go away, and Ben's resemblance to Ken was making my emotions all wonky. The apricot soy latte I'd downed out of desperation actually seemed to have made my caffeine-cravings worse and now I was getting the third degree.

Well I wasn't afraid of Ken's angry caterpillar expression, and I certainly wasn't going to cave to his sister either. Dad was picking up on the suddenly tense atmosphere. His breath came in agitated, short gasps, eyes rolling like marbles underneath his eyelids.

"Look, I only learned about this, the Kind, like a couple weeks ago. Since then I've been busy with an Armenian sea-dragon trapped in a human myth and his evil human servant who kidnapped my sister. Not much chance for quality daddy-daughter time."

"If Herai-san can no longer eat dreams, then all this is for nothing. We will—"

Pon-suma interrupted. "There's another way." He indicated me with a jerk of the chin. "She's Baku."

"Only a Baby Baku," I said. "Completely inexperienced."

"Baby?" repeated Ben.

"Kwaskwi's nickname."

Pon-suma made a little negative waving motion under his nose.

"Herai Akihito was Baku here in Japan for over half a century before he abandoned his homeland. Once he understands what we are working toward, he will not refuse," said Ben. Something vibrated loudly in Ben's shirt front pocket. She gave a startled smile.

The extra-long curves at the corners of her mouth, visible only with the smile, and the easy familiarity of her expression was a dead ringer for Ken's salesman face. The elegant, long fingers and strong wrists also made me think of Ken. I had a thing for hands. That made me angrier.

"Who is the Black Pearl? Tell me what you want from Dad."

Pon-suma shook his head and reached down to take Dad's pulse again. Ben slipped a Docomo phone out of a pocket. She swiped a few times. "My brother is quite persistent today. Is there something I should know about your relationship to him?"

"Don't change the subject."

"Ken usually gives me a little more leeway."

"You said he wouldn't follow right away," said Pon-suma in that calm voice. I wonder how angry he had to be to lose the serenity.

"Yeah, well," Ben shrugged. "I didn't know we'd be stealing the Baby Baku as well."

"You are planning to bring Dad to Herai-mura to eat the Black Pearl's dreams?"

Pon-suma nodded at me. Still no smile, but he seemed to approve of me figuring out stuff. "And the Council *doesn't* want him to eat the Black Pearl's dreams?"

"You could frame it that way," said Ben.

"What the hell *is* the Black Pearl? A Kitsune?"

Ben gave a delicate snort. "No, not a Kitsune. She is a far more powerful ancient one. The Black Pearl is a river dragon. The Amur

River, or the Heilong Jiang, depending on what century you're talking about. It borders Mongolia and China on the East coast."

A river dragon. One of Ullikemi's fragments flashed through my head. Strong, sinuous body in blue-black ocean depths, straining upwards with a terrible yearning for a glimmer of sun.

Ullikemi was also an ancient spirit. His dreams packed quite a wallop. Kind dreams were so vivid I couldn't fight them off during the day, as I did with human ones, but Ullikemi's dreams had been completely overpowering. Like getting a fire-fighter's hose in the face; myself, Koi, my own feelings obliterated. The only reason I'd survived our encounter was because Ullikemi had needed my help to be freed from the prison human myths had made of the Vishap Stone.

Now there was another dragon. No wonder Dad had seemed desperate in his warning. "I am not exactly a dragon expert. I'm not sure I'll be able to help."

"Well," said Ben. "I guess we'll find out. This is Herai village."

Rice paddies and some other small-plant crop had surrounded us for the past half hour. Now we drove under a white highway sign that pointed to the right and said "Grave of Christ" in English and Japanese. Midori turned onto a city street of concrete public buildings interspersed with bipolar traditional but modernly sided two-story houses. Their curved, ceramic roof tiles in blue, ochre and sometimes pink, smugly regarded us from both sides. We turned again, and then pulled onto a private drive in front of a brick building with a white awning and a gigantic white cross on the roof.

Museum of the Legend of Jesus read the sign out front.

"For real?" Marlin would have loved this. Too bad I couldn't message her a pic.

Pon-suma gave another serious nod and then slid an arm under my semi-conscious Dad. He wrestled him out of the van and force-marched him into the building. I scampered behind. A *noren* cloth hung in the inner hallway, jarringly embroidered with white crosses and the ancient Buddhist symbol for temple—a red swastika. Beyond the *noren* was a room dotted with display cases and posters chock full of dense text. I only got a glimpse as Pon-suma and Ben bypassed the main hall to enter a "staff only" door to the right. This led to a large room with a cluster of desks covered in the usual busy-office piles of paper on one side and a low table made of polished wood surrounded by *zabuton* floor cushions on the other. No land lines on the desks. I sighed. Everyone had a cell phone these days, even Jesus museums.

Midori stepped into the room behind me and indicated the *zabuton* next to where Ben and Pon-suma had propped Dad.

"Sit. I'll make tea."

"No chance you have a Keurig or Nespresso hidden somewhere?"

Midori flashed a patently false smile and then went to the wall and slid open a panel to reveal a small kitchen-cubby with sink, microwave, and a hot water pot. While she fussed with loose-leaf tea and glazed ceramic cups that looked like they should be on display in an art gallery, I sat down, stretching out my legs. Ben entered the room through another door, accompanied by a man. He was much older, hair grizzled gray and cropped short like a marine.

"So you are Herai Koi? I am Murase Ayumu. Welcome to the town of Jesus' Tomb."

This was so weird I let the whole wrong-last-name thing slide. "Yes. Okay, we're here. Now what?" It struck me that Murase was the name Princess Stewardess had thrown at the airport attackers, threatening them that Murase wouldn't be pleased by their attack. Was this their second kidnapping attempt?

Murase's placid expression did not waver. "Now we drink tea, and I tell you why The Eight Span Mirror needs a Baku."

Midori came over with a loaded wooden tray. She knelt in a graceful motion and then set the cups in front of everyone, including Dad. Murase continued as she poured. "Fujiwara-san has told you about us, already, yes? That we are Kind who do not see eye to eye with the Council?"

Fujiwara? Did he mean Ben or Ken? "Sort of. Your welcome envoy at Narita didn't leave the best impression."

Murase's eyes narrowed. Despite Princess Stewardess invoking his name, none of these people were Red Shirt or any of the other attackers. "I apologize if your first experience in Japan was unpleasant, but The Eight Span Mirror are not to blame."

Yeah, right. I waved to indicate the room. "Not sure what Jesus or mirrors have to do with the Kind."

"Technically, this isn't about Jesus," said Ben.

"But it's important to understand the context." Murase sipped his tea thoughtfully. "In the early nineteen hundreds, the Herai villagers began to have weird dreams. They had an overwhelming desire to bathe their newborn children in the river. Babies were toted around in rush baskets commonly found in the Middle East. Men grew beards. Women wore veils and felt a strange sadness when they went to the village well for water."

I wrapped my hands around the teacup, hoping the warmth would anchor me. Fatigue, my mini-migraine, and the total crock of shit this Murase was peddling made this all feel dangerously unreal. Like a hallucination. It was hard to take any of it seriously. Midori had returned to the table with the biggest, reddest apple I'd ever seen. She knelt, took out a pocket knife and cut a long, unbroken single spiral of skin. The firm flesh struck me with its sweetness from across the table.

"And this was because Jesus was buried here?" I couldn't help the incredulous tone. My mouth literally dripped with saliva now from the smell of the apple.

Midori slid toothpicks into the perfect, white slices of apple and placed them in a cut-glass dish in the center of the table. "Aomori regional specialty," she said.

Ben and I reached for apple at the same time. She gave me a grin—again so much like Ken I wanted to smack her. It was hard to remember I wasn't supposed to trust her when she kept setting off reactions mistakenly stemming from the intimacy I shared with her brother.

"It's unclear where the anthropologist who discovered the ancient texts alleging the graves are those of Jesus and his brother, Isukiri, got his inspiration. But it was a convenient cover for what really happened."

"The Black Pearl," mumbled Ben through a mouthful of apple.

I bit into a piece and had to take a beat to appreciate the single most delicious piece of fruit I'd ever experienced. Like I'd been eating cardboard all my life until now. What the hell was in the water here?

"You're familiar with events leading up to the Great Pacific War and the North China Incident?" Murase asked, steepling his finger over the steaming teacup.

"I think Americans call it the Boxer Rebellion," added Ben.

I nodded my head slowly. "Bunch of foreign powers invaded China. Something about peasants rebelling."

Midori muttered something under her breath about Americans and ignorance. Ben gave her a wide-eyed quelling look. Murase just continued. "Japanese troops went inland as far as Hokushin, North China. I was a sergeant in a troop that made it all the way to the Heilong Jiang." He lifted his chin in Dad's direction. "Herai Akihito was my captain."

Something heavy settled in my belly: the tea's bitterness suddenly unpleasant. I knew Dad was older than he appeared, but I knew nothing of his life before Portland. This didn't sound good. Where was Kwaskwi when I needed a sarcastic quip or snarky banter to deflect what I suspected was a heavy, emotional freight train of a revelation barreling full speed my way?

"We were soldiers caught in a nationalist fever of the Meiji Restoration. The ignorant Yihequan, the Boxers, massacred innocent Christians. Our job was to create a lasting place of peace and prosperity in the Pacific Basin."

"I'm sure Koreans and Filipinos would have a different view of that," I said, suddenly uneasy that Yasukuni shrine, the headquarters of the Kind Council, was a place not only Kamikaze pilots were honored, but also generals who most likely were responsible for things like raping Nanking or massacring Manila.

Ken couldn't be blind to that history. So either his loyalty to the Council meant that Kind had nothing to do with World War II military decisions or that Ken was mixed up in a Council that condoned bayoneting babies. *Oh crap.* What was the name Ben had called Rockabilly? Tojo? That had to be a common name. Rockabilly couldn't actually be the World War II prime minister convicted as a war criminal. *Right? Please!*

"The army had to cross the Heilong Jiang, but the Black Pearl lashed out at any Kind who dared come near. It wrecked the army's boats and sabotaged bridges. Pressure from military headquarters, both Kind and human, was mounting, and then the Council gave permission to remove the threat of the Black Pearl permanently."

Midori and Ben both looked overcome with sadness. The Kind turning against an ancient spirit. Even with as little as I knew about Kind history, this seemed wrong.

"So they sent Dad."

"Yes," said Murase. "Captain Herai boarded a raft, waited for the Black Pearl to show itself, grabbed its tail, and hung on for dear life. I was standing on the far bank, well away from the water, and I was soaked to the skin by the time the Black Pearl stopped lashing Captain Herai around. It went quiescent. Captain Herai convinced the rest of the Kind in the army that we couldn't kill it. That it was valuable. We coiled it up into a railroad car and shipped it back home."

"Here?"

"The Council wanted the Black Pearl far from the population and their base of power in Tokyo. But not too far away. This was unprecedented, keeping an ancient one from another country prisoner. Your father brought him back to his hometown."

"Dad stayed in Herai village to keep eating the Black Pearl's dreams? Then how did he get to the states?"

Murase sighed. "Captain Herai spent the end of the Pacific War eating many grievous dreams. The fall of Manchukuo, the bombing of Hiroshima and Nagasaki, the post-war famine."

"The only thing Dad ever told me was he couldn't take living in Japan anymore, but it wasn't just the war suffering here, was it?" I imagined eating the dreams of starving children. I'd wanted to throw up after experiencing Professor Hayk's memory-dream of his murder of a boy. What would it be like to be surrounded by soldiers whose dreams were all atrocities?

Ben shrugged. "He disappeared after MacArthur and the Occupation left."

"He ran away from the Black Pearl?"

"I think so," said Murase. "But only Yukiko-san and Kawano-san know for sure."

"A pair of fascist fools," said Ben.

Midori returned the wide-eyed quelling look to her with interest, but Ben was on a roll. "No sense of shame. No sense of responsibility. Stupid old traditions blinding them to the changing world. If the Americans hadn't forced a no army constitution down Hirohito's throat, we'd still be marching toward Northern China—"

"I'm sure Miss Herai doesn't need a politics lesson."

Time for some straight answers. "I don't. But you obviously need me and Dad. You need a Baku. Why now?"

Everyone but Murase suddenly couldn't look at me. Ashamed? Murase sipped his tea noisily, straining it through his front teeth. Stalling. Ben broke the silence. "You and Herai-san are the last known Baku to exist. There's no one left strong enough to hold a dragon—and the Black Pearl is restless, possibly waking from her long, quiet sleep completely. If she isn't freed, they'll either kill her trying to keep her here, or she'll die trying to free herself."

The last Baku? My sinking feeling turned into a full-blown heart drops to your stomach, roller-coaster dive. So many questions. I was temporarily paralyzed. Why were there no other Baku? Why was the Black Pearl waking now? The Council wanted Baku to eat the Black Pearl's dreams to keep it quiet, but The Eight Span Mirror wanted Baku to eat dreams for some other reason?

While my thoughts swirled around and around Murase's face seemed to relax, grow fuzzy at the edges, and then resolve itself into a gentler, more symmetrical arrangement. A salesman face like Ken used when he wanted to make me trust him. Murase was Kitsune. Or was he *Hafu* like Ken and Ben? "You must be tired and hungry, let's get you some of Midori's famous cold noodles in sesame sauce."

"I would literally kill for noodles in sesame sauce right now. But I'm going to walk out of here and flag down the first person driving past if you don't stop stalling. Just tell me what you want me to do!"

The corners of Pon-suma's mouth twitched. Murase sighed. "The Council wants to keep the Black Pearl sleeping. It's one of the most powerful dragons in the Pacific Basin. The Black Pearl's ambient magic ensures the Council's powerful position. Japan lost the war, but the Council still rules. The Kind influences human politics. As long as we hold the ancient one, China's growing global ambition will be held in check. North Korea won't dare attack us."

"We used to be able to rely on our treaty with the U.S.," said Midori. "But who knows what will happen there, now. Okinawa keeps protesting. The Philippines are kicking out U.S. bases. Your politics are growing insulated and prejudiced. The world is turning isolationist."

"Brexit isn't our fault. And we didn't elect the Filipino President, either." I was a little stung by the dig at America. As if some long-dormant patriotic gene came awake the moment I left my own country.

And the U.S. was my country.

Ben pushed her teacup away. Her gaze, as annoyingly dark and penetrating as Ken's, fixed on me. "The Armenian dragon in

Portland. You released it, didn't you? That's what Ken said."

Was that a good thing? I nodded slowly. Ben's palm slapped the table, making the cups clatter. "Let's bring her now. She can do it. She's Baku!"

Murase sucked air through his teeth. "It's too soon."

"Ken is on his way," said Ben.

"What?" said Pon-suma.

"I forgot to turn off my own cell phone. He tracked me here," said Ben.

Pon-suma gave a disgusted snort. Midori shook her head. Ken was on his way. Relief settled over me like one of mom's brightly patterned island quilts. On the heels of the relief came prickling pride. Stupid to feel relief at the thought of Ken being here. I couldn't trust him completely after his actions with the Council and his not telling me all this Eight Span Mirror nonsense. There was an Eight Span Mirror somewhere in the Amaterasu goddess myths. It was annoying not having my phone to look that up. "Do what? What's too soon?"

"Touch a sleeping dragon, take the dreams into yourself," said Murase quietly. "And then use that power to release her."

Her. A female dragon. Well that was new. And somehow worse in some tangled, sexist way I didn't want to acknowledge to myself. "So my crash course on Kind politics didn't cover this, but you said the Black Pearl has ambient magic? She'll what, take that back to China? Won't that upset the balance of power?" *Way to go, Koi. Using phrases like balance of power. As if you understood what was going on. Fake it til you make it.*

"Now you see why the Council is so keen on making sure Herai-san is under their control," said Ben.

"The Council's ambitions are thinly disguised fear," said Murase. "Fear of having to listen to new voices, fear that their outdated world view will crumble. If we release the Black Pearl, the Council loses the luxury of fear. They will be forced to find a more inclusive way to survive."

For a moment, I wondered at the passion behind Murase's words. I had an inkling of what it must be like to be ethnically *Hafu* in Japan—I'd heard the stories about the Zainichi Korean, the second largest ethnic majority that was still treated like outsiders. Was it the same for Kind *Hafu*? Did the Council unfairly treat those with a human mother or father? Ken had never talked about that. Like he never talked about a lot of things. Important emotional things.

I bit my lower lip. *Okay, Dad. Now would be a massively superb time to wake up.* But no, relying on Dad was just as bad as waiting for Ken to rescue me.

"Let me talk to my father. When he wakes up, I can ask him the same questions."

"Yes, but he may not wake up for hours," said Ben. "You are awake, here, now. Ken just texted me two minutes ago. He's already in Morioka. We need to do this."

Murase gave me a smile with eyes filled with slow-moving currents of grief. "It's time for you to meet the Black Pearl."

CHAPTER EIGHT

"Dad seemed desperate to avoid this," I said.

"Herai abandoned his responsibilities. He left," said Ben. "Will you also turn your back on an ancient one's suffering?"

"Look, you don't know everything about me," I said. "Back off."

Midori put a gentling hand on Ben's arm. Murase drained the dregs of his tea. "You will have to excuse Ben-chan's passion. The Eight Span Mirror has lived with the Black Pearl's pain for a long time. You will understand when you see her."

I can do this. I can make decisions about who I will help. And figure out who is right and what is wrong. But first there needs to be coffee.

"Is there time for coffee first?"

Murase blinked. Ben gave a scoffing sigh but stopped bristling like a hedgehog.

I couldn't take Dad with me. He'd been so afraid of the Black Pearl. I'd tasted Pon-suma's dream. The nature of it made me trust him on an implicit level I didn't trust Murase and Ben. I looked to the silent young man, sitting correctly erect on folded knees. "Will you make sure nothing happens to my father if I go with them?"

Murase answered. "You will need Pon-suma. Can you be content with Midori's care? She is a trained nurse. You have my word no harm will come to him while you are gone." He extended his hand palm up on the table. "If you wish to taste one of my dreams to see if I speak true, I consent."

"No thanks. That isn't really a good idea right now."

He withdrew his hand, bushy eyebrows drawing together in a disconcerted way. *Yeah, well, this didn't make me happy, either.* But him offering had to count for something. All eyes watched me, the weight of unspoken hopes and Ben's edgy excitement almost a palpable roughness on my skin.

"Don't make me regret trusting you," I said. I'd tried for a gangster threat, but my tone was more of a plea. Midori busied herself making Dad comfortable in a reassuringly grandmotherly way.

Pon-suma, Murase, and Ben herded me into a small, black sedan with Pon-suma at the wheel.

We pulled out of the private drive and drove past a few residential streets where aproned women were hanging sheets from second floor verandahs and old men puttered around in carefully tended gardens behind latticed concrete walls. We hit the *Shotengai,* the main drag lined on both sides by stores and slightly rundown mom-and-pop cafes. Pon-suma maneuvered into an impossibly small parking spot between planters full of blooming cactus and a lavender backhoe. Ben kept up a stream of directions and comments until Pon-suma sighed in frustration. "Stuff it, Kitsune."

"It's my car, I should be driving," said Ben.

"No!" Murase and Pon-suma yelped in unison. Pon-suma kept the keys after we got out of the car.

We walked along the street until it narrowed into a covered walkway. Shopkeepers were just lifting the sliding shutters over their stores despite it being almost ten o' clock. Drugstores and convenience stores were interspersed with more colorful rice cracker vendors, tea, and cake shops that called out to me with perfectly wrapped, glistening cakes flavored with matcha and lychee. Colorful banners and vending machines crowded every spare inch between stores.

At last, Pon-suma lead us around a corner and into a nondescript, wood-shingled store with no banner or sign. Inside was a narrow, long room with three bistro tables on the right and a mad chemist's wooden counter on the left. Test tubes, Bunsen burners, burlap sacks, and tubes intertwined around gleaming brass stands.

There was not a menu or sign to be seen inside the shop, either. Murase cleared his throat. At the far end of the counter a man pushed through the hanging noren doorway curtain and stepped stiffly into the room. "*Irrashaimase*," the man gave the usual shopkeeper welcome. "Who are your friends, Murase-san?"

"Just museum flunkies plus a visitor from America."

The man stepped carefully closer and gave a slight bow in Murase's direction. His eyes didn't seem to focus. I realized he must be blind.

"Welcome," he said this time in English without a trace of the usual Japanese issue pronouncing 'l'. "May I make you some coffee?"

"To go, unfortunately," said Murase.

The man sucked air through his front teeth in disappointment.

Coffee! Saliva filled my mouth. "Yes, please," I answered back in English. "Can you make lattes?"

This time Murase hissed in disapproval. "Herai-san, we will trust Enoshima-san to make us delicious coffee without interference."

Enoshima reached for a burlap bag with confidence, knowing exactly where it was. The sleeve of his soft, gray Henley rode up at the movement, revealing wrists with the kind of intricate colorful dragon and cherry blossom tattoo I'd only seen in *Yakuza* movies. He poured beans into a grinder and arranged test tubes and water in one of the contraptions in a flowing, deliberate tea ceremony way. In no time at all, the most heavenly aroma filled the room.

Ben fiddled with her phone, and then shuffled closer to Murase with a serious expression. She tilted the screen for Murase to see.

"He's close now," Ben said quietly. "Maybe twenty minutes away."

Ken. My heart gave a little flip. The smell of coffee and Ben's disturbing resemblance conjured him out of thin air. Dark-on-dark eyes, the sly arch of one eyebrow, the way his breath always smelled like kinako cinnamon. I couldn't stop the upswell of relief at the knowledge he'd soon be here, even if I did intend to make my own decisions about the Black Pearl and these Eight Span Mirror nutzoids.

The man poured coffee into porcelain travel mugs, somehow judging when they were full without seeing or touching the coffee. No Styrofoam or paper cups for Mr. Coffee Whisperer.

A thick crema sat on top despite the lack of added dairy product.

"Enoshima-san," said Murase. "Forgive us for hurrying your art."

He went to the counter and made the *goodbye* hand wave that meant *come here* in Japan. Just as I reached for a mug, Enoshima pushed it forward—our fingertips brushed.

The tingle up my spine and a flash of warm, espresso-scented darkness told me I'd gotten a fragment. Funny how it seemed so weak in comparison to the Kind fragments I'd been getting lately. I probably wouldn't even experience it until I next slept, whenever that would be. I used to freak out about such casual touches, and now it seemed about as annoying as a mosquito.

No money exchanged hands, but Mr. Coffee Whisperer stood back, hands clasped behind his back in military style. "Your American guest will have to return the mugs and tell me if my coffee satisfied her craving."

Ben and Pon-suma got their own mugs and then hustled us out the door back to the car.

Ben and I settled in the back seat and the most beautiful, dark, rich, smell I had ever experienced wafted up from my mug. Like someone took windblown moors and angsty, aristocratic British actors in period costume, covered the entire thing in dark chocolate, and then somehow distilled the whole mess into an essence, and that essence was the exact color and compelling promise of Ken's eyes.

I gave myself a little shake and brought the mug to my lips.

This was the most delicious coffee I'd ever put in my mouth. It was as full-bodied and complex as the scent, as deeply satisfying as a physical embrace. A wave of peace, like my entire body exhaling this trip's accumulated stress, swept me from head to toe. I sighed, feeling tears well up behind my eyes. All these years I'd been drinking lattes and missing out on this little piece of distilled heaven?

Overly dramatic much? I must be ovulating.

We'd left the *Shotengai* and seemed to be headed back to the museum. Sure enough, we pulled into the tree-lined lane leading to the main building, but instead of pulling up in front of the entrance, this time we passed the museum and entered a narrow, dirt track with a faded wooden sign I couldn't make out.

Pon-suma drove slowly through the trees, the car jiggling over ruts as we all frantically balanced our mugs in the air to keep coffee from spilling. He pulled onto an area of flattened grass. "Bring the coffee with you," said Ben as he opened the door.

"As if I'd leave liquid gold behind." What were those test tubes? Why didn't Stumptown in Portland work alchemy with their coffee in test tubes and Bunsen burners?

Beyond the scruffy grass was a concrete path bordered on both sides by carefully tended clumps of spiky grass and purple pansies. We followed the path for a few moments, all of us contentedly sipping. It was the first time I'd seen Pon-suma's alert calm relax. The path passed by a pond deep enough to be home to some truly monster koi fish, and then emptied out into a bigger clearing with agricultural fields on the far side. In the middle of the clearing were two big mounds of grass-covered dirt encircled by low, white-picket fences and topped by huge wooden crosses.

"Jesus's tomb," said Murase, all seriousness.

I stifled an inappropriate desire to guffaw. This was all so nutzoid. The large, wooden sign board to the left of the biggest mound detailed more or less the same story Murase and Ben had told me—this was the final resting place of Jesus of Nazareth and a brother who had spent their last years here in Aomori as rice farmers.

Ben swung a culotte-clad leg over the fence and got down on her knees in front of the cross. For a horrified moment, I thought she was going to start praying, but after bowing her head, Ben clicked something at the base of the cross. A large panel of grass at the top of the mound slid away, revealing a hole just big enough to fit one, typically-sized, slim Japanese person. Ben held her phone out, so the light could penetrate the hole and reveal steps leading downwards.

"Oh, hell no."

Murase gently tugged the empty coffee mug from my resisting fingers. "The Black Pearl."

"Under Jesus's tomb? Just like this? No guards? No password, nothing?"

Pon-suma made a clucking noise. "Doesn't need a guard."

Does he realize that makes this worse?

Ben made a hurry-up waving motion.

I was entirely unprepared. I had agreed to meet the Black Pearl and perhaps try to release her as I had Ullikemi but all of a sudden it struck me that I was about to go down a hole in a mound in Northern Japan with people who, granted, knew how to score orgasmic coffee, but had kidnapped me and Dad.

"I'm kind of having second thoughts. I'm sure Ken will be willing to listen to your concerns. Can't we wait just a little bit for him?"

Murase and Ben exchanged a loaded look. Murase's eyes flickered toward Pon-suma. He sighed, rolled his shoulders like a professional wrestler, and bared his teeth in an expression not at all a smile.

"Here," he flung his mug at Murase who scrambled to juggle all three, grabbed my arm above the elbow in a grip like a blood pressure cuff and pulled me over to the fence.

"Sorry," said Ben, with a cute, sheepish grin. *God damn Fujiwara siblings can go suck eggs.* "The Council will be hot on my brother's heels. We can't risk them stopping us."

Pon-suma's other arm scooped around under my knees and I was lifted bodily over the fence and shoved feet-first into the hole.

Oh god, oh god, oh god. I twisted and kicked but the boy was built like a wiry Mack truck; all ropy muscle and fierce will. He propelled me further down the steps by simply advancing.

Ken had called him a wolf, but he was more like a wombat or badger in his den. The boy's abs were seriously of steel.

"Sorry," said Ben again from above. I glared up. She gave a little wave and then slid the panel shut—leaving us in utter darkness.

I halted. "What the hell?"

Pon-suma stopped pushing me. I immediately sat down on the step, my heart beating a mile a minute. "This isn't making me sympathetic to your cause."

"Doesn't matter now." Pon-suma's voice rose in the darkness. "Black Pearl knows we're here. She will get restless if we do nothing."

Pon-suma must have pulled out his phone because a rectangle of light appeared, casting just enough illumination to show a metal door at the bottom of the long flight of wooden stairs. I briefly fantasized trying to grab the phone and rushing past him up the stairs but who was I kidding? Pon-suma was too strong. And I had no way to get Ben to open the panel at the top, anyway. I rubbed at my arms, feeling an itchy, rising panic.

"Why aren't Murase and Ben coming?"

Pon-suma gave a little cough. "Kitsune are susceptible to the Black Pearl's atmosphere. I am Horkew Kamuy, born of the eternal snow and perma-frost of the great North."

Ah. There is that overly dramatic Kind-speak I was missing. So Pon-suma was some kind of superwolf? And what did he mean by atmosphere?

But I already had an inkling. I had been rubbing my arms so

vigorously that I was causing a rug burn, but the prickly queasy feeling had spread, like slime-covered ants crawling all over my body.

Pon-suma manhandled me down the rest of the stairs and reached past me to wrench open the metal door with a painful squeal of protesting hinges.

My lungs couldn't seem to get enough air, my heart pounded fit to break a rib, and a chill sweat broke out at my temples. Inside my belly was what felt like a frantic gerbil desperately clawing to get out and *run the fuck away.*

"No," I said, but Pon-suma pushed us through the door. I gave a kind of strangled yelp and froze, trembling.

Dark, a cavernous dark. And cold. Like walk-in freezer cold. Long stripes of faint, green light in unimaginably huge, tangled coils filled the space. Each of my inhalations brought in the smell of moldy old socks cut with fresh *wakame* seaweed miso soup. Our breath formed ghostly clouds around our mouths.

Pon-suma's phone-light flicked off. "Bioluminescence," he said. "Beautiful."

So glad his immunity to the slime-ant distress gave him the opportunity to appreciate biodiversity. Somehow I couldn't summon up the same appreciation.

"What's that?" A soft, moist sound was growing louder and louder. The coiled green began to slide in all directions. I shivered. Pon-suma coughed again in answer. The door rattled as if Pon-suma clutched the handle for support.

He is scared. The superwolf is scared. Awesomesauce.

My eyes were adjusting. The green streaks of light resolved into an understandable whole—the giant coils of a snake as big around as a sequoia tree trunk. My memory flashed to the final confrontation with the dragon, Ullikemi. He'd taken the shape of a giant snake in the dream world I'd created out of Ken's forest fragment. But this was real, this was here and now, not a dream.

"Go on. Do it."

"Do what?"

"Most likely she's not really aware of us," said Pon-suma.

"Most likely?"

The soft sliding stopped. "She never fully awakens...yet. She is lost in dreaming. But in her half-waking restlessness she strikes out at petty annoyances."

"I'm all good with not being a petty annoyance." I stifled my own bout of coughing. It was truly rank in here. A bunch of friends had joined the terrified gerbil in my belly, and my lungs felt raw from trying to breathe the thick air.

I really, really, really do not want to touch that giant snake. But Pon-suma was between me and the door, and this imprisoned dragon situation wasn't right. No one should be locked in an underground cave.

Okay, time to put my Baku where my mouth is. I could touch this monstrosity, take in some dreaming, and figure out if The Eight's version of what was going on here rang true or not. And maybe consume enough of the dream to get the strength to barrel straight past Pon-suma and back to Dad.

No one will get hurt. Not like sucking the energy out of Dzunukwa 'til she almost died or Thunderbird trying to drown me in his own dreaming out of a desire to control.

I tiptoed closer to the nearest coil and reached out. My fingertips made contact with freezing, wet leather. I gasped, wanting to jerk away, but the world was spinning, and I was hammered by the deluge of a gale-force fragment. Awake, I dreamed a living dream—the Black Pearl's memory dream.

Pressure on all sides. I swam through murky, deliciously cool shadows. The sun's scalding heat sent fingers of light to glimmer in shifting patterns in the uppermost layer of water. Muscles flexed in a ripple up and down my spine, tail thrashing back and forth to startle a school of *bang huahua yu* flitting away as fast as their spotted bellies and tails could move.

The dream froze, then the world juddered around me, seeming to skip. Now there was blood in the water, more salt-copper than I'd drunk in years. Men in machine-made cloth, not tanned fish skins, fought along the river. With them invader Kind floated on flimsy rafts of brown bentgrass and young ash. I would taste the flavor of outlander blood.

Another skip in the dream, a different group of men with guns in invader blue lined the banks. Yet even now, *Abka Hehe* heeded my prayers. She sent the hairy, slow-moving *Nari* and the sleek, spotted *Kesike* to nibble at the ranks of invaders as they slept in their cots last night. There were fewer campfires along the south. Anger curdled my insides. I would pray for hail and punishing rain, and chase them all away, including the Kitsune who did not fear me as the humans did. And did not respect me like the shamans.

But today, I was careless. I swam close, too close, to a whirlpool eddy. An invader stabbed down with a bayonetted rifle. There was a sharp pain. I reared out of the river and crushed the invader in my jaws, more blood coating my fangs and polluting the swift run of the Heilong Jiang's current. But he was only a distraction. There was another invader, reeking of Kind but not Kitsune or shaman, and he reached out with a hand and caught the tip of my tail. Sharper pain arced through me, like a bayonet through the spine to my brain.

A pasty, human face contorted in a rictus appeared, and then I was heavy, sinking down into the water, draining of vitality and drowsy. The human-shaped Kind eating away the mighty, river-heart of myself, eating away the very name *Muduri Nitchuyhe* until I was but a small consciousness, a Black Pearl—

Dad.

Awareness struggled to the surface, a small flame flickering barely, some consciousness other than of the great river-dragon, something that recognized the face not as an enemy. It was human, familiar, bringing a surge of anguished longing.

I was human.

Another stutter in the memory, a skip, and now I was in a great, metal box. It was cold, so cold. I was so tired. It was so hard to fight the invader the others called *Baku* in my dreams. They took me so far away from my river, even *Abka Hehe* would not hear me across this ocean. Sleep. I could sleep, and the Baku would siphon my dreams, a slow death, a peaceful death, but better this than becoming a tool of the blue-uniformed invaders, becoming their weapon—

"Koi."

Sleep tugged at me, whispered from the four corners of my brain, weighed my eyelids, vibrated along my curved spine, even as I knew sleep meant an eternal rest, no exit—

"Wake up!" A stinging on my cold-numbed cheek.

Cheek?

Human, not dragon. The small flame of awareness burst into life again, and I knew what *Koi* meant. It meant me, but I couldn't take it in, couldn't force the meaning into the oddly-shaped container of flesh and bones. Longing for the sun-kissed whorls and eddies of my home raged like a flood along my veins, and I could not consume the enormity of her, the dragon.

The voice spoke again, urgent words that were meaningless syllables even as the timbre and vibration of the voice awoke the fierce ache of deep regret. It was too hard to fight, though, too hard. The dream was a spigot open to a torrential stream of the Black Pearl's memories, and I was weary. It was easier to sink back in the depths on the cooling, rocky bed of mud—

A warm pressure this time, followed by a kinako scented whisper. "Take my dream, Koi. Let it bring you back to me."

The soothing water blurred from muddy browns to bright, mossy green. The sharp scent of pine needles and last season's leaf cover decomposing to dust under my feet.

Feet?

With a jolt, every muscle in my body spasmed in exquisite, stretching torment and a blossom of pain burst into life at the base of my neck. The world spun, a sharp 360 degrees blurring into a kaleidoscope of colors, slowly, slowly resettling into the shapes of trees. Cedars reached towering branches to a bright, star-lit sky, and I was running, running—

Ken? This was Ken's dream, the very deepest fragment of him dreaming himself. But, how?

No energy to waste on how. The Black Pearl's river still flowed around the bubble Ken's fragment had woven around me. I was Koi Pierce. I was Baku, and I had to eat this dream or drown, my own self-flame extinguished forever.

I pictured the flame inside me bursting into life like a roman candle on the Fourth of July. There was a strangled yelp not my own—Ken!—as I drew in, inhaling like a cigarette; the forest, the running, the pine needles. I consumed it in a burning flame, feeling the draw on Ken's very spirit as his strength drained into me. The bubble held as the Black Pearl's river flowed through us. The pain blossom at the back of my head unfurled great petals of hot agony. I shivered, but held on, burning, burning.

Another rapid series of stinging slaps on both cheeks this time, hard enough to wrench my whole head. I jerked away in indignant surprise and found myself back in the cave, Pon-suma grasping me by the shoulders in a bruising grip. Ken lay crumpled and shivering on the floor as the Black Pearl's tail lashed overhead.

CHAPTER NINE

"*Ramusak Ceh!*" yelled Pon-suma directly in my ear.

I ripped my hand from the Black Pearl's skin with a wrench that rocketed from palm to heart and down to my gut, like ripping my tongue from a frozen lamp post. "God damn it!" I pushed at the middle of Pon-suma's chest, and he went flying, skidding away across the slime-covered floor. The giant tail came down on Ken with a sickening crunch, too loud in the dark space. My heart clenched. Static, along with pressure rising inside my skull, clouded my eyesight.

I hesitated.

Ken's scream of pain penetrated the fog. Tugging my sleeves down to cover my hands, I pushed with all my might at the nearest dragon-coil. It shifted with a muffled thunder. I dropped to my knees, half-blind, searching with fingers for Ken's face.

The scream stopped. "Don't." Ken's words came out strangled through gritted teeth. "Don't touch me."

I pulled back hands sticky with blood, pressing fists into my sides instead, trying to contain the ballooning pressure. *So cold. Why is it so god damn cold?*

"Move the dragon," said Pon-suma. It had shifted, now blocking our exit. On hands and knees, I scuttled between the dark blob that was Ken and the coils of green light where the Black Pearl had settled again.

"*Shikari shite,*" I said. *Hold on.* Panicking, I shoveled my hands between the nearest coil and the floor. With another full-body muscle spasm the Black Pearl's dream crashed over me in a flood of sun-kissed water, ratcheting up the pressure ballooning my already full insides. The kernel of Koi-flame flared bright with Ken's strength, his forest dream bubble holding against the Black Pearl's torrent. I jerked the coil back with all my might, going ass-over-teakettle. I clocked the back of my head on the cave floor.

A pair of hands lifted my shoulders gently. Pon-suma's voice said softly, "We have to carry him out together."

I stood with his help, head reeling, static scrawling across my vision. "Too dangerous. He's hurt."

"He'll die of hypothermia."

"No," said Ken, teeth chattering so hard he could barely speak. "Koi can't—"

Whatever he was going to say was cut off with another muffled groan of agony as Pon-suma grabbed his shoulder and beckoned me over. We gripped forearms and slid Ken onto our makeshift sling, careful not to brush bare skin. He groaned again, a sound that ripped my already tender insides to shreds, but the solid weight of him straining my arms was an anchoring release for the pent-up energy of the dreaming twisting my guts like ropes.

Pon-suma managed to hold Ken one-armed while he wrestled the door open. As the door closed, the slithering, moist sound of the Black Pearl's restless coiling chased after us, but the dragon didn't try to follow. Halfway up the stairs, Ken bumping and limp between us like a broken rag doll, Pon-suma leaned against the rock wall. "Murase-san! Ben!"

There was no answer from the darkness above. The door was closed, the rectangle of light gone, but at least it was warm on the stairway. Ken lost consciousness. I bent my head to his face, relieved to feel his breath warm on my cheek, but I couldn't keep hold of one thought for very long. My brain was filled with a whirling chaos of fear; the Black Pearl's river, a stabbing bayonet, the bone-deep terror of seeing the Black Pearl's tail come down over Ken's body. *What just happened?*

Pon-suma moaned and muttered something in that strange language he'd yelled earlier under his breath. *Ainu? Stupid. Ken is dying and you're wondering what language that is? Pull yourself together!*

"Why is it so cold?"

"Yukiko-san. This cave freezes energy," said Pon-suma.

No time to unpack that information; we had to get Ken further up the stairs. Pon-suma's foot slipped on something fluffy covering the top stair, and he came down hard, spilling all of Ken's weight into my arms. Luckily the wall was there to keep us from falling any further. I barely managed to hold us both up, even with borrowed unnatural strength flowing through me from dream eating. Soft things floated in the air, stirred up by the draft of our movements.

Pon-suma reached out and plucked one from its lazy trajectory, comical in his dismay. It was a feather. A blue jay feather.

"Kwaskwi, open the god damn door or I will rip your head off," I yelled.

The door slid open with a jolt, and a familiar wide grin in an oversized face blocked the sunlight. "You wound me, Koi. No thanks for the rescue? Imagine how tedious it was to travel hours with an angry Kitsune. And only J-pop on the radio!" Kwaskwi gave an exaggerated shiver.

Good to see you, too, Asshole.

"Help!" Pon-suma lifted Ken up, and Kwaskwi stepped back, allowing us to bundle ourselves back out into the fresh air. The pain blossom in my head began to wither, but I was still angry at

Kwaskwi, myself, the stupid cave floor and the dent it put in my head, not to mention Pon-suma and the rest of his gang.

"We need to get Ken to the hospital," I said, as we laid him gently on the grass. In the sunlight he was pale, bright spots of red high on his feverish cheeks, eyes working madly under shut lids and pant-legs frozen solid with blood or dragon slime.

"No hospital," said Pon-suma. "Midori." He glared at Kwaskwi. "What did you do to them?"

Kwaskwi gave an innocent shrug and pointed back down the path. Ben and Murase sat, tied to the historical marker signpost, blue feathers scattered all around them and poking out from their mouths like a gag.

Ben's left eye sported a darkening bruise. Parallel, angry-red scratches marked both forearms, but Murase looked untouched.

"Ken, not me," said Kwaskwi. He had on his creased leather jacket, chains, and royal blue flannel shirt, so couldn't quite pull off innocent. "He might have been a little mad."

"Let them go," said Pon-suma.

"Anything for you, princess."

Pon-suma ignored the accompanying smarmy grin and went over to Ben and Murase to begin untying them. With a retching gag, the two vomited up black bile and feathers, coughing as Pon-suma pounded them on their backs.

Kwaskwi put a careful hand on my shoulder. "Ken will be okay."

All I wanted was to melt into that touch, give up fighting the pain and the pressure of the dreams I'd eaten, and let Kwaskwi take over, but I didn't quite trust him. I wasn't sure who anyone really was here in Japan.

Despite the fact that Ken had come for me, run into the Black Pearl's den and now lay wounded on the grass, bleeding and unconscious, I wasn't sure of him, either.

I wanted more than anything to believe Ken had done that out of caring for me. But he'd given my name to the Council. There was a betrayal here, and I didn't know how deep it ran. I was shaking and starving and bone-tired and didn't know how long I could stave off the tell-tale tremble of my lower lip.

Kwaskwi pulled me into a tight, one-armed hug, burying my nose in the warm leather of his jacket which smelled of Old Spice and sunshine. He let me go just as Pon-suma approached, Ben and Murase in tow.

Ben ran to her brother and knelt, checking Ken's pulse at wrist and neck. "Steady, but weak."

With a groan, Ken's eyes fluttered open. "Don't, don't make Koi touch the Black Pearl! Ben, she's not ready."

"Too late," said Kwaskwi. Ken tried to sit up, and groaned, clenching his fists around Ben's wrists at the pain.

"What happened?" Ben demanded.

"The Baku couldn't handle the Black Pearl. The ancient one broke the Bringer's legs," said Pon-suma. "We need to get him to Midori."

"I'll bring the car," said Murase, and took off at a fast jog back toward the field.

"Koi?" Ken's eyes were open, but he still seemed confused. I knelt on the other side of him. "I'm here. It's okay." I ached to touch him, to feel his solid reality, to reassure myself he was here, breathing.

"I found you."

"Yes," I said.

"I'm sorry. My sister is stupid."

"Yes."

"Savage," said Kwaskwi. He stuck one arm out and bent his head into the crook of the other one. *Dabbing? Seriously?*

"Hey!" Ben protested.

I gave her my best Marlin Pierce stare-of-disapproval. "You kidnapped us."

"Still!"

The car bumped over the grass and maneuvered past the sign to

91

stop close to the white picket fence. Pon-suma and Murase came over with a blanket to improvise a sling. Ken reached out, grasping my sleeve. "She stays with me."

"We're all going the same place," said Murase. We rolled Ken onto the blanket and into the back seat of the car, me squishing in awkwardly with Ken's head on my lap. Pon-suma and Murase got into the front seat.

"What about me?" said Ben.

"You can go to hell," said Ken in a voice like he'd swallowed gravel.

Murase rolled down his window. "Rendezvous at the museum."

Ben looked at Kwaskwi. Kwaskwi gave his trademark grin and made little flapping wings at his sides. "I'm covered."

"Let's go!" I said. We pulled away, leaving Kwaskwi and Ben staring after us. I wanted to ask Ken if he'd found my rest stop message, what he'd had to do to reach me, and why he hadn't told me of the Black Pearl, but he was in pain and that wasn't a conversation anybody else needed to hear. Pon-suma and Murase most definitely spoke some English, so there was no private language for us. My whole life I'd had Japanese to talk about secret things with Marlin and Dad. This felt like a gag, words building up in the back of my throat.

"You're okay?" Ken's face looked oddly alien upside down on my lap.

"It was like Thunderbird," I said. "I couldn't break free. But your forest, it grounded me, helped me funnel the Black Pearl's dreams around the core of myself..." I trailed off, aware of Pon-suma's eyes watching us in the rearview mirror.

Ken blinked very slowly, and strength drained from his features, as if he was finally letting go of urgency. He was slack, exposed. "This wasn't how it was supposed to go. I knew you were strong," he whispered. "Your ability to take power from a waking dreamer, it caught me off guard. So deep, so quickly. But you're fine. You came back."

He let a finger hover over my wrist tentatively. Asking permission for touch. His ability to touch me without forcing weird fragments on me was part of our growing intimacy. I got flashes of his forest, but I'd dreamed them so many times, they were almost my own. I gave him a nod letting him know the touch was okay. Nothing would transfer anyway, most likely. I was burned out.

I'd hurt him by drawing on his forest dream to break free of the Black Pearl. Is that why he didn't want me to touch him in the cave? I pushed damp hair from his brow, and he turned into the caress, lips brushing my palm. *Not afraid now.*

"You have explaining to do," I said sternly, but couldn't stop the answering ache rising from inside me. Out of the Black Pearl's cave, Ken's inner nuclear reactor was back in business radiating that delicious body heat. Even hurt and helpless in my arms, his eyes, irises wide and pupils spilling over into the whites, made twin slashes of primal dark that speared right through me.

"Don't let Murase-san or the Council bully you into anything more tonight."

"I'm more afraid of what you can make me do," I whispered.

Ken's brows furrowed deeply. "Yes, there is that."

That broke the spell of his eyes. I gave him a light smack. We were pulling into the museum's circular drive. The bumpy ride over uneven concrete made Ken close his eyes and gasp in pain.

Midori held the front door open. Pon-suma and Murase lifted Ken from the car, leaving behind an empty, cold feeling on the front of my body. I followed after them back into the tatami kitchen room. Midori had them lay Ken out on a low table where she'd already arranged a bewildering array of first aid bandages, iodine, splints, sprays, tubes, and syringes.

"Your text said broken legs?" said Midori.

"The Black Pearl," said Pon-suma.

Murase looked grim. "He shouldn't be this hurt."

"Yukiko-sama's freezing of the Black Pearl's cave drains energy as well," said Midori in a lecturing tone. Then in a softer, more worried voice, "you've lost a lot of blood, young man."

Ken closed his eyes again, skin pale and clammy. Midori turned on Murase. "Where is Ben?"

"She's coming with the Siwash Tyee."

I have to ask Kwaskwi what Siwash Tyee means. Later.

Pon-suma picked up one of Ken's hands and held it out to Midori. "Blue-tinged fingertips."

"He's at risk for hypovolemic shock."

"What's wrong with him?" My question came out a bit hysterically high-pitched; I couldn't seem to get a handle on the inner pressure of the dreams I'd eaten. I needed to go punch something or someone.

"Midori-san and Pon-suma-san are trained nurses. Ken will be okay."

"You're not O positive, are you?" Midori asked me.

I shook my head mutely. Ken needed the hospital if he was so messed up! Why were they all just standing around staring down at him? He was going to die! And they were all a bunch of heartless, manipulating *creatures* who couldn't be trusted. They didn't care Ken was literally fading in front of them!

"Koi," said a voice suddenly behind me. Startled, I swung around, all my worry and fear and the restless energy I'd taken from the Black Pearl's dream surging through me in a black roar of emotion that ended with my fist flying out in a punch. It connected to the middle of Ben's face.

Ben went flying across the tatami. "Fuck!"

"Language," said Midori.

"She punched me! On the same eye Ken did."

My knuckles throbbed. I tried to make my angry face into one of apology. Midori bustled over to help Ben stand up, and then took her by the elbow. "Ken needs a transfusion. Go wash your hands and arms in the sink with antibacterial soap."

"Silver cannula?" said Pon-suma. Midori gave a brisk nod, and then the two began breaking open antiseptic bottles, surgical tape, and other implements of torture.

Kwaskwi approached from the door with his hands held up in the air. "Don't attack. Innocent bystander, here."

I gave him the Marlin death-glare.

"Koi. You're reacting from eating the Black Pearl's dreaming. Do something with the energy, walk it off." Ken's quiet voice pulled me back to him. I reached for his hand, still hanging over the side of the table where Pon-suma had abandoned it.

Ken opened his eyes. "Go with Kwaskwi. I'll be fine. Ben and Midori won't let anything happen to me."

He didn't include Murase in that. I put my hands safely behind my back. "I can handle it."

"If you're leaving, leave," said Midori. She was all gloved up holding a syringe filled with a clear liquid. Pon-suma slipped a large needle into a vein in Ben's hand while pushing me aside with his bony hip.

"What, I'm free to go now?"

Pon-suma gave me an irritated look.

"We could go hit a bakery and get you some curry bread or chocolate croissants," said Kwaskwi. "They might have mochas."

My mouth filled with saliva. But no. No running away from this mess. Not even for a mocha. I shook my head.

Murase gestured over to the other table. "Let's sit, then. We should discuss what happened."

No shit, Sherlock.

Kwaskwi settled down next to me on the tatami while Murase fetched a small, traditional, long-handled *kyuusu* and looseleaf tea from the kitchenette. He poured water over the leaves from an electric hotpot and then set out a different set of tea cups of fine, green porcelain. The one nearest to me had a thin web of cracks in the side that had been plastered with a shiny, gold substance.

"We're not the enemy," Murase said.

Kwaskwi gave a laughing scoff.

"You kidnapped me and put me in a freezing cave with a giant dragon."

"I don't think she appreciates your flavor of friendship," said Kwaskwi.

I punched him in the shoulder, making his chains rattle. "You also kidnapped and tried to force me into Thunderbird's thrall when we first met."

"True," said Kwaskwi, utterly non-plussed. He turned to Murase. "So there's hope for you yet."

I punched him again.

"My eldest interrupted at an inopportune moment."

"Wait, your *eldest*?" I repeated.

"That's an interesting wrinkle," added Kwaskwi.

Murase stiffened, giving a little nod. Murase was Ben and Ken's father? He was full Kitsune, then. I glanced to where Pon-suma and Midori were finishing up binding a splint along Ken's left leg while Ben sat quietly on a chair tethered by a tube to her brother's inner elbow. Ken's face showed a glazed, relieved expression. That syringe must have contained some bomb-ass pain killers.

Dad came walking slowly and stiffly into the room, the left side of his face creased with sleep but his eyes clear.

"Dad," I said, pulling a few more *zabuton* cushions over next to me. "You're awake." And lucid. He nodded in response, eyes flickering over my torso and face.

Murase offered Dad tea in the gold-webbed cup with precise movements redolent of ceremony. Dad received it in both hands and bent over, bathing his face in the fragrant steam. "This cup is cracked and repaired, different from its brothers—it wears its unique history. Now it is more beautiful because it was broken."

Was Dad having one of his confused spells? But he seemed so

himself right now. Tired, yes, but inhabiting his body with the military posture he was known for before Alzheimer's, or actually the fog that came from refusing to eat dreams.

"If only we all wore our histories so visibly," said Murase.

"You already know I am broken, don't make the mistake of thinking it has made me weak. If you take her to the Black Pearl again, you will make me your enemy."

Something warmed inside me at the strength in Dad's voice. He was almost the gruff Master Sushi maker behind Marinopolis' busy sushi counter again—doling out commands to be acted upon at once or else. Murase stiffened, his face as grim as Dad's. "We are organized far beyond what you remember, Herai-san."

It was a threat coated in formal calm, and the hairs on the back of my arms stood to attention.

"Your family has done enough damage," said Dad. "Don't embroil Koi further in your politics."

"You brought the Black Pearl here," said Murase. "You gave the Council access to its dreaming. Your family created these *politics*."

"No longer," said Dad gravely. "I came back for my daughter, not to continue this travesty of what they call *survival*."

Funny, I thought we were here to cure his Alzheimer's dementia. What did he mean for me? It wasn't me with the massive problems. Okay, some problems. But I was well on my way to my accounting degree and getting my life in order when *his* secret Baku past caught up with me.

"We strive not at cross-purposes, old friend," said Murase.

Uh-oh. Breaking out the overly dramatic and formal Kind-speak meant things most likely were going to hit the fan. I sat up, trying to simultaneously weigh the meaning of Midori and Pon-suma's fierce whispers behind us.

"I turned my back on the Council and its domineering, narrow-sighted machinations."

"We are not the Council."

"Then why do you engage in the same underhanded arbitrary strategies?"

Living with Dad had equipped me well for discerning Japanese-old-man seething under a calm exterior. Murase hadn't moved, not a blink, in the past minute. Under Dad's scorn he was frozen as a statue, holding back a great rage.

I wasn't the only one who noticed. Midori came over, removing latex gloves streaked with Ken's blood, and put a hand over Murase's clenched fist.

"Forgive our ignorance and foolishness, Herai-san. We regret placing your daughter in danger."

"We are all in danger," grumbled Murase under his breath.

Kwaskwi pulled a steamed cheese-bread out of his pocket like a magician with a rabbit. "Well, you Eight Span Mirror folks are definitely in for it. Ken and I were only the vanguard." He ripped open the plastic and set the cheese-bread on the table, giving me a sly sideways look like he was daring me to take it.

Midori exchanged a worried moment of wordless communication with Murase. An instant later she unhooked Ben from the makeshift transfusion. Pon-suma slapped a Band-Aid on her hand.

"What?" said Ben.

"The Council is coming," said Ken. He yawned, eyelids slowly lowering over feral slits of darkness, a full Kitsune face.

"Go now," said Midori. She ripped off her gloves and pushed Pon-suma between the shoulder blades.

Kwaskwi stood, stretching nonchalantly, but he wasn't fooling anybody. He was preparing for a scuffle. I nabbed the abandoned cheese-bread. Kwaskwi didn't react at all. His focus was solely on Pon-suma.

"Not running," said Pon-suma.

"Tojo can't find you here," said Midori.

"I'm not afraid of the Kappa or the Snow Woman," said Murase gruffly. "We stand our ground."

Kappa? Seriously? Kawano was a half-froggy river sprite?

Midori knelt again next to him. "We lost our gamble they would only send the Bringer to retrieve the Baku, but we pledged no direct confrontation. If Kawano-san and Yukiko-san come here, they will have no choice but to punish our challenge to their authority. At least for the kidnapping."

"Not if there was no kidnapping," said Kwaskwi.

A bit of cheese-bread went down my windpipe. A coughing fit overtook me until Kwaskwi leaned over and thumped me on the back, hard.

"Hey!"

"You're interrupting the criminal strategizing."

"Dad?" He'd kept silent, but the set of his mouth and the glint in his eyes told me he was deeply unhappy. "Do you trust them?" I didn't know if I meant The Eight Span Mirror or the Council.

"Give me your word you will not ask Koi to touch the Black Pearl again and we will lie for you," he said quietly. "I brought Koi here to show her my hometown."

It was hard to remember that this was actually Dad's hometown, like a hundred years ago. "Are you sure?"

"Keeping you ignorant of Kind all these years, of what it means to be Baku, was a mistake. I thought I could protect you. Keep you from my troubles."

And I ended up a socially awkward hermit afraid I was schizo.

"Isolation isn't the right answer for the Council or for *Hafu*," said Murase. "That is why The Eight needs you, Herai-san."

"This is why you need them, Koi-chan," Dad echoed.

"We are your people," said Ben. "We'll help you."

"Unless the Black Pearl drives you bat-shit first," said Kwaskwi.

"And you," I asked softly, letting Dad's familiar care-worn face block all the rest. "Where are your people?"

Dad stared straight back, challenge and sadness tangled in his words. "Gone. They're all gone."

CHAPTER TEN

Ben and I, designated most harmless in appearance to Ben's obvious disgruntlement, were dispatched to the front hall of the museum to await the Council's arrival. We were to sit around a metal bistro table drinking more tea and nibbling on crustless cucumber-and-cream cheese sandwiches Midori had hastily whipped together.

Midori argued that if the Council saw me and my erstwhile kidnapper just hanging out, they wouldn't come in guns blazing. She and a belligerent Pon-suma watched over Ken in the backroom where Dad and Murase still traded calm, deadly-sharp barbs about The Eight's goals, ready to provide backup if things went pear shaped. Kwaskwi flitted back and forth between the groups, ferrying updates and napkins.

"Herai-san is right, you know." Ben grinned around a mouthful of sandwich. "You need us."

"Please," I snorted.

"I can't imagine growing up without knowing what you are. It's hard enough growing up *Hafu* and knowing both sides."

Silly girl doesn't know the Hafu of it. Try growing up mixed race-wise as well as mythological creature-wise. "You and Ken are half-human, right? And Murase's your father?"

Ben nodded. "But Midori isn't our biological mother, obviously. She's father's second wife. My mother passed away a long time ago." Sadness was in her voice, but only the echo of a once-sharp grief, now a familiar companion.

"Oh, I'm sorry."

Murase and Midori are together? That makes sense. A Kitsune genealogy chart appeared in my brain. Murase and Midori at the top with Ben and Ken as their children.

"Don't be. She had a full, human life."

Human life. How long ago was she talking about?

Kind lived longer. Did that mean Ben and Ken outlived their mother by decades?

I thought of the vision Ken had given me back in Tokyo. His mother had been wearing a quilted kimono jacket, no electric lights, holding a dying man on a cobblestone street. Definitely pre-World War II. So how old was Ken? He was more experienced relationship-wise than me, of course. But *how* experienced? Like was he hundreds of girlfriends experienced?

Something tightened in my chest. *And what about Marlin?* She was completely human, at least I thought so since she didn't grow up flinching from casual touch. But she was Dad's daughter, too, so she was at least *Hafu.* My chest tightened at the thought of Marlin not getting any Kind genes at all—outliving her by decades was unthinkable.

Kwaskwi sauntered in with a plate of apple slices cut so that the divided red peel on one end stuck up like rabbit ears. "So," he said to Ben, overly casual. "Talk to me about Pon-suma-san. Think you could ship us?"

Ben put down the last sandwich. "You want to hook up with the white wolf?"

Kwaskwi gave his trademarked big-toothed grin, but for the first time, a hint of boyish hopefulness peeked through the arrogance. "He has a partner already?"

"Ah...no... He's a *wolf of the North*." Ben paused, waiting for that to sink in. "He may be *Hafu* like the rest of us Eight Span Mirror, but his human people have been gone as long as my Mongolian ancestors have been in Japan."

"Nice," said Kwaskwi. "I can work the indigenous connection."

Ben shut her mouth like she'd suddenly realized she was handing Pon-suma over on a silver platter to a seasoned player.

"What happened with the Black Pearl?" said Kwaskwi, clearly changing tack. He pulled up a metal-wrought bistro chair, flipping it around and resting his crossed arms on the back. "Can you set it free?"

"I don't know," I said. "She's very strong, but not exactly awake. She doesn't seem to understand where she is. At least Ullikemi wanted my help."

"Murase-san promised not to ask Koi-san to touch the Black Pearl again," said Ben. "And the Council won't want her near it until they can confirm her loyalty."

"Why do you care?" I asked.

"You know me," said Kwaskwi, producing a tall stalk of something like pampas grass from under the heavy fall of black hair over one ear. He stuck it between his teeth, the very picture of a country hick. "Always looking for an angle."

Ben stood up, hands gripping the metal edge of the table. "They're here."

"You should probably sit back down," Kwaskwi drawled. "Aren't we all supposed to be friends on a sight-seeing tour?"

Ben sat down and picked up her abandoned sandwich. My mouth was dry, but my cup of tea was empty.

The museum door slammed open with a bang. Three wiry young guys dressed in black suits and gray ties strode in and took up wide-legged stances in a defensive triangle formation. Their faces had that sharp, feral quality I associated with Ken's Kitsune face. For an instant, I flashed back to Narita and Red Shirt. But none of them looked familiar. As soon as the lead black suit set eyes on me, he touched a hand to his ear and began muttering rapidly into a mic.

Bald Monk, who was actually Kawano the Kappa, and Tojo came in followed by Yukiko gliding behind like a ghostly snow queen.

"Fujiwara Kennosuke," demanded Kawano as if Ken were actually standing there instead of the three of us, "what have you allowed The Eight Span Mirror to do?"

Ben stood up again, but Kwaskwi tugged her back down one-armed, still leaning casually on the back of the chair. "Late to the party again, Kawano-san?"

Tojo ignored Kwaskwi, striding over to Ben and gripping her collar in both hands. He jerked her from the seat, twisting the collar so Ben's airway was painfully constricted. "You have gone too far. You've crossed Kawano-san's line."

Kawano was silent and still. Waiting for Ken to magically appear and explain? He was utterly unperturbed witnessing Tojo manhandling Ben.

Ben took on the feral Kitsune face, and the guards all tensed. She arched back, tendons straining in her neck, and then smashed her head into the bridge of Tojo's nose.

Tojo released her with a grunt.

I stifled a cheer. Tojo really was a jerk.

Ben stared defiantly as Tojo put a hand to his nose. "We can't stand idle and let a group of old fools decide the fate of our Kind."

"Kind?" Tojo spat, a trickle of blood forming on his upper lip. "I'll show you *Hafu* what an old fool can do."

Flames burst into roaring life around Tojo's shoulders, arcing into a fiercely burning aura like he was an ancient statue of Amida Buddha on his throne. He grabbed Ben again and the flames traveled onto Ben's arms where they *burned.*

Ben flung herself away, rolling on the floor and moaning as the sickening smell of charred flesh filled the room. I shrugged off my cardigan and began swatting the flames.

"Enough," said Kawano.

Tojo grimaced and the flames completely disappeared.

Ben fended off my cardigan. "I'm okay, stop!" She pulled at her shirt, popping off buttons to reveal a black sports bra, but there wasn't a mark on Ben's chest. Her neck and arms were smooth and untouched.

Illusion? That was a hella stronger illusion than I'd ever seen Ken use—I'd smelled the burning and felt the heat from the flames. Tojo wasn't *Hafu*. I was realizing that might mean Ken's face illusions were a limited version of what a full Kitsune could do.

What the hell have I gotten myself into?

The noise we'd made had summoned the reinforcements. Murase stood in the hall, dignified and grave. He conveyed deference in the slight arch of his neck, but not a drop of fear.

"Kawano-san," said Murase. He bowed to Tojo and Yukiko as well. "You are joining Herai Akihito on our tour of his hometown?"

Tojo gave an exasperated huff. The three black suit flunkies hurried to form a triangle behind him. From his diminutive height, Tojo sneered down his nose at us as if we were a pack of filthy children caught with hands in the cookie jar.

"You kidnapped the Baku. Produce him and the Bringer now," said Kawano.

Kwaskwi jabbed me hard in the ribs. "Kidnapped?" I said, voice breaking in the middle of the word. "Dad decided he wanted to show me around Herai-mura."

Yukiko glided closer to Murase, pinning him with a cold stare. He cleared his throat, and gave way a bit. "Herai-san is in the back room." Yukiko exchanged a nod with Kawano and then glided down the hall toward the back room.

Kawano waved his hand at the whole room. "The Eight Span Mirror courts war," he said. "The Black Pearl was endangered. You used Herai Akihito-san."

"It was me." The words burst out. "Dad told me about the Black Pearl and I was so curious. I didn't mean to upset anyone."

Tojo folded his arms. "More lies."

Kawano held up his hand in a quelling motion. "You tried to eat its dream?"

"I'm not sure what happened. The Black Pearl's dreams were very powerful. I became a bit...stuck. Then Ken came and unstuck me."

"And bagged two broken legs in thanks," Kwaskwi added.

"The Bringer is injured?" Tojo sounded more miffed about the possible inconvenience than concerned. *I don't think I like this guy.*

"Midori is taking care of him. He's in the back room, too."

One of the guards stiffened. Another one shot a worried look at Ben and Murase, who had at some point moved to flank Kwaskwi and me. Five against four in this room, and the guards were worried about an injured Ken appearing?

Kawano considered each of us in turn, disapproving of Ben and Murase, but blank for me. He settled on Kwaskwi. "Your stake in this is unclear, Siwash Tyee. Will you interfere with the Council's right to retrieve Herai Akihito?"

Should I be irked or relieved that I am not valuable enough for his notice?

Kwaskwi flicked away his piece of pampas grass. Somehow it landed on Tojo's shiny, leather shoe. "Why would I jeopardize our mutually beneficial relationship?" The lazy, sarcastic tone made a muscle in Tojo's cheek twitch. "But maybe one of you should ask *her* that question," he said, jerking a thumb in my direction.

"I, I don't know if Dad's tour was over," I stuttered. I really, really didn't want to go anywhere with the black suit guards or Tojo. We weren't fooling anybody with this cover story, but for diplomatic reasons of their own Tojo and Kawano were playing along.

"The American Herai are welcome here as long they wish to visit," said Murase, folding his arms behind his back. "Our agreement still stands. The Eight Span Mirror will keep watch over the Black Pearl without directly challenging the Council's decision to keep her in Herai-mura."

What does he call all that "release the Black Pearl" crap he threw at me?

Tojo was obviously fully aware of Murase's sketchiness—for a short guy, he could certainly suck in all the air and attention in a room, standing there red-faced with arms crossed. "How long will you allow this?" he said in a low voice pitched to be heard by the entire room.

Kawano ignored him. "Our agreement is unchanged, but it does not include the Baku or the Bringer. We will take them back to Tokyo now."

Murase shook his head slowly. "It would be rude to drag Herai-san and his daughter away."

"This is not a negotiation. The Bringer is ours, and we require the Baku as a gesture of good faith."

"Strange how the quality that makes the Bringer valuable to the Council is one you ignore in the rest of us," said Ben. She had readjusted her clothing, but restlessness spilled off her like heat from a motor engine.

Kwaskwi's smile broadened and he leaned back in his chair, clearly amused by the verbal tussling. Of course, he had all the background context for this political dingleberry. I did not.

The black suits were shifting around and Tojo's frown grew fierce.

I am the Bringer. I bring Death. Ken's anguish when he talked of what he was capable of back in Portland, that he could take Kind life though it was anathema to all Kind, had been real. But Ben implied all *Hafu* could kill. That gave a different sheen of power to The Eight Span Mirror.

"And Koi's got it, too," said Kwaskwi, making a show of plopping down into the chair opposite of Kawano and resting backwards, hands clasped at the back of his neck. "Bet nobody put that together yet."

No wonder Kwaskwi was tickled. Tojo's pure Kitsune illusion was just a party trick. A painful party trick, true, but making someone think they were burning to death if that person could stab you in the chest for realsies was still just a trick. *Hafu* were dangerous.

"I want to stay here," I said. "I don't think Dad will go with you, either."

"He must!" said Tojo.

"We will formally request his presence," said Kawano. He jerked his chin at the front door, and the three young black suits hurried out, looking relieved. "A gesture of good faith."

Murase bowed in acknowledgement.

He stood up, clearly expecting us to lead him to Dad.

Kwaskwi couldn't contain his glee. "Oh, please, let's all go see Herai-san." He stood up and strode down the hallway whistling.

The back room felt stifling and over-stuffed with ego, self-importance, and cranky men by the time we all filed in, crowding around the low tea table where Dad still sat with his tea. It steamed, untouched, in front of him. Yukiko sat motionless beside him, eyelids at half-mast, her hand on Dad's shoulder. Ken, Pon-suma, and Midori made a startled tableau on the other side of the room.

Ken tried to sit up, supported on one side by Pon-suma. Kwaskwi's sudden look of concern was comical, and he made his way swiftly over. Propping up Ken's other side apparently involved a lot of touching Pon-suma's arm and hand. The white wolf of the North gave an exasperated huff of breath and then began an implacable, relentless stare on Tojo. He really didn't seem to like Tojo at all.

He's not the only one.

I knelt at Dad's side. "Dad?" His neck, stiff as clockwork, swiveled my direction.

"It's okay, Koi-chan. Yukiko-sama's cold makes the dreams sluggish and dim."

Murase, Ben, Kawano, and Midori joined us at the table in a

flurry of rearranged *zabuton*. Tojo remained standing behind Kawano, arms still folded, an angry guardian deity.

"Herai-san," said Kawano. "You have seen the Black Pearl?"

Asshole. I told him it was me. Apparently I was not to be trusted.

"No," said Dad, yawning. "I wish to stay far away. That is why I left Japan."

"Then it is time to return to Tokyo. I know how proximity to the Black Pearl pains you."

"Not yet." Dad drooped forward over the table, catching his head in his hands. "Listen to Murase-san. It's time to consider releasing the Black Pearl."

Tojo made a disgusted sound. "Nothing has changed. Our numbers shrink each year. Only those living close to the Black Pearl here in the Kanto region have pure-blood children."

"The Eight Span Mirror have children in every prefecture," said Midori.

Tojo kissed his teeth in displeasure. "*Hafu* breeding like rabbits will not save the Kind."

"I was in Nagasaki," said Kawano in a tone that held actual weight and heft. All eyes went to him, including Pon-suma and Ken from across the room. Even Kwaskwi turned uncharacteristically serious. We were all glued to his words. "No one believed what the Americans had done at Hiroshima, details traveled too slowly. The stories that it was gone, just smoke and wreckage, were insane." He looked at Murase. "I survived because I was on the Uragami riverbank when the air raid siren went off. We'd been bombed so many times before, it was instinct to submerge in the river."

No one moved. I felt a squirming awkwardness. Dad tied me to Japan, but I was American. It always birthed a weird mess of conflicting butterflies hearing about World War II atrocities no matter whose side was the villain, but Kawano wasn't done. "I came up near a bridge. There were dead people with blackened skin. As we walked out of the city, some came to us asking for a drink of water.

They were bleeding from their faces and mouths, and they had glass sticking in their bodies."

"No *Hafu* or Kind are born in or around Hiroshima or Nagasaki," said Murase quietly. He drew in a shuddering breath, the weight of the world on his shoulders. "And Fukushima is starting to experience the same thing since the tsunami damaged the nuclear power plant."

"The Black Pearl is waking up," said Dad in a sleepy voice. His eyelids were at half-mast again, but not fogged with dementia. Ever since we'd arrived in Herai-mura he'd been lucid.

"We have been without a Baku for too long," said Tojo. "We have no way to keep the Black Pearl here without a Baku to soothe its restless dreams."

"North Korea has nuclear weapons, but doesn't want to anger China. China won't risk North Korea destroying the Black Pearl. Without her here as insurance," Kawano spread his hands and shrugged, an oddly American-looking gesture, "the Council doesn't have the power to control the Pacific Basin, let alone our own country."

"Would that really be so awful?" said Ben.

"Shush." Midori made a chopping movement in the air.

"We need you, Herai-san," said Kawano. "We need you back where you belong, here, with your own Kind. With you in control of the Black Pearl, we could heal Fukushima before even more babies go unborn."

"My own Kind?" Dad had turned pale, a sheen of clammy sweat across his brow. Yukiko withdrew her hand, resting it gracefully on her folded knees. She was regal and untouched by Kawano's emotional stew, a storybook noblewoman from one of Dad's historical dramas.

Dad's hand shook, the contents of his tea cup dangerously close to spilling over. "Tojo Hideki, Yamada Otozo, Ishii Shiro-sensei with his experiments in the war. You sent all the Baku and Tengu to Manchukuo and the Philippines and used us all up. Grabbing land

and power. For Japan's *peace* and *co-prosperity*. And now all you have left of our hubris is the Black Pearl. Can't keep her much longer with just Yukiko-sama's power. What will you do, Kawano-sama? Yukiko-sama, you and myself: we are the only ones left in Japan with power that is more than illusion."

"Hmmm, that's not actually true," said Ken in a groggy voice. Startled, we all looked over to where he drooped between Kwaskwi and coldly furious Pon-suma. "Now we have Koi-chan, too."

CHAPTER ELEVEN

Kawano, Tojo, and the black-suit boys left to find a *minshuku* hotel to stay overnight, after ridiculously overly-formal Kind speak promising no one would mysteriously disappear or mess with the Black Pearl. At one point Tojo seemed about to pull out a knife and demand a blood-promise. Not that he needed one in order to keep me away from the Black Pearl.

Yukiko and Dad would not be persuaded away from their endless cups of green tea at the table. Dad was half-comatose anyway, but Midori and Murase, and more importantly to me, Pon-suma, obviously trusted her enough that after the others left they didn't hold back an explosion of heated arguing right in front of her.

Uncomfortable with any role The Eight Span Mirror was trying to force me into, I scooted away from the table toward where Pon-suma and Kwaskwi had abandoned Ken on a pile of *zabuton*. He lay there quietly. I thought him asleep, his chest rising in a slow even rhythm, his legs bulky from the splints underneath a knitted afghan. I slipped my hand down in my cardigan sleeve and put it to his forehead, relieved to find no evidence of fever. Ken's eyes popped open.

"No, don't," he said when I pulled my hand away. "You smell so good." *Okay, now I know he is delirious.* I was pretty sure I smelled like sweaty gym socks. I was starving, and so far beyond exhausted that gray static hovered at the corners of my vision. But Ken captured my hand and placed it over his heart, sighing peacefully, and closing his eyes again.

"Why did you bring me here?" I asked, softly.

Eyes still closed, Ken's mouth, the generous lower lip looking even puffier than usual after his battering, pursed in thought. "To fix things. For your father. For you to learn about being Baku."

Midori's drugs were making him drop his guard. Was it taking advantage if I dug deeper to get to the truth? I thought of how he'd given my name to the Council, how he'd seemed so reserved since we came to Japan.

Fuck it. I was on shaky ground, and so far Kwaskwi was the only one who was still solidly Team America. I needed every advantage I could get. "No, Ken, that's not the truth," I said gently, brushing stray strands of the thick, slightly wavy hair through my knuckles he usually had moussed up into trendy spikes at the top of his head— not something I could ever do if he were all the way awake. Not only because I wasn't touchy-feely, but because reaching out for Ken felt too much like an open admission of how much I enjoyed touching him. "Because the Council told you to?"

"The Council doesn't know about you." *Okay, so maybe Ken's brain is actually still caramelized.* The Council definitely knew about me now.

"Why not just bring Dad, why me, too?"

Ken turned his head away from me, the pressure on my hand lighter. He was going to sleep. "Because," he said in barely audible English, "I can't let you go. You can make everything better." He went limp, and something fluttered from his other hand. A small scrap of paper. A white mountain with a crudely drawn fish and the word Herai. Ken had found my stupid rest-stop clue after all and carried it all the way here.

God damn it. I swallowed back a torrent of confused words stewing in the back of my dry throat. *This boy!* His chest was warm against my palm, and though the pressure of those octave-spanning, strong fingers no longer bound it there, the force of that confession was a steel band.

Starry-eyed ingénue, I was not. Maladjusted, sometimes morbidly paranoid, yes, but also painfully self-aware. A side effect of growing up with no defenses against other people's psyches invading your own through dreams. I distanced myself from anyone but Marlin and Mom, but that didn't mean I wasn't aware of what normal looked like. Now that comfy isolation was a fatal flaw—anyone who managed to get past my defenses loomed larger than life.

He's using you, said Survivalist Koi.

But he doesn't want to leave you, whispered the girl whose heart pumped fervent blood, growing too tender, too large for its flesh and bone cage.

Wanting to trust Ken, no *aching* to trust Ken, and being able to trust Ken were different things. Kissing him felt like a refuge, a safe, breathing place for me to touch and feel without guarding against invasive fragments. His forest fragment was so innocent, so familiar that it had *refuge* flags planted all around it in my head. But had Mangasar Hayk's murder-dreams scared me into blindly trusting the first guy who came around with peaceful forest dreams, dreamy, moka-roast eyes, and an unbearably sly arched eyebrow?

Survivalist Koi spun Ken's protection not as caring, but self-interest. Ken was keeping his assets close. We Herai Baku were obviously valuable to both The Eight and the Council—and I didn't like how that made me a pawn.

Only Marlin gets to manipulate me. She'd earned the right by putting up with me all these years. I was definitely not going to melt into googly-eyed mush just because half-baked Ken said he *couldn't let me go.* If he was super old like Dad, then maybe he'd used that line a hundred times.

I disengaged my hand from Ken's chest and stretched out my aching legs. Sitting *seiza* was definitely painful on the knees, even with the *zabuton* cushion bunched up under my butt like Kwaskwi did.

A cold draft wafted down my spine and I looked up to find Yukiko sitting next to me, waiting patiently for me to meet her gaze. I flinched. Her eyes were the transparent blue of compressed glacial ice. "Oh, hello," I said, blushing.

Outside distant thunder rumbled, and the hushed murmur of a spring rain shower gathered across the museum's ceramic tiled roof.

Yukiko nodded slightly, raising both elegantly plucked albino eyebrows. *Asking me what I am doing?* She hadn't ever spoken a word in my presence. Non-verbal communication wasn't my strong suit.

"Ken seems fine. He's a little foggy from the drugs, but resting peacefully," I told her.

Yukiko shook her head, lips slightly pursed in disappointment. "Thank you for…for taking care of Dad. He seems peaceful, too." The glacial eyes unwaveringly pinned me in place, making me uncomfortably aware I was missing something important.

"…we gave our word," Murase was saying loudly at the table. "It can't be *Hafu* that break the peace."

"Why not?" Ben jumped up with fists clenched at her sides. "We've tried following the Council's rules, and it's only gotten us meaningless meetings. All the while the Black Pearl suffers. It's not right."

"It's kept us alive." Midori reached out, but Ben shook her off. With a determined glance my direction, she stalked off, muttering.

"Kids these days, what are ya gonna do?" said Kwaskwi in English.

I sighed. Yukiko's motionless silence was more than I could bear. Her waiting tugged and pulled at me, like the nagging frustration of trying to recall a fabulous dream after being startled awake. I was desperately close to babbling nonsense out loud just to fill the void.

She stretched out her hand, palm up.

"I d-don't think that's a good idea, actually," I stuttered. *No way in hell. Frozen fragments are not on the menu today.* Shivers whispered down my spine.

Yukiko looked down the line of her aquiline nose, daring me to touch her. I wasn't going to fall for that. I had nothing to prove. I'd survived Hayk and Ullikemi and the Black Pearl. I just wasn't in the mood for mental frostbite.

Thunder cracked directly overhead, startling me into a flinch. Kwaskwi spared me a sideways smirk, but Murase, Midori, and Ponsuma didn't pause their intense argument.

"Excuse me, but I think I'm going to go interrupt the huddle over there. I'm literally starving and—"

Yukiko, quick as lightning, darted forward on her knees, capturing my head between two ice-cold hands and pressing her forehead to mine. She breathed out a chill mist that obscured the air, enshrouding us in a blanket of hushed cold.

My heart seized painfully like I'd jumped in the water at Cannon Beach in February. Then, with enormous effort, it began beating again, but slowly, ever so slowly. Sounds came through distorted, Murase's voice impossibly deep like James Earl Jones, and the Sanrio Kerropi frog character clock on the wall ticking out the seconds at a sonorous, geriatric pace.

The transition to Yukiko's dream was unlike any I'd experienced before. No, spinning, no jerk. Just a slow fade to white. The thunder, heartbeats and clock sounded further and further away as if I were moving through a long tunnel. Kind dreams were vivid, and the white was unbearably so, but there was no way to squint or close my eyes. Slowly, the quality of the white resolved into a million specks of frost, widening, spreading into the most beautiful, intricate laced patterns. Lace-frost spread into my peripheral vision, and I found I was able to turn my head. My exhalations left my body and became crystalline beauty, adding to the pattern.

Quiet. And still. Between one heartbeat and the next, everything stopped. No fear, no worry, just...silence. And beauty.

And then the frost cracked, ugly jagged breaks that felt like the edge of a knife trailed down my skin. The cracks widened, and yellow sun shone through, melting it further. My breath came in huffs, too fast, my hands uselessly clutching at melting patterns in the air.

A long, low moan rent the whiteness, catching it in a grip of pain, squeezing the air from my body, and smashing me down to the earth. I raised my head to find myself on my knees next to a mound of grass-covered dirt. *No cross, no white picket fence, but this is the Black Pearl's prison.*

The moan came again, not heard, but a dark vibration felt through my knees and palms pressed to the earth. I lifted my head, long white hair swinging over my face, and stood. There was a door, I knew this, and a staircase, and at the bottom a creature in terrible agony—a wrongness that made my teeth ache—unraveling the pure beauty and stillness of the frost patterns in my boundless white.

I found the first door, opened it, glided down the stairs, and opened the door at the bottom. A horrible, awful stench assaulted me, but I surged forward. A clean-cut Baku in military uniform stood, arms in a wrestler's grip around the neck of an old one, a dragon, born of earth and water far from the islands. Foreign. The dragon thrashed, but the Baku drained it, consuming its ambient magic, and it *hurt*.

This is Yukiko's dream-memory. It was Dad, eating the Black Pearl's waking dream—consuming the kernel-self power of the dragon. I didn't want to experience this. *Enough! I get it!*

I was done being forced. Reaching for the Koi part of myself that still burned steadily deep within my belly, I coaxed the flame into a short-lived spurting flare. *Burn.* The flame eagerly consumed Yukiko's dream. As soon as I felt the icy agony being drawn into me, the world spun on its axis, the white disappeared, and I was lying on tatami next to Ken, staring up into Midori's worried face.

"Are you okay?"

No. Not okay. Very far from okay, thank you very much. I tried to sit up, and instantly wished I'd kept one of the airplane sick bags.

"What were you trying to do?" Midori demanded of Yukiko. She sat regally, hands on her folded knees, expression serene. Whether she meant to hurt or control me with that dream I didn't know, but I suspected it wasn't something she worried herself over. I'd gotten her message, though.

Yukiko was from the Council, but she pretty clearly felt the same way as The Eight about the Black Pearl. Her vision of Dad eating the Black Pearl's dream was suffused with a dark, treacly *wrongness*, which left a burnt espresso grittiness on my tongue. And it had hurt, as if that wrongness was the force disrupting the chill, peaceful beauty Yukiko carried within her.

Oh Dad. What did you do?

It hadn't really hit home yet that the Dad I knew from Portland when I was growing up was actually a reinvented man. I didn't want him to be the man from Yukiko's memory. It felt like betrayal. But how could I be angry at him for stuff he did before I was born? I had enough anger on my plate from him keeping me ignorant all these years, even if it was out of love.

"I think she's on your side," I said in a husky voice. Midori held out a glass of chilled *mugi-cha*, barley tea. I grimaced. Dirty dish water appealed to me more.

"She talked to you? You communicated with Yukiko-sama?"

"In a manner of speaking."

Murase came over and folded himself into a mirror of Yukiko's formal seiza. "You feel it, don't you? The Black Pearl has turned dark. Despairing."

Yukiko turned the glacial ice on Murase, and gave a long, slow nod.

"But what of Tojo and Kawano-san?"

Yukiko lazily blinked, and though I swore not a muscle moved in her face, when her eyes opened, her expression was of disdain.

"I don't think she's afraid of the Council," said Kwaskwi from the table, propping up his head on one fist.

"How can you be sure?" Murase asked of me. "Maybe you misunderstood."

"It tasted true," I said. "I think it was a memory-dream. I've never encountered a false memory-dream before."

"If you're willing to help us, that changes quite a lot," Murase said. Midori tried to urge the *mugi-cha* on me again, and I gave a little wave under my nose to signal no thanks.

"Isn't it almost dinner time?" said Kwaskwi. His fingers tapped a thoughtful tattoo on his skull.

Dinner time? No wonder my tummy feels sloshy and empty. I guess we skipped lunch. I sat up, relieved when the room stayed firmly still and the bit of energy from Yukiko's dream fizzed and popped along my limbs instead of creating a migraine.

Kwaskwi gave a slow grin. "Pon-suma should drive me into town to get some food for everyone. Then you'll have time to scheme."

Pon-suma did not look pleased by the idea, but Midori and Murase quickly gave instructions for a local supermarket that did dinner bento and handed him a sheaf of pink and blue yen notes from which dour bald men glowered.

After they left, Midori went to find Ben, leaving me with Murase, Yukiko, and my two comatose guys on the floor.

"Herai-san has to go back to Tokyo with the Council," said Murase. "Kawano-san and Tojo-san will not agree to anything less. And I admit I didn't realize the extent of Herai-san's deterioration. There are facilities in Tokyo that can better care for him."

Yukiko gave a slight dip of her chin.

"But if you could get them to leave Koi-chan here..." Murase trailed off.

Yukiko pointed her chin at Ken.

"The Bringer is a complication. Maybe we could keep him here as the Council's eyes and ears?"

This time she responded with an arched eyebrow.

"No, he's too weak, isn't he? Tojo won't allow it."

This is the weirdest war council. One-sided conversation didn't seem to faze Yukiko and Murase, but I was antsy. And tired. And hungry. "Look, I'm *Hafu*, but don't automatically assume I'll blindly follow your agenda. You kind of wrecked my goodwill by the kidnapping and tricking me into touching the Black Pearl."

Murase stiffened. "Surely you see now why that was necessary? We are at odds with the Council—forced to keep an ancient one imprisoned solely for their own moribund, blind goals. They care solely that Japan has the Black Pearl's power."

"And I care solely for Dad!" *Well, and Marlin. Maybe Ken.* But Murase and Yukiko didn't need to be all up in my romantic business. "You just said the Council can take better care of him!"

"You are one of us no matter what you feel, a mix of human and Kind. Growing up with that experience gives you the same empathy, the wider understanding of the beautiful diversity of the world and how it is changing, as *Hafu* born here."

Wrong. I am not the same.

Coming to Japan, embracing the Baku part of myself like Ken urged; this was somehow magically supposed to make me belong, integrate into a group, a family, I'd always been missing. The Kind. But I was realizing that I'd been naïve on several levels. The more the Kind's political cracks were revealed, the more I didn't quite fit with either The Eight Span Mirror or the Council. I'd grown up believing myself entirely human. Whatever *wider understanding* Murase referred to, I'm sure it wasn't this "I'm just a human girl with a side of psychotic break" thing I had going on.

"I'm not saying I won't try to help, just that I'm unclear about everything. You can't just pack Dad off to Tokyo with the Council. I will not be separated from him again."

"You have to stay here." Murase was getting quite agitated.

Yukiko's icy regard swiveled his direction. Pursing her lips, she gave him an obvious *chillax, dude* look.

Before I could try to explain my inner ball of tangled feelings again, Kwaskwi swept into the room with two plastic shopping bags bulging with square containers and a pouty expression I'd never seen before. "Come on, Koi, let's ditch this Popsicle stand."

CHAPTER TWELVE

"What's gotten your feathers in a twist?" I asked.

Pon-suma padded into the room, implacable as always, but decidedly *not* looking at Kwaskwi. Kwaskwi dumped his bags onto the table. A heavenly aroma comprised of equal parts something fried and something pickled wafted my direction.

"I've had enough of what passes for *hospitality* here," he snapped. "White Fang over there gave me the keys to the guest shack. Let's go eat somewhere not drenched in duty and honor and politics."

Was that a blush pinking Pon-suma's cheek? *No way.* Had Kwaskwi made some kind of stupid move and been rebuffed? I couldn't think of any other cause for the tetchiness. But I wasn't about to look a gift blue jay in the mouth. "I'm not leaving Dad and Ken here to their tender mercies."

Kwaskwi made an exasperated sound and threw his hands up in the air like Mom when she faced Dad's stubborn silence during an argument. He sauntered around the table, giving Yukiko a wide berth, and then bent over and slipped his arms under Ken's back and legs, lifting Ken as gently as if his tall frame weighed no more than a

Teddy Bear.

"Be careful!"

"He's out cold, feeling no pain. Don't fret."

"I can't carry Dad by myself."

Yukiko lifted a hand. Murase startled, but she rested it on my clothed shoulder. Even with the cotton barrier, a numbing sense of chill spread down my shoulder into my chest, slowing my heartbeat for a long, stretched-out moment. Murase cleared his throat, breaking the spell. "Yukiko will see that Herai-san rests until you and the Council return tomorrow morning."

I leaned over the table and Yukiko's hand fell away. I'd tasted her dream. She would protect Dad because he could help the Black Pearl. It was Murase I needed to be sure of. "Nothing disturbs Dad. If you want me on your side."

Murase nodded gravely. I knelt next to Dad fussing with the cotton towel covering him, making sure his pillow was plumped.

Kwaskwi made an impatient clucking noise and headed toward the door. Scared he was going to bash Ken's splinted legs on the door frame, I jumped up and wedged myself in between the frame and the boys.

"What about dinner?" I said in English, the consonants feeling oddly harsh in my mouth after so much time spent in Japanese.

"It's already at the guest shack."

"Should I be scared you keep calling it a shack?"

Kwaskwi gave his trademark wide grin, showing more front teeth than usual. I followed him out the main doors and onto a little path curling around the back of the museum leading into a thicket of towering cryptomeria, needles bristling ominously in the gathering twilight. Japanese beeches shivered and rustled beyond.

The Eight Span Mirror's guest shack was a hunched over, traditional cedar-beam and earthen-walled box, thatched with a steep roof mossy with neglect and likely housing a horde of mice and spiders.

"Seriously?"

"Oh, it gets better," said Kwaskwi maintaining that over-sized grin.

I skipped ahead to open the sliding outer door and help Kwaskwi wrangle the unconscious Kitsune inside. We found ourselves on a packed-earth genkan entrance with a built-in shoe cubby and a huge step up to the raised tatami mat floor of one big room. Kwaskwi started to lay Ken down.

"Whoa, not there." Toeing off my shoes, I hopped up onto the tatami and made a beeline for the sliding doors on the far side I guessed were hiding a closet. *Bingo.* Japanese style folded futons in a dyed-indigo pattern and fluffy, white comforters covered in clean-smelling cotton were neatly stacked inside the closet shelf. I lugged out a futon and spread it near the floor-inset charcoal brazier at the center of the room.

"Please tell me this isn't the kitchen," I said.

Kwaskwi carried Ken over. Only a slight gasp marked Ken's transition from arms to futon, but he did not lie peacefully. His breath came unevenly and his hands made jerky clenching movements. Midori's drugs were wearing off.

"Okay, I won't tell you the only way to heat water is the brazier. Or about the Japanese-style squatter toilet in the outhouse."

"Sure know how to butter up a girl," I said, settling down cross-legged at a low *kotatsu* table laden with more convenience store plastic bags. The heater slung underneath was sadly not turned on. I started rifling through the bags: convenience store pasta carbonara in a plastic tray, tonkatsu pork cutlet sandwiches with crusts removed, and konbu and pickled ume plum rice balls. No way was I going to fire up that charcoal for the pasta, so I snagged the sandwiches. The salty-sweet Bulldog sauce created a harmony of pork goodness in my mouth and the cutlet was soft as butter. The first bite woke up my stomach. I was ravenous.

Kwaskwi watched me gobble down the sandwiches. When I

reached for a pickled plum rice ball, he covered the pasta container with crossed arms. "Mine," he said. "But this," he held out his hand palm down, concealing something with his sleeve, "might make up for lack of a real toilet. Thank me later." He flipped his hand over.

My cell phone! "How did you…?"

"Pon-suma slipped it to me." With deft chopstick action, he began slurping cold pasta carbonara directly from the tray.

Yikes. There were thirty texts from Marlin, ten from my Portland Perlmongers contact, Ed, offering gigs, and two from Ken. Feeling disloyal to Marlin, I opened Ken's first.

I'm sorry.

Koi, hold on, I'm coming. Trust me.

A tear welled up hotly and dripped down my right cheek, a salty condiment for my rice ball. I snuffled.

"Not the thanks I was looking for," said Kwaskwi. I wiped my nose with a sleeve and then reached out to squeeze his clothed arm.

"This is…you don't even…I could kiss you."

"Whoa there, little lady," said Kwaskwi with a sudden John Wayne accent. "Not that the thought didn't cross my mind before, but now I have colder, less damp fish to fry." Kwaskwi gave my arm a little pat, and then pushed my hand off his arm. Beside us on the floor, Ken gave a deep groan.

Oh you silly, silly boy. What are you doing? Why did he change so much when we got to Japan? It was a constant ache inside my chest that he seemed more a tool of the Council than the generous, strong man who helped me handle a murderer and a dragon in Portland without trying to control my Baku decisions or man-splain the Kind world. I waded through Marlin's angry texts, and wrote a long message back telling her Dad and I were fine. But my thoughts kept returning to Ken.

He had come for me. And now he lay there, broken. This wasn't the first time he'd walked into danger for me, either. When I was under Hayk's control back in Portland and I'd barely known Ken seventy two hours he'd rescued me too. More tears trickled down my nose. The rice ball was gone, and there was no more Oolong tea left in the bottle Kwaskwi had handed me after the sandwiches disappeared.

Food couldn't be my distraction anymore. I had to decide who I was going to trust. The Eight Span Mirror? Ken? The Council? Weird that the man sitting across from me, still slurping spaghetti carbonara like his life depended on it, was already in the trust category.

I'd never touched Kwaskwi's bare skin or experienced his fragment but I felt in my bones that broad grin and restless energy were backed by a fiercely loyal heart. Naïve? Probably. I'd even googled his name, and found nothing but Google Books versions of Abenaki and Algonquin dictionaries. Apparently "kwaskwi" meant either *push forward* or *run through*. I'd also googled blue jay tricksters and suspected the Salish tribe stories like *Blue Jay Finds a Wife* were closer to Kwaskwi's origin than the plains tribe verb definitions. Really, I knew very little about him.

I understood he wouldn't always choose my side or even jump in to protect me if it meant ripping his leather jacket, or went against the interests of the Pacific Northwest Kind, but Kwaskwi had always been straightforward. He didn't hide the fact that he saw me as a little Baku feather in his Siwash Tyee cap—an asset for the U.S. Kind.

He hadn't outright defied the Council yet, but there was definitely antagonism there. Maybe Kwaskwi and his people were tired of living under rules made by a bunch of cranky, old Japanese men. I'd lived in America all my life, and despite having Japanese heritage, the fact that Kwaskwi was from my side of the Pacific meant something. "Why do you defer to the Japanese Council?"

Kwaskwi looked up, noodle suspended mid-slurp. He coughed and had to take a swig of his Cherry Coke before he could speak. "Why do you?"

Because I don't know anything, and I was trusting Ken to do the right thing. "I didn't think I was."

"You trailed after the Council's lackey like a Belieber with a backstage pass, and now The Eight Span Mirror has you feeling up the Black Pearl without foreplay or even dinner first." Kwaskwi rested elbows on the table, steepling his hands together and fluttering his fingers like a movie villain. "Question your own issues with daddy figures lately?"

"Oh, totally." I sighed. "I just can't decide on which daddy figure to latch onto. Murase? Kawano? How can I decide when I don't know the history? Isn't there a textbook or a Kind Wiki I could read?"

Kwaskwi pointed a chopstick at my nose. "You are funny. It's why I keep you around."

"I thought it was because I'm Baku and owe you a debt."

Kwaskwi cocked his head at an angle, almost like a blue jay eyeing a delicious worm. Exhaling slowly, he laid palms flat on the table. In a series of infinitesimally small changes—angular, muscled shoulders sloping down, lips closed in a smile, a widening of dark irises, and jarringly uncharacteristic stillness—he took on an aura of seriousness. "*Hafu* like Midori or your sister Marlin who don't manifest Kind attributes sometimes are raised ignorant of their true parentage, but you are unique. You are powerful Kind. Like the ancient ones: Ullikemi, the Shishin, and the Black Pearl. It's easy to forget how much Akihito kept from you."

Oh great. Pulling out the overly-formal Kind-speak. Serious Kwaskwi meant things mattered more than I had the energy to care about.

"Japan's Greater Asian Co-Prosperity Sphere from World War II was built as a mirror to Kind politics. They wanted to create a bloc of Asian and Oceanic nations independent of European influence. The U.S. Atlantic states are autonomous, beholden to neither Europe nor anyone else, but the Pacific Seaboard bows to the Council."

Another history lesson. "But the Allies won. And you have Thunderbird! How can the Japanese Council have so much power over the U.S. Pacific Northwest?"

"Thunderbird is *free*," said Kwaskwi, a cutting edge to his voice I'd only heard once before back in Portland, when he'd berated me for betraying his name to Mangasar Hayk. It was easy to be fooled by that wide grin and his easy-going wit and forget that Kwaskwi was the boss of the Portland Kind. He most likely had a dark history of his own. "I forgive your insulting question because you are so cute. And ignorant. Our ancient ones are revered and not kept as magical batteries to swell the power of beings who were never meant to wield it." Kwaskwi's upper lip pulled up into a sneer. "We do not keep comfort women or force prisoners into death marches, or rape cities."

I was too weary for Kind politics or more World War II talk. Especially since I'd left my cardigan in the museum, which meant my Tcho Mokaccino bar was out of reach.

Wait, I'd already eaten it back in the van. Without chocolate, the world was a meaningless, howling void. Rummaging fruitlessly in the plastic bags, I asked, "Is it like Kawano said about the low birthrate for you guys, too? Are there no baby blue jays or baby bear brothers running around Portland?" I put my head down on a pillow of crossed forearms. I needed chocolate, and I had to pee, but exhaustion weighed my shoulders like a clumpy, old comforter. There was no way I was going to visit a stinky outhouse before I fell asleep.

"Portland is different," said Kwaskwi. "We are a vital community. You'll see when we get back."

If we ever get back.

CHAPTER THIRTEEN

Darkness. Complete and utter darkness. My eyes were open, but I couldn't see a thing. My heart pounded rapidly, and a strange awareness prickled over my skin as if I were hyperaware of air currents.

I am dreaming.

The delicious, nutty richness of roasting coffee beans filled my nose with each inhale. The flavor coated my tongue like sipping freshly roasted coffee. A warm blanket of peacefulness descended. The darkness was not fearful at all, but strangely alive with possibility and shaped by unseen energy currents.

Coffee. Darkness. This is Enoshima's fragment.

I startled awake with a massive flinch like jumping backwards off a cliff and hitting bottom—every muscle in my body clenched in charlie horse agony for a brief instant. My ragged pony tail stuck to my clammy neck, and my heart pounded a drum line competition beat.

Where am I? I propped myself up on an elbow, frantically trying to find meaning in the steep shadows of the thatched ceiling and the musty-smelling futon underneath. My bladder broadcast a message of bloated urgency. Half a gray-mottled moon, fuzzy like mothwings, loomed in the sky visible through a low window. The shack. That's right.

I put a fist to my heart, pressing firmly to slow the drumbeat, and sat all the way up, untangling what felt like a terry cloth towel from my midsection. The last thing I remembered was falling asleep at the *kotatsu* table.

Underneath the window to my right, Kwaskwi lay half-naked on a futon with arms stretched out like wings, his sculpted chest gleaming faintly in the moonlight.

"Koi."

I gave a startled yeep. Ken sat at the table eating a rice ball, hair gelled into perfect, upright spikes, dressed in jeans and an unbloodstained gray Henley open at the throat. He arched an eyebrow and finished off the last bite, licking his fingers free of sticky rice bits.

"What?" I managed to gasp.

"You look a little frazzled," he said in his slightly accented English.

"You're sitting up?"

Ken put a finger to his lips and gave a melodramatic glance at Kwaskwi. I gave him the Marlin death-glare, eyes wide. My body was coming down from full panic mode and I really, really needed to find that outhouse, but the boy had serious explaining to do.

"Come outside," he whispered and stood. *Stood!* He obviously favored his right leg, hopping along to the *genkan* in a painful-looking way. I grabbed my phone and shuffled after in the unreal-feeling moonlight, the tatami rough on my bare feet. I half-slipped on my sneakers, heels crushing the backs, as I followed Ken out the door. It was chilly, I wished I had my cardigan. Ken was definitely limping and after a moment's search, he hopped off the path, leaned over, and picked up a sturdy branch. With his makeshift cane he surged forward on the path.

"You have two broken legs."

Ken stopped, turned around and looked down at me, eyes shrouded in moonshadows and inscrutable in the darkness. "Outhouse or Museum?" he said.

"Museum, of course. Don't dodge my question."

"Kitsune illusion."

I grabbed the crook of his elbow. His skin was as hot as a *kotatsu* heater turned on full blast through the Henley sleeve. "You *faked* broken legs? How is that even possible? Wouldn't the other Kitsune have seen through it?"

Ken started walking again, tugging me along like a broken children's toy. "Midori isn't able to inhabit her Kitsune self, Ponsuma is oblivious, and Yukiko-sama doesn't care."

"You fooled me, too."

"Yes, surprisingly," he said gravely.

"You made Ben give you a blood transfusion!"

"Actually, that I needed. I lost a lot of blood."

The museum's cement walls and incongruous white church steeple reared up suddenly before us. Outside lights clustered over the doorway were abuzz with clouds of flying insects I hoped weren't mosquitos. Crickets or locusts thrummed loudly in the grass.

Inside the building it was dark. Everyone was asleep. Still, I felt the need to tiptoe to Ken's obvious amusement.

I let go of Ken's arm and turned down the corridor leading to the restroom. A bright green exit sign and that crazy moon provided enough light that there was no need to flip the light switch. I beelined for the blessedly Western-style toilet at the end of a row of Japanese squatter stalls. Relaxing on the electrically warmed seat melted away the last vestiges of sudden waking panic.

The toilet flushed automatically when I stood, the loud sound making me flinch. Ken had fooled us all into thinking he was heavily wounded, but more importantly, had fooled me. I mentally swatted away implications about not realizing your love interest was faking broken legs. *Clueless, taken to a new level.*

What about the parts where he was supposedly unconscious? I replayed the conversation I'd had with Kwaskwi last evening, squinting into the mirror. Had I said anything I'd regret Ken hearing? I pulled the band from my ponytail in a painful clump of broken, sweat-tangled hair. I finger combed my hair loose around my shoulders, unable to see more than a dark blob in the mirror.

When I returned to the corridor, Ken had magically conjured up lattes in a cardboard drink carrier. "Peace offering?"

"Those better not be illusion, too, asshole."

"I don't have a death wish," he said. "We have to get going."

"Going? Where? Hell to the no. First you tell me why you were playing wounded martyr. I wasted guilt on you."

Ken handed me the drink carrier so he could give me a one-armed shoulder squeeze. Just like the very first time he'd ever touched me in front of Marlin's apartment back home, a warm wash of heat enveloped me, tinged with the illicit excitement of physical connection after a lifetime of avoiding human touch.

"Trust me, Koi," he whispered, breath missing its usual delicious kinako scent, but making my toes curl with its familiar bitterness. "I'll explain everything in the truck."

"Truck?" I hesitated. I was no fool. He knew what effect sudden touches had on me. Should I trust him? Something hinky was going on here. I didn't want to believe I was being hoodwinked into something, but then again, he could make me believe anything, apparently.

"The Council will return in a few hours. They will take your father back to Tokyo just to keep him far away from the Black Pearl. It's unlikely they'll leave you here, too. This is our only chance."

"Chance?" God, I was repeating words like an airhead ingénue in an action flick, but things were moving too fast for me to keep up.

"To release the Black Pearl."

CHAPTER FOURTEEN

Ken grabbed a black windbreaker from the coat tree near the door and went out. I thought about his text while creamy, bitter, microwave-hot coffee warmed my throat. That little flush Marlin got from her second glass of Pinot Noir, but that I got from a really good latte, soothed away the last bit of chill.

I'm sorry. Trust me.

Clearly that apology was for far more than letting me be kidnapped by The Eight Span Mirror. Should I go back and wake Kwaskwi? Refuse to play along with this dangerous game? Or should I follow Ken? I'd known him for bare weeks, but until now, I'd never doubted what he did was done out of caring. Japan had changed that. The face he wore in Portland was only the one he'd chosen to show me, and despite his confessions of angst over being the Council's Bringer, somehow I'd overlooked what being the Bringer meant. It meant killing. Ignoring his motives for doing the Council's dirty work meant now I was paying the price.

And there it is. My morbid, paranoid, old self. Getting in the way of midnight adventures.

Ken stuck his head back in the doorway. "Iku zoo." *Let's move it.*

The tangled mass of emotions writhing in my chest like a bunch of poisonous snakes was paralyzing. I couldn't go forward, yet it was too late to go back.

"How old are you?" I blurted, and then clapped a palm over my mouth.

Ken made an exasperated sound. "Older than I look."

"How can I trust you are who you say you are? You're a Kitsune. And probably a hundred years old. Oh god, were you married?"

Pushing up a sleeve, Ken grabbed my free hand and pressed it firmly onto the bare skin of his wrist, tugging me outside into the chill night smelling of pine and the spicy smoke of someone burning incense.

I gasped. With his other hand he cupped my cheek and drew me close enough to press his forehead against mine with a little rolling motion. "Look. I get it. Just go ahead, you can see for yourself."

The world spun 360 degrees as Ken's deepest dreaming entered through our bare skin connection. The latte dropped from my hand, but I barely registered it. The dark night, the even darker danger of Ken's eyes, the fuzzy moonlight blurred to a kaleidoscope. When things stopped spinning, the colors deepened into the vibrant greens and browns of an ancient cryptomeria forest at dawn, the sharp, clean scent of crushed evergreen needles stinging my nose.

This dream was like coming home. It had saved me from losing my primal, kernel-Koi self when I'd touched Ullikemi and the Black Pearl.

I was running, flying through the forest on sure feet, dodging stray branches, leaping over gnarled, exposed root clumps, and chasing the rising sun. At the center of my chest, within the striving and the rhythm of the pounding feet, was an utter peace, a centered knowledge of the rightness of the world.

Using this dream to get my trust isn't fair. Heady stuff, yes, rooted where this journey started, back in Portland, and with the growing feelings between us, but could I trust the dream? What if this peace was an illusion, too?

Survivalist Koi spoke up, quelling the morbanoid part. *I would know.*

Then the dream changed. I burst from a copse of trees into a clearing containing a small village lane lined by traditional wood and thatch houses encircled by watery paddies and narrow strips of vegetable gardens, the lacey, green tops of daikon radish sprouting like mohawks from tidy, mounded dirt rows.

What is this? I've never seen this before.

A younger, less grizzled Murase stood in mud-streaked *jinbei* pajamas and traditional split-toed, black work boots leaning on a hoe. Beside him, beaming, was a short, round-cheeked woman with long hair pulled back into a messy bun at her neck. It was the same woman with the quilted vest from Ken's dream fragment back in Tokyo.

Mother.

She cuffed me on the shoulder and complained with affectionate irritation about my lateness. Overwhelming love for this human woman and the small toddler clinging to the bottom of her gray linen yukata struck me.

Ben. She was such a cute baby.

The dream changed again.

I knelt in *seiza* in a room with a green-eyed tiger, emerald-feathered pheasants, and a long and sinuous dragon coiled in black-scaled rings on the walls.

I've seen this before, at the airport. This was the same room as in the stewardess' dream.

But something felt weird, the angle from which the dragon stared down was shifted to the right. Across from me, sitting in the rows of robed people with bowed heads, I recognized Princess Stewardess but also Yukiko, Murase, and the black suits, now sporting indigo-dyed kimonos. Even Red Shirt was there sitting way in the back. I lifted my eyes to the lord on the raised platform. Tojo. Parallel feelings washed over me: a clenched misgiving in my chest and the swelling of prideful elation.

Ken's feelings in this memory-dream.

I rose in a muscular, fluid movement to approach an old man that I recognized as a human servant sitting off to the side. Next to the man was a clean, metal tray with bundled steel needles attached to bamboo handles—*tebori*, or traditional tattoo instruments. I knelt in front of him and pulled open my formal, black kimono at the neck, shoving it down around my shoulders. I bowed, forehead touching tatami between the triangle my carefully placed palms made, and spoke in the most formal old-fashioned inflections. "I accept."

Accept what?

The man's eyes were cloudy with cataracts, but his hands were steady and sure as he picked up a bundle of needles, used one hand to spread the skin of my chest, and the other to tattoo the character that would make me Bringer.

I, Fujiwara Kennosuke, once scorned with all my siblings as cursed with a weak and diluted bloodline, was now the Council's most respected servant. I'd shown everyone how dangerous *Hafu* could be—a flash of memory, a man with his throat cut, blood on my hands accompanied by a wave of revulsion and grief—*I will be their sword. I will be their Justice.*

I made my vows to the Council in a steady voice, despite the burning in my chest, despite Tojo's angry glare, despite the meaning of the words made heavy by the weight of Kind power. I renounced all contact with my human mother, cleansing her taint from the pure line of the Fujiwara. A heat flared within, a flame that burned hungrily the fuel of my pride, the triumphant anger—

"That's enough." My voice, sounding oddly thin and reedy. Not from my own throat. Ken's voice. Ken's *present day* voice.

The world shuddered, fractured into spinning pieces of darkness, and then I felt hands on my shoulders, pushing me away. I was Koi again, standing in moonlight watching Ken gasp, sweat pouring from his temples, wilting his hair-spikes, bent over in pain. "No more. I can't—"

I pushed past his arm outstretched to fend off the monster that I was, ripping living energy along with the memory-dreams from the very heart of my victims, and thrust two hands at his throat. I tore open the collar of his shirt. My foot squelched the abandoned latte cup, but I stared at Ken's chest.

The dark strokes of the tattooed sigil showed stark on exposed skin. Worse than a secret marriage or the fact that he was old enough to be my great-grandfather.

I am not the only fucking monster here.

Migraine gathered at the back of my neck, gray static buzzing at the corners of my eyes. I hadn't recognized the old-fashioned kanji character back in Portland. Now I knew it was two characters, artfully painted, one inside the other in an old style of kanji as it had been imported from China: *Dorei.* Slave.

"What did you do? Why did you?" Anger choked my throat, coated my mouth with bile. The Council's slave. Not the sensitive, funny, loyal Ken I'd come to know in Portland. *Rejecting his mother? Murdering?*

Ken moaned low in his throat, taking my punishing fingers scraping his flesh, not trying to escape the grip twisting his collar into the vulnerable skin of his throat. "I was proving something to the Council. Becoming their servant made *Hafu* valuable. I was convinced I could change the way everyone treated us."

Tears streamed down my cheeks. Icepicks speared halfway through my temples. My heart was in shreds. I wrenched away, leaning against the doorjamb to stay upright.

That terrible joy at cleansing away the taint of his human mother somehow overlay my hospital memories of my own Mom. They were tangled together. As if Mom was garbage because she was human and not Japanese. As if I would throw her away or avoid her when she was dying in the hospital, all bones and loose skin and sores. Ken rejected his mother. Marlin accused me of rejecting Mom, just like Dad, by leaving at her first invasive ductal carcinoma diagnosis.

No. It wasn't like that. Mom had released me—given me a priceless gift. She kept me from her hospital room at the end because neither of us knew what it would mean for me to follow her into that last, dying dream. She'd never been bitter about Dad leaving, either. That required a strength, a generosity of spirit I could only hope to emulate. It was a gift I could never repay. Nothing, no one, not Dad, not Tojo, not a lifetime's supply of free lattes, could ever make me renounce her.

"This dream-memory is supposed to make me trust you?"

Ken began buttoning his shirt, covering the sigil. Teetering on one leg, he spoke in Japanese. "I didn't choose what dream to show you, Koi. Even Kitsune can't fool a Baku in the dreaming. What you saw was truth."

"That you're Tojo and Kawano's slave?"

He flinched. My fists curled and uncurled, aching to hurt him, make him feel the pain blossoming inside me. "Bastard. How much of Portland, how much of *that* was real?"

Ken looked up sharply. "All of it." He reached out to caress my cheek, but I batted his wrist away.

"You told me the Council could help Dad, help *me*. You—" I swallowed a sob, damn him for seeing me vulnerable like this, "slept in my bed."

Ken clasped his arms behind his back, making himself non-threatening, and then ruined it by stepping too close. Even with the limp and a wince he couldn't hide, he radiated a hot menace that set off alarms all up and down my spine.

"Look at me," he urged, the planes of his cheeks sharpening under the bruises, bridge of his nose thinning, eyes going dark-on-dark feral. "I did not fully explain the political landscape, but sleeping next to you, *kissing* you, was never part of any illusion."

"A distraction, then, so I wouldn't question your true intentions."

"Not even Kawano-san dictates where I sleep," Ken's voice came out low and rumbly. He leaned closer, lips millimeters from my ear, but hands firmly clasped behind his back. "I don't share a futon lightly."

The past few weeks' closeness had lulled me into relaxing, accustomed me to touching without invasion of my deepest, most private self.

I had to remember his nearness wasn't safety. It was precarious. I teetered on the edge of a high cliff with only jagged rocks at the bottom.

I'd been changing my life back in Portland just when Ken appeared; finishing my accounting degree, working out a long term plan for Dad with Marlin, going outside my apartment every damn day. The Kind and the revelation I was Baku eclipsed all that hard work. Somewhere, deep down, I feared that agreeing to come to Japan was just another sly way to avoid real life. Piggybacked on the ache to trust Ken clung all my fears, but was it because I couldn't trust his motivations or my own?

"You were proud of becoming the Bringer." *A slave. A killer.* Naïve fool that I was, I'd dismissed his tearful confession of that as more Kind over-dramatics.

"Yes."

The night was growing colder. Every inch of my skin shivered with chill prickles except where his breath caressed the delicate outer shell of my ear. "Did you see your mother again after renouncing her?"

"No."

I turned away from that heated breath, from the compelling draw of his eyes. "That's not the answer I was looking for."

"Too bad," he said and then drew back my hair with one hand and pressed his lips into my neck. Instantly I flushed head to toe under the chill, the migraine forgotten. On the heels of eating that memory dream there was no hidden danger of another fragment in this skin-to-skin touch. It took everything I had not to turn around, grip those wilted spikes of hair in both hands to hold his head steady so I could lose myself in the blissful sweetness of his mouth, feel the broadness of his chest like an anchor in the midst of this hurricane.

Instead, I took a deep breath. "You're such an asshole."

Ken nibbled my earlobe and then pressed his cheek to my temple. "Ben warned me you would see things that way," he murmured in Japanese.

"Ben? So now you expect me to believe all this time you two have been thick as thieves? Secretly in cahoots?"

Another kiss at the nape of my neck, nudging away tangles of hair, and then Ken's hands and lips dropped away. "It's true. Ben and I have always been close. Like you and Marlin. Though the last decade we had to pretend otherwise."

"Why aren't you waking up Murase and Midori and Pon-suma? This is what they want, right? To set the Black Pearl free?"

"There's no time to prove to them I'm not working for the Council here. Only Ben knows the truth." And how much pain did that simple phrase conceal? *His own father thinks him the Council's toady?*

"They need to know!"

"Too much explaining. I will not put them in danger for defying the Council's direct orders while Tojo is right here with his black squad. Now there really is no time. We have to get to the Black Pearl."

I shivered. The migraine-vise had returned as soon as Ken's lips left. My back was cold, goose pimples popping out all along my arms. *So cold.* Like this conversation extinguished some sure, steady warmth I'd taken for granted until it was suddenly gone.

"Ah," said Ken in an entirely different voice. "Good Evening, Yukiko-sama."

I jerked around. Yukiko stood under a copse of trees, dressed all in white robes like a shrine maiden, and dangling a silver key on an oversized ring.

CHAPTER FIFTEEN

"Truck key, I presume?"

The corners of Yukiko's mouth curled up ever so slightly. Amusement at the situation she found us in? Or something else? *I refuse to feel like a teen caught making out on the front stoop.*

Ken bent down to pick up his dropped makeshift cane. "Lead on."

Yukiko's expression didn't change, but the air grew a bit sharper with the scent of icicles. Ken's breath made a frosty cloud. Slowly, Yukiko raised her other hand and pointed a slender, bone-white finger tipped with a sharpened, crimson-painted nail in my direction. *She doesn't want me along?*

Ken shook his head, eyes pleading, but Yukiko did not relent. Her hand closed into a fist like she held something by the handle, and then jerked toward her chest in a flap of billowing sleeve.

Again Ken shook his head.

The Rebel Alliance are not all on the same page.

"What does she want, Ken?"

Ken sighed, bringing his free hand up in a fist to rub his eyes, flinching at the pressure against the darkening bruise on his cheek.

He squared himself off against Yukiko. "The Black Pearl has waited long enough. Do you really want to risk Murase-san or Tojo-san discovering us while I explain? We won't get another chance."

Yukiko tossed the keys toward Ken. He snatched at them, but they fell just out of his reach into the wet grass. With a grunt, Ken leaned over to pick them up. Anger propelled me forward, stepping on the keys before his fingers could touch them.

Ken looked up with a confused frown.

"I am going nowhere without explanation."

"There's no time."

"Make. The. Fucking. Time."

Yukiko arched an eyebrow in utterly condescending amusement.

"The Council never asked my opinion. Murase didn't tell me what he was sending me in to. *Dad* never explained. You all just assumed the good little Baku would march blindly along with your plans. Well, not tonight."

Ken straightened, eyes flickering from my mouth to Yukiko to the trees and back like he'd get burned if his gaze settled anywhere too long. "We have a truck," he said quickly. "You and Yukiko-sama will keep the snake weakened long enough for us to muscle it into the truck. We will drive to the Aisaka River where we can release the Black Pearl and wake her completely from your father's Baku-induced dream prison with some level of safety. From there it's downstream to the Pacific Ocean at Hachinohe, and then through the Tsugaru Straits and west to Sakhalin Island where she can enter the mouth of the Amur River."

"The detailed itinerary wasn't the problem I'm talking about."

Ken hobbled closer. "I know what the problem is. It's not trusting your own heart. I know you, Pierce Koi AweoAweo." My full name in that husky voice made little hairs stand all up and down my arms. "Your loyalty, your true caring. You are horrified by death. You value people, even ice hags and dragons. You freed Ullikemi from his long imprisonment, even though it cost you. You forgive, you are not overcome with bitterness and recrimination, and your intentions are without malice or greed. This gave me hope. For me. For the Black Pearl."

"Hate to interrupt the Oscar-worthy monologue, but Tojo's *kempeitai* patrol is about to get lucky." Kwaskwi dropped down from a low-hanging branch of the tree nearest Yukiko. She nodded gravely when he flashed her his usual wide grin. He nodded at Ken. "Looking mighty hale there, Lazarus."

Ken used my momentary confusion to tap me between the shoulder blades so I stumbled forward on the path.

"Et tu, Brute?" I said to Kwaskwi. He held up his hands in surrender. "Whoa there, I'm just eavesdropping. I'm not mixed up with Emo boy's nefarious plans."

"Now's not the time for your brand of joking, Siwash Tyee," Ken said gravely.

Yukiko glided after Ken, unconcerned about our latest addition.

"So you knew nothing about this?" I waved in Ken's direction.

"Just following along for the ride," said Kwaskwi. "And protecting my assets." He cuffed Ken's shoulder. "Massive points for fooling the trickster."

"This is not your fight," said Ken formally, but he continued herding us forward with his stick and palpable urgency.

"I am a stakeholder," said Kwaskwi, showing even more teeth. "And I'm curious, too—I can't imagine any scenario where this plays out without you getting your asses handed to you by Tojo."

If only this headache would go away. It was hard to think, to muster up and arrange all the things I wanted to batter Ken with before I followed him to the Black Pearl.

In my heart, I knew from the first time I touched her that I couldn't leave the Black Pearl dragon chained here for Tojo and Kawano to use. She was a prisoner, in pain. It was wrong on so many levels and I couldn't leave her without trying to help. For the same reason I couldn't ignore Ullikemi's wild ache to be free. But was I strong enough? Ken seemed to think so.

Mom had also called me strong way before I believed it. When she was trying to tell me it was okay to leave the hospital, escape her dreams of dying. She'd been unable to sit up, but I'd tucked the Captain Adriamycin red satin devil pillow Marlin sewed for her underneath her head so she could look at me without craning her neck.

"Do you know why I named you Koi?" she had said. "Because you were always so sturdy, so strong, even when you were just a keiki. And I wanted you to remember, when it got hard." Here, Mom's voice had cracked. She coughed, and I took her water tumbler from the side table and carefully held the plastic straw to her lips, inflamed with mouth sores despite the Biotene the nurses urged on her.

She swallowed with such obviously painful effort my own throat ached.

"Koi can live on any continent, in almost all temperatures. Survive even in the muddiest water. And that's what you've got, yes?" I looked through the glass window where the OHSU nurses in their annoyingly flower-patterned scrubs hustled back and forth down the corridor.

"Muddy water," Mom repeated.

"It's okay," I said, pulling down my sleeve to hold her hand again.

She batted weakly at my sweater-covered fingers. "You've got to take care of yourself when you spend all day stirring up what lies on the bottoms of ponds."

I hadn't understood then, just thinking she was spouting more of her Marine biologist pop psychology. But she'd been alluding to the family monster in the room: Dad's and my weird dreaming.

Then Mangasar Hayk shattered my careful world of denial and took Marlin to force me to help him use Ullikemi's power to wield magic that messed with people's memories. I got Marlin back and set Ullikemi free with a little help from Ken. Now I truly *believed* in my own strength. But that strength came with some attached strings that

I don't think Mom would ever call *good*.

My Baku hunger had almost drained Kwaskwi's friend the ice hag, Dzunukwa, of her life. The heady rush of energy I got from eating a living, waking Kind dream was invigorating and terrifying. Dad had chosen to stop eating dreams for years and risk living in a senile fog rather that give into the hunger for the Black Pearl. What was the Nietzsche quote? *Whoever fights monsters should see to it that in the process he does not become a monster.*

I shivered, wishing I had my cardigan or that terry cloth towel-blanket thing. Ken and Yukiko walked forward utterly focused, their eyes sharp as glass with determination.

Why did I think Japan would hold the key to helping me figure out the Baku bits of myself when Dad had run away from Kawano and the Council decades ago?

No more running away. That was my mantra now. No more hiding out in my apartment. No more relying on Marlin for social interaction. I was inextricably tangled in the Kind zaniness, unable to go back to my normal life. *I have to see this through. Just not sure I know what I'll be when I reach the other side.*

We emerged from the wooded path onto a gravel road. Everyone's footsteps but Yukiko's crunched jarringly loud despite the night chorus of crickets in the tall, plumed grass lining the sides of the lot.

Restlessness like biting ants crawled up and down my spine, the energy from eating Ken's dream fizzing and popping inside me like Marlin's eighth grade experiment dropping mint candy into cola.

I needed to *do something.*

In the shadowed far end of the lot under drooping beech trees squatted a wattle-and-daub walled, traditional Kura storage building with a peaked roof of curved tiles. One high dark window peered down like an eye.

All my years of horror movie watching told me this was the last place I wanted to be, but Ken strode confidently around the corner so I followed reluctantly, hoping spiders were the scariest thing the Kura contained.

The other side of the Kura sported a weirdly modern, metal sliding door. Ken and Kwaskwi raised it slowly, minimizing the noisy rattle, to reveal the cutest little truck I'd ever seen. Covered in a green tarp on top, the bottom was yellow with the picture of a surprised Panda with huge eyes and 'Sakai Moving Company' emblazoned in hiragana block letters.

"Get in the passenger side," said Ken.

"You're driving with that gimpy foot?" said Kwaskwi. He exchanged a concerned glance with Yukiko. "We'll meet you at Jesus' Grave."

The two waded into the plumed grass and then disappeared under the beeches' shadows, Yukiko a flash of white that was suddenly swallowed by the warm darkness. A flock of jays lifted in an eerily silent cloud from the tree canopy and headed east toward the sliver of rose horizon. Morning was upon us. Ken opened the driver's side door. "Please, Koi," he said in English. A concession. "This is not the way I wanted things. I regret much, but I can't regret you being here."

The base of my throat tightened with anger, with a torrent of hot words about illusion and mothers and what else he could regret, but I was already moving toward the truck. He swung himself up into the cab. I slid into the passenger's seat. Instead of buckling in, I sucked in all that Baku restless energy from eating his dream and slapped Ken across the face with an open palm.

His head cracked satisfyingly against the driver's side window, the red imprint of my palm rising up like a sunburn over the indigo bruises.

There's my strength, my pure heart. Bastard. "I regret being here."

Ken sat up, head bowed, breathing in gasps while his hands gripped the wheel so tightly his knuckles turned white. Hurting.

What am I doing?

Part of me was glad. Glad to wield physical strength against him, while the sane part of me urgently whispering about becoming a monster was drowned out by the rush of satisfaction. Let him feel pain. Ken had muddied the water here, it was his fault we'd come to this. I was just taking care of myself.

Without a word, he turned the ignition key, and pulled out of the lot slowly.

The truck's motor and open windows made talk blessedly difficult. The slap had released the pent up energy from dream-eating, but blowback hangover was happy to fill in the vacancy. Eating powerful Kind dreams made me super-cranky, kind of like PMS on steroids. If only I could remember that.

My stomach informed me it was ravenous, and my throat felt dry and scratchy like I'd contracted strep. We jostled and jounced our way to the Tomb of Jesus while I pulled out my phone and caught up on Marlin's texts. She was a shade less histrionic with the emojis since I told her Dad had several lucid periods. She had messaged a snapshot of Dad's prescriptions and pill schedule laid out on her kitchen table. The familiar pineapple and palm-leaf patterned tablecloth underneath made my heart give a little twinge. I missed her affectionate bossiness but was simultaneously heartily relieved she wasn't here. One less Pierce-Herai to worry about.

Gosh, Dad hadn't had his pills in over twenty four hours. They were back in Tokyo with our luggage. But did it matter? Yukiko's freezing magic seemed to work better than actual Western medicine on keeping the not-eating-dreams-induced dementia at bay.

The truck came to a stop. We were here. Ken pulled onto the concrete path leading to the grassy mounds and cut the engine. "You don't," he swallowed audibly. "If you are afraid—"

"Keep digging that hole, buster," I cut in. Then modulating my tone to something less knife-edged, I looked out the front windshield. "Don't patronize. Don't pretend this isn't exactly why you cozied up to me in Portland. It's insulting." Ken reached for my hand, I snatched it away, pressing it close to my chest. "What the hell? No touching."

"There's so much I want to…"

The boy seriously needs to finish his sentences. "I get it. We're here to release the Black Pearl before the Council can stop us. I don't like how I got maneuvered here, but it's clear this is the right choice. Tojo gives me the creeps. But somehow, despite the kidnapping, I like Midori and Ben."

"That's good," said Ken, folding his arms across his chest. Probably consciously mimicking my body posture or some other kind of psychological bullshit. At least he wasn't using Kitsune illusion to make his face prettier. "So you'll try?"

"Yes, I'll try. But don't take it the wrong way. I'm not doing it for you."

"I know," he whispered in Japanese. "But that doesn't stop me from wishing…from wanting to be near you, or loving how you can't keep from helping. No matter what happens, I wanted you to know that."

"Aw *hell* to the no." I jammed the door open and dropped out of the truck. He did not get to pull out the L-word. *Not kosher.* It was time to get this freak show on the road and deal with Ken and the angsty turmoil later.

Yukiko stood motionless by the mound with the biggest cross, while a dozen jays perched on the crossbeam above her. She nodded as I scrambled over the white picket fence, and then she glided over and put a hand on my chest bringing me to a sudden halt.

"What?"

Those glacier eyes caught my gaze, enfolding them in icy attention that momentarily soothed my aching head. Then chill breath slithered down my neck and arms. It felt like I was being probed body and soul. Unwilling to risk accidental skin-to-skin contact, I waited. She arched an eyebrow and tilted her head to one side like a quizzical bird.

"It's okay. Yes, I do this willingly," I said. "Even if the pretense that brought me here was a lie."

She nodded again, lowering her hand to my stomach. She tapped it twice, the corner of her mouth raised ever so slightly.

Ken had somehow maneuvered himself over the fence. "She's telling you to eat something before you go down there."

Still caught in Yukiko's gaze, I answered sharply, "Great idea. Who's got a breakfast buffet hidden in their pockets?" The jays lifted, jostling each other and ruffling wings in silent laughter.

"Actually..." Ken stepped up. "I was saving this for an emergency," he said, pulling a thin rectangle from his magic pocket. "And I guess hoping for forgiveness points."

"Shut up and give me chocolate," I said.

"Right."

I am really angry and betrayed and food will not make me forgive you.

But Ken had brought Dagoba Xocolatl, not only artisanal but *Oregon* chocolate. The bar loaded with my heaviest emotional baggage about food, Dad, and the break-up of my family.

Marlin and I inherited our need for theobroma cacao straight from Mom, who scorned the typical Hawaiian milk chocolate macadamia stuff as tourist fodder and taught us to eat bean-to-bar chocolate from a small company on Kauai. Dad, on the other hand, would grumble in surly, male Japanese the equivalent of *real men don't eat sweets* at dessert time.

Except for Xocolatl.

For some reason both Mom and Dad loved the chili bite. Even when Mom was nauseous from the Adriamycin, she could keep that down. And Dad would literally snatch the last square from Marlin's palm if she was inattentive.

The wilds of Aomori didn't contain a store that sold this, so Ken must have brought it all the way from PDX. *Chocolate doesn't give him the right to use the L-word. This doesn't make up for manipulation.* But I was horrified to discover tears welling up in a hot veil over my eyes.

Chewing the dark spiciness, the exact shade of Ken's eyes, I hid my stupid reaction by tugging at the grass panel at the top of the mound I knew hid the secret entrance. The jays suddenly lifted away from the crossbeam, flying in a swarm clockwise around the cross and then shifting counter-clockwise: a swirling, blue-feathered funnel. They released a piercing cry and then pinwheeled out in all directions, revealing Kwaskwi leaning casually against the cross, arms resting on his chest. *Such a drama queen.*

"Having trouble with the secret lever?" He reached down and pushed at something at the base of the cross. The panel slid open, revealing the narrow opening. Yukiko floated into the opening with boneless grace and disappeared down the stairs. I coughed, the delicious chocolate bitterness turning to a chalky bile.

"Are you coming?" I said to Kwaskwi, jerking a thumb at Ken. "He's injured."

"I'm sensitive to cold. It gives me a sinus headache."

"You don't need the trickster," Ken scoffed.

"You were planning to send her down into the icy cave of an ancient one with only Yukiko?"

"She's Baku, she is strong."

"And you're several kinds of idiot, Bringer."

Ken bristled. "I do what I have to do. Don't doubt Koi. She's more than capable of eating a few dreams to make the Black Pearl groggy enough not to lash out but still awake enough to move. I'll come down as soon as Yukiko releases the cold."

"Without even giving her a jacket?"

Ken sheepishly shrugged off the windbreaker and held it out to me. I gave him an incredulous look. "Keep it."

"You're mixing politics with your love life, and we all know that usually turns out rosy," Kwaskwi muttered.

I shoved a hand in the direction of both boys. "Enough. Kwaskwi are you in or out?"

"Is this a favor you're asking? If so, I'll need a token."

I glared at him. *I am so not in the mood for this.* "You're doing this out of the goodness of your soul. Also so I won't grab your smirking face and eat the dreaming heart right out of you."

"Ah," he said, smiling even more broadly. With a courtly bow and overly grandiose sweep of his arm toward the entrance he added, "If that's the case, after you, madam. The Black Pearl awaits."

CHAPTER SIXTEEN

Damn my pride. I should have taken the windbreaker. Yukiko's presence made the underground passage not just cold, but arctic. Polar. Beyond freezing. My teeth started clattering before we even made it down the stairs. The metal door at the bottom stuck to my nervous fingers when I turned the handle.

Good thing I don't have to lick it.

Infuriatingly, Kwaskwi had on a thick, flannel shirt, leather jacket, and fur-lined black leather boots. He whipped out a slouchy beanie of startling blue and shoved it on his head. "I am always prepared," he said as I gently disengaged my fingers from the door, leaving a top layer of skin cells behind. "I would not send my girlfriend down a frozen tunnel to capture an ancient dragon. Especially without a coat or hat."

I don't see you sharing your hat now. "You want some kind of award? Pon-suma isn't even here!"

"Never know who may be listening," he said, nodding at Yukiko, waiting impassively. Kwaskwi gave an exaggerated sigh and reached around me to push the door open.

Ah, eau-de-Black Pearl, how I've missed you. I'd forgotten what a delight this cave was. The only illumination came from faint light leaking down the stairs behind us and a vague, hazy shimmer hovering around Yukiko like a ghostly double.

"I'm gonna just stand here and look pretty while you girls do your stuff to calm the Black Pearl down enough for transport." Kwaskwi shoved his hands into his pockets, stomping his boots for warmth.

"Where is she?" I asked Yukiko.

She held up a hand, opened her mouth wide, and *hoovered* in air like her lungs were balloons. The cave temperature rose noticeably, enough to stop my teeth-clatter.

A stripe of green lit up the darkness, slowly advancing in long curves, tracing the Black Pearl's large coils—eerie bioluminescence.

"Baby's waking up," said Kwaskwi, pulling out his hands. "Better get Baku-ing." A harsh, scraping sound echoed through the cave, making me startle. Yukiko, mouth firmly pressed shut, lowered her arm and indicated the closest green stripe with her chin.

Okay, I got this. I am Baku. I released an ancient dragon before. The first time I'd touched the Black Pearl I'd been taken by surprise. Now I knew what she felt like. All I needed was a little bit of her dream, just enough to weaken her a little. Plus, I had Ken's forest fragment handy to help me focus.

I rubbed my cold-numbed palms together and blew on them for luck. Stumbling forward with outstretched hands, I reached for the green light.

Fingers connected with rough leather, a feeling like rock pressing in all sides compressed my lungs, and then I was in her dream.

Warm silty water caressed the long, sinuous stretch of spine from head to tail as I swam into an eddy shaded by the leafy boughs of an ash. Tiny *bang huahua yu* darted back and forth to catch insect larvae stirred up by my passing, their small collisions against my scales the slightest tickle. I was tense and listening for the blue uniforms encamped in this area. Anger flared at what I had seen on the

153

riverbanks this morning—the limp and breathless bodies of the spotted feline servants *Abke Hehe* had sent to help me against the invaders. Even the spotted feline *kesike* fell to the blue uniforms and their guns. *Abke Hehe* could not help any further.

A flame, not anger, flickered to life inside. *Koi. I am Koi.* The river, the fish, the layered glassy light overhead rippled for an instant, a prolonged moment between one breath and the next when I was fully aware of my double existence: I was Koi in a cave now, I was the Black Pearl in the Heilong Jiang long ago. This knowledge spawned Baku hunger. A gaping maw opened, waiting to be filled. I ached to take in this dream, the kernel-self of the Black Pearl, the dream she returned to day after day, struggling to hold herself together deep inside the chilled ground of her prison. The flame brightened, and grew bigger.

Burn, little flame, burn.

The flame consumed the dream, heat flowing into all my limbs in a delicious pulse. Now it was me swelling, bloating with the Black Pearl's life-energy, a pressure building at the base of my throat and underneath my ribs. A glorious fullness of ecstatic warmth and power.

I should stop. But the dream was very seductive, and there was room for more within me. My hunger was cavernous, my body ample, and the ancient one had so much to give. Just a little more, just a little longer.

The Koi part of me remembered the ice hag Dzunukwa lying haggard and wilted on the Pioneer Square brick and the awful guilt of how close I'd come to killing her. *I will not do to the Black Pearl what I did to Dzunukwa.*

I willed the flame to shrink. *Koi. I am Koi, in a cave.* It worked. The Baku hunger subsided back into my own human limbs. A disjointed, loose-boned feeling lingered, the aftereffect of trying to move my human neck like the Black Pearl's flexible spine. Moving through a sea of molasses, I slowly dragged my arms back, aching in every muscle. Pain spiked at the base of my skull. My heart tried to batter its way out of my chest.

"You holding it together?" Kwaskwi's voice.

Why is it so dark? Ah, my eyes were screwed shut. I cracked them open, the faint light of Yukiko's glow too harsh to look at directly.

"I'm here."

"Nice job not sucking the dragon to death. She's gone quiet. Let's get her up the stairs."

Yukiko glided over to the door. Kwaskwi moved to my side while I tried to keep my bulging insides in check by pressing hands along my ribs. "You sure you ate enough that this bad girl won't object to manhandling?"

"Of course not!" My voice exploded in anger. "I'm not sure of anything!"

"We will try anyway," said Ken. I peered at him, outlined in dawn's glimmer at the bottom of the stairs. Yukiko must have warmed the cave enough for Ken to handle. "I'll take the front end in case she wakes up."

"Always the butt end, never the bride," Kwaskwi grumbled. I elbowed him in the ribs. "Aw come on, mortal danger is way more fun with a little levity."

Ken fiddled with something by the door and red emergency lights flickered to life along the perimeter of the cave floor. It was my first real look at the dragon. She was beautiful. Black scales rippled with a rainbow iridescence that grew lighter at her tail and her head sat upon an arched neck like a seahorse with a rounded, elegantly long snout and huge eyes swirling in intense shades of blue, turquoise, and indigo. She had small webbed forelegs near her head and tiny vestigial legs near her tail that looked more like clawed wings.

As I stared into her eyes, she blinked, slowly, and the delicately scalloped protrusions forming her eyebrow ridges twitched. She was half-awake, but weakened. I flushed from head to toe, sweat breaking out at my temples despite the lingering cold.

I had done this. Me. *I am not the bad guy. This is not an attack.* But a part of me reveled in the tight fullness of my belly and the jittery trembling of my arm muscles from stolen power coursing through them.

Yukiko and Ken stepped to either side of the Black Pearl's head and embraced her around the neck; their hands barely reached around to grip each other. A grunt of pain ripped from Ken as they lifted her head.

"You can't!" I blurted, stomping over to elbow Ken aside. "Just give me the damn windbreaker."

Ken was stupid and injured. Better I use this borrowed strength to actually do something helpful this time, otherwise I would have to slap someone again. A muscle ticked along his jaw as he handed over the jacket. Ken's long limbs meant the jacket sleeves hung well past my fingertips—perfect for keeping away from bare contact. I gripped Yukiko's hands through the windbreaker, and bent my head so a curtain of hair covered my cheek. The Black Pearl's scales were strangely soft through the protection of my hair, like a rough chamois, and her moldy sock smell overwhelming. The smell stung tears from my eyes as we heaved the Black Pearl's head and neck toward the stairs.

The Black Pearl's forelegs scrambled on the stairs as if eager to escape the cave. But two layers of eyelids fluttered down over the mesmerizing tapestry of her eyes, one translucent, another cloudy milk. She wasn't truly awake.

Halfway up the stairs, the coils pulling straight behind us, Ken and Kwaskwi began lugging the tail end as well. A strange, melodic moan filled the stairwell, like whales singing. It vibrated up from the depths of the Black Pearl's body directly into my bones. An overwhelming wave of loneliness rode the song, so intense it stilled the breath in my lungs, froze the tears in my eyes, and tightened a burning belt around my heart.

I shut my eyes against welling tears. I crouched naked and alone, shivering in a dark place not my home, feeling the raw festering places all over my soul where river, friends, *Abka Hehe's* love had been ripped away and would not heal.

"Yukiko-sama," said Ken, gasping.

I wailed, a long low cry like a solitary wolf in a vast forest. Then my breath frosted over, cold encasing me and the Black Pearl's head in a muffling, protective shield.

Yukiko to the rescue.

The whalesong stopped just as we reached the top of the stairs. I rested the Black Pearl's head on the grassy mound with Yukiko, leaning over, elbows on my knees, crying. "Oh god, she's so sad."

"We're getting her home," called Ken from halfway down the stairs. "Just a little more to the truck. We're almost there."

The truck was a million miles away. I sniffled. Yukiko reached down and wrapped her arms around the Black Pearl's neck, clearly unmoved by the whalesong or my breakdown. I gripped her hands again and heaved, borrowed power still giving me the muscle strength of a bodybuilder.

Luckily, the strength lasted until we reached the truck where Kwaskwi's jays circled relentlessly overhead. If Tojo and Kawano were on the lookout for us, the jays were a dead giveaway, but no one else seemed to care.

"Now what?"

Ken climbed onto the back of the truck and unfastened the tarp. "She goes in here." I bent to lift her head, but couldn't even straighten my legs. My arm muscles had turned to limp noodles.

"I'm tapped out." I stepped back so Kwaskwi and Ken could move in. The three of them managed to push the Black Pearl's head to the front of the cargo space. Then working together while Ken leaned on his stick, every line in his face stark with the strain, we tugged the long coils up and packed them in the tight space.

Yukiko gracefully smoothed the bottom of her robe to one side and then nestled herself in *seiza* amongst the dragon folds. She nodded to Ken.

He beckoned the rest of us out of the truck and then refastened the tarp. "You coming with us to the river?" he said to Kwaskwi.

"I guess so."

"You going to ride in the truck cab?"

"No, you lovebirds have all kinds of fun issues to hash out. Lies. Suspicions. Betrayal." He peered into my face. "And she desperately needs a tissue. I'll follow."

The circling jays began chattering excitedly. They exploded in all directions, one zooming down like a missile headed straight for Kwaskwi's head. With a grunt, he lifted an arm parallel to the ground. The jay pulled up at the last moment and settled on his wrist, cawing. Kwaskwi's upper lip lifted into a sneer. "Tojo is at the museum." He pulled off his beanie and crumpled it into a pocket.

Ken limped over to the driver's side without a word, starting the truck before I had even gotten halfway through the door. He put the truck into reverse and skidded out of the parking lot. Kwaskwi disappeared from the rearview mirror as we bumped and jostled our way onto the main road. Three black cars were parked at the museum's front door with their headlights turned on. As we passed, someone slammed a car door.

Driving through town, we were both quietly tense, expecting any moment to find Tojo or Kawano glaring back from the rear view mirrors.

Ken slowed down for a toll gate machine and handed me a ticket without comment. We entered a highway bounded on both sides by metal, corrugated walls.

"What does the dragon dream of?" said Ken quietly.

"Home."

"And the war?"

"Yes."

"Are you going to talk to me in more than single syllables?"

"No."

"You can't avoid me forever."

"I have hella good avoidance skillz. Queen of denial."

Ken gave me a hopeful glance, probably latching on to my deceptively light tone. It was taking everything I had to keep myself together. He arched an eyebrow in that sly fox way that usually made me melt. *Not now, jerkface.* "When we reach Aisaka River you'll have to release the Black Pearl."

"Oh my god, what did we *just* do? Didn't we *just* release her from the cave?"

"Yes," said Ken gravely. "But she's been in a deep, deep dreaming state for decades and frozen by Yukiko for decades more. She isn't completely free yet, that's going to take more work."

"And?"

"And what?"

"There's an unspoken *and* there."

"Why do you say that?" Ken's brow furrowed in a really cute, perturbed way.

"There's always an unspoken *and* with you. Something dangerous or terrible."

"I don't lie to you, Koi."

"No, you're just king of the partial explanation." *What a dysfunctional royal pair we make.*

There was a deep, muffled thump from the back of the truck as Ken swerved suddenly onto an exit ramp, hugging the sharp curve. I was thrown to the left, brushing against his arm before I could use my grip on the dashboard to right myself. When we straightened out onto another smaller highway with no sound barrier walls, Ken sighed and rested both elbows on the steering wheel. For a moment, the road was clear, the silence fraught, and the scenery a soothing blend of pastoral lands dotted with the dark outlines of traditional peaked-roof houses.

"Do you remember how Ullikemi's human servant, Mangasar Hayk, cut you and Marlin? How he used your blood in his word magic?"

"Of course I do." My fingers rose to trace the faint seam Hayk had left on my cheek with his knife.

"I explained before that magic beyond our individual Kind nature requires blood. And great magic requires a release of essence—a birth or a death."

"No one died when I released Ullikemi, I think. Not even Hayk."

"Yes," said Ken. "That was unexpected." I wondered if that was what had caused him to covet me for the Council. Or wait, not the Council after all, but The Eight Span Mirror's plans to release the Black Pearl. It was all so messy and I longed for someone to just tell me what was right and who was wrong. "Recall that you had just drained Dzunukwa close to death—"

"Unintentionally!"

"—as well as being under Thunderbird's dream influence."

"An ancient one like Ullikemi and the Black Pearl."

"Herai-san believed the combination of Dzunukwa's life-essence and the eating of two ancients' dreams—Ullikemi and Thunderbird—provided enough power to release Ullikemi from the prison of its human myth form."

I'd also eaten Ken's dream at the end. A dream of me, a vision in the primeval forest. That image anchored me at the crucial moment when I was so full of dreaming that I was in danger of following Ullikemi into oblivion. *Funny how he isn't mentioning that.*

"You don't happen to have an extra ancient one hidden up your sleeve?" I glanced at an earthquake emergency-vehicle corridor sign we were passing featuring a simple cartoon of a giant catfish. Mom's childhood was spent hearing tales of Madame Pele stomping her feet when quakes rocked the Islands, but Dad always blamed Oregon's quakes on giant catfish who lived in fault lines.

I pointed at the next earthquake sign. "Wait. That's not for real, right? There isn't actually a giant catfish living underground in Aomori?"

"Of course not. That's just plain myth." The boy was too serious. He didn't even arch an eyebrow at me this time. It didn't bode well for whatever he was not telling me about the Aisaka River plan.

"We need a bunch of life essence? You, me, and Kwaskwi slicing open a volunteer vein won't cut it?"

"Unfortunately," said Ken with a somber gravitas that made my teeth hurt, "someone's going to have to die."

CHAPTER SEVENTEEN

"You're just bringing this up now?" I screeched. All the curses and foul names I could come up with seemed tame compared to how I felt. He'd unlocked a whole new level of jerkface. He couldn't trust me with this vital information until the very last second? I clamped my mouth shut and pressed fists to my eyes, holding back another useless round of angry tears.

Ken put on the right blinker and took the next exit, Towada High School.

He pulled up to the pay machine at the deserted exit tollbooth and twisted in his seat so he could give me that perfectly calm, absolutely irritating regard that boxed me into the role of emotional wreck. His eyes captured mine in dark, fathomless pools of complicated emotion.

I couldn't stop the jitters boiling up from the nauseous mess of my belly. "How are we doing this, then?"

Ken pulled the ticket out of the visor and fed it into the machine along with some yen notes. The gate lifted, and he wrenched the truck into gear with more force than necessary. "You will eat my dream, the life-essence of my very primal self, and when I'm near true death, Yukiko-san will freeze me."

"That is the stupidest plan I have ever heard. Are you kidding me?"

"It's our one chance. To break Tojo's power. Force Kawano-san out of his outdated view of the world. To right a terrible wrong. Isn't it worth risking the Bringer's life for that?"

"You don't get to make me a monster! I won't risk being responsible for your death—even if you are a jerkface."

Ken pulled into a big parking lot while I breathed in outraged gasps. Turning off the engine, he bowed his head, staring intensely at his open palms resting on the steering wheel. "I'm responsible for quite a few deaths."

I'd just called him a monster. I'd shoved his guilt and anguish over what he'd done as a Bringer back into his face. *That's not what I meant.*

"This is suicide."

"Yukiko-sama will freeze me in time." His voice was steady and underneath that calm was a terrifying acceptance.

My door opened. Yukiko stood outside the cab, undeniably imposing even though I was several feet taller due to the height of the cab.

A streak of blue plummeted down from the sky in a long, ear-splitting scream. The sound abruptly ended, and Kwaskwi stepped out from behind her with hands on his hips. Crow's feet and smile lines created deep grooves in his tanned skin, making the trickster appear old and tired for the first time since I'd met him. The pronounced cupid's bow of his upper lip was obvious without his characteristic grin, giving him a full-lipped pout that felt too intimate outside a bedroom.

Even Kwaskwi is worried.

"The natives are restless," he said. "Chop-chop."

Yukiko craned her neck to look back over her shoulder where the sprinkling of trees dipped down an embankment of cat tails and tall grasses along a slow-moving, greenish-brown mass of water. Aisaka River, I presumed.

We were well into the morning now. Sunlight warmed my face. "Are we carrying the Black Pearl all the way down there?"

"Once Yukiko unfreezes the Black Pearl, the river *should* draw her to it," Ken answered.

Kwaskwi jumped backwards with arms raised and palms outward. "No way. I know where this is going."

"But if she doesn't head to the water," Ken continued, "someone will have to act as bait."

"Just had to go and get your leg injured, huh sly fox? I hate being bait. Bait always ends up crushed or dead. Why can't Yukiko be bait this time?"

Yukiko did that odd thing where her head twisted on her neck like a snowy owl so she could tilt her head up to unleash her full icy stare at Kwaskwi. Her lips retracted in a grisly caricature of a smile, revealing pointed canines and a glistening pink tongue.

Kwaskwi lowered his hands and cleared his throat. "Okay. Not Yukiko-san, then." He gave me a hopeful, puppy dog look and then spat on the ground. "Forget it, baby Baku. You're no good either."

Yukiko reached out a closed fist as if she were about to salute Black Power, and then slowly, slowly opened her hand. A sound like a carpenter sanding—no, like a dozen carpenters sanding—came from the truck and the tarp poked out in a dozen directions. The Black Pearl was waking up.

"Maybe we should—" With a pop, the tarp lifted free of its rivets and the Black Pearl burst from the truck, heading straight for us like a black, shimmering ginormous arrow. Ken jerked me out of the dragon's path by the arm. I was mesmerized by the shifting aquamarine, teal, emerald-blue of her eyes. Double-eyelid membranes fluttered open and shut while the Black Pearl writhed coiling and uncoiling, her tail whipping back and forth wildly.

Yukiko avoided the tail by shifting instantly from place to place, not a hair out of place, but Kwaskwi had a harder time, hopping about like a mad momma-jay to keep from getting crushed.

"Now would be a good time," Ken observed, "to run to the river."

Kwaskwi twisted to dodge a lash of the Black Pearl's tail, but instead of hopping away, he grabbed the tip and stomped on it with his steel-toed boot. The head stilled and then curled back on itself, regarding Kwaskwi with unblinking eyes.

Something powerful welled up inside my ribs in response to the glow of the Black Pearl's eyes. An aching, precarious pressure, like the thrill of being upside down at the top of the Looping Thunder coaster at Oaks Amusement Park. The mysterious depths of her eyes called to me, promising hidden treasures. I stumbled forward.

"Koi!" Ken tugged at my arm again. I tried to escape his grip so I could get closer to those beautiful eyes. "What is it with you and ancient ones?" He slapped a palm over my face, breaking the spell.

"What?" I wrenched his pinky finger back to force him to release his hand.

"Don't look at her eyes." Ken's hand dropped away.

Kwaskwi was waving his hands and yelling. "Come on, you overgrown, snake-headed monster. Over *here*! That girl is not the bait you're looking for—all tendons and bones. I'm very meaty." He jogged a short distance toward the river. The Black Pearl wavered, bobbing back and forth as if she was reluctant to tear away from our mutual stare-fest. Finally her eye membranes fluttered as if she were drowsy. Her neck drooped and her snout swung around to track Kwaskwi.

"How much did you take when you ate her dream?" Ken's eyebrows knit together like worried caterpillars.

Released from the Black Pearl's spell, I shivered, pins and needles running up and down my limbs as if they'd fallen asleep and only now reawakened. I scoffed. "Hell if I know. Dad hasn't had a chance to cover dream eating measuring cups with me yet."

"This part of the Aisaka is shallow. There used to be a fishing weir here for Ayu sweetfish. We have to get the Black Pearl into the river to release her, but we don't want her to drown."

"Release her in the river?"

"The river is her element. If there's any chance of the Black Pearl returning to herself…" Ken trailed off, his attention caught by the fact that the Black Pearl's initial frenzy had completely dissipated. Her head lowered to the ground, opaque eyelids closing.

Kwaskwi quit waving and stood with his hands on his hips. "She's seriously lost steam, dude."

Yukiko glided over next to Kwaskwi, pointedly looking at me and then the Black Pearl's massive head in turn.

I remembered the sleek leather of her scales, and the moldy sock smell, and the gorgeous depths of her eyes. Her song had been so, so sad. She couldn't give up now. The thought of the Black Pearl locked away again inside the cave made my chest hurt. I moved carefully over to her whiskered snout where it lay crushing dandelions on the lush grass. Ken sucked air through his teeth. "Be careful."

"Unnecessary warning." I pushed back the long windbreaker sleeve. Recently eating her dreams meant I could *probably* touch her without getting overwhelmed by her dream. There was really no other choice, though, I had to try. I rested the back of my hand on the tip of the Black Pearl's snout. Movies and European fairy tales taught me that dragons gave off ambient heat, but the Black Pearl's shimmering scales, streaked with purple and crimson at the snout, were cold. On the heels of that thought came a quiver of the whalesong from before.

"Wake up," I said softly, prodding stiff fingers into the hollow underneath her ear wells. "Go to the river." The whalesong vibrated more strongly up through my fingers, into my lungs and down to my belly, a current of sound flowing in stuttering ripples and eddies. I placed both palms along the scales underneath the Black Pearl's right eye and took a deep breath. "Time to go home."

The world began tilt-a-whirl spinning, but just as trees, river,

Black Pearl began to blur together into dream colors, fear spiked through me and I jerked my hands back to clasp them at my chest. *Not yet. We're not ready for the full monty. Just a little prod to get you going.*

The Black Pearl opened an eye, nostrils flaring in and out with silt-dank breath. Or maybe that was actually the Aisaka River, I couldn't tell. Just an instant, long enough for a stray thought, and already I was leaning closer to the mesmerizing, shifting blue. Straining like I was carving a line through butter instead of air with my eyes, I turned away. Yukiko was frowning. Clearly unhappy. What was I supposed to do? Let myself be drawn in?

This is what Ullikemi had done to Hayk, what Thunderbird tried to do to me back in Portland. At first a seduction, a promise of beautiful connection, but then it would turn to control. I remembered Hayk's glowing green eyes and the rasp of his voice when Ullikemi rode him. Morbanoid Koi spoke up. *How different is that from dreaming the Black Pearl's most intimate dreams?*

"Touch her again," said Ken, coming closer.

"I will drown if she lunges for the river with me attached."

"I won't let that happen."

Kwaskwi gave an impatient huff. "Oh, here we go. Come on kiddles, can we skip the part where the Kitsune attempts to make you trust him again despite his secret motivations for bringing you to Japan?"

I stabbed a finger in his direction. "You are not helping."

Kwaskwi shrugged. "This isn't about me, Koi. Or Ken. Choose. Either you're in or you're out."

He was right. The hurt part of me was holding on to these doubts because I wanted to lash back at Ken. He should feel the same precarious feeling I had in Japan, so far out of my comfort zone I might as well be moon-walking. But Kwaskwi was right. This wasn't about me putting all my trust eggs in the wrong basket. It was about the Black Pearl, and on a deeper level, about whether I could live with myself if it was my fear that made us fail. I had to go deeper into her dreams as Baku.

Face carefully averted from the mesmerizing eyes, I put my palms on her scales again. Ken gave a surprised cry just as the world blurred, spinning on its axis. Underneath my hands the Black Pearl shifted, trembles rippling up and down her scales as I took from her the waking dream.

CHAPTER EIGHTEEN

I was swimming again, the warm water of late summer caressing my belly and sides. The light glimmered above.

Somehow, underneath the pleasing rhythmic strength of my body I sensed an urgent need to keep going. I had to move forward. The pleasant hum of the sunshine on my back slowly faded. A chill crept over me, and an odd, bitter taste to the water flowed through gills on either side of my neck. Craning back, all I could see at first were the ripples, bubbles and disturbed river-mud marking my passage. Was that a shadow? An unfamiliar outline of something bigger than a river trout or eel?

The little Koi-flame, the buried awareness of my true self, flickered to life. *Keep going. To the river. We have to get to the river.*

But I am in the river.

Frustration rose up from my belly. That was definitely a shadow behind me, human-shaped.

Human?

I remembered blue coats and being stabbed and the terrible weight of the Baku in my mind, crushing the frantic beating of my heart.

Danger! Human-shapes were dangerous and I had to get away. I flexed the powerful muscles along my spine to put on a burst of speed, but they reacted only limply, strangely atrophied as if I'd spent too long stagnant and slumbering. The bright, mammal scent of crushed grass coalesced out of the strange bitterness in the water. Not water. I was on land, and there was danger—

"There she goes!"

I opened my eyes, human eyes, as the Black Pearl gave a wobbly lurch toward the Aisaka. "You did it," Ken said.

"She's still half-asleep, seeing her own river dream. There was something weird in the water in her dream, but I didn't do anything, really."

Kwaskwi waved his arms and gave an ululating yell. Yukiko's eyes went huge in surprise and she silently darted after the Black Pearl's wildly thrashing tail while Kwaskwi scrambled backwards madly, trying to channel their zigzag progress toward the Aisaka.

"There's something odd about the river in that dream and how much it looks like this one," I said wearily. Ken threw me a questioning look over his shoulder, but when I didn't elaborate, he hobbled after the dragon parade.

The slight widening of the river at the closest bend looked as shallow as Ken had promised, but even water that rose only to my knees could hide treacherous currents. Ken said he wouldn't let me drown, and I believed he meant that, but he was injured.

Kwaskwi reached the top of the embankment just in front of the Black Pearl's sleek head. He held out his arms wide, crouching low. "Come on, girl. Almost there." With an astounding leap, Kwaskwi flew into the air on legs like coiled springs, reaching for the upper branch of a grandfather willow tree halfway down the embankment. He caught the branch and swung round it like an Olympic gymnast. On the last upswing he curled himself into a ball and landed perfectly balanced on the branch.

Crouching jay, drunken dragon.

The Black Pearl couldn't halt her headlong rush to the river and flopped into the water with a splash that sent droplets pattering down over everyone.

"Swiftly, now," said Ken, wiping the back of his hand at water collected at the corner of his eyes like tears. "Before she gets her bearings."

Kwaskwi sat on the branch, swinging his legs in the air, and pulled out his cell, orientating it landscape as he snapped pics of the coiling Black Pearl. I shot him an *are you kidding* look.

"What? The guys will never believe this otherwise."

Yukiko started down the embankment and Ken tugged us after her, carefully gripping my clothed wrist. The wet grass was slick on the way down, and I found myself wishing for Dad or for Marlin; someone bossy who I could trust to know the right thing to do. Because even if it involved giant dragons and imminent drowning, at least I would be confident I wasn't utterly mucking things up. This whole operation pinned too many hopes on me. Without a lucid Baku, The Eight wouldn't be challenging the Council or possibly sending the entire Kind population of Japan into a fatal population tailspin.

No running away.

Maybe if I repeated it another hundred times I could control my racing heart and the urge to jerk out of Ken's grasp.

"You're sure this is the best way?"

Ken maneuvered us closer to the water. "She can't be free until you break her out of the dreaming. She's suffered long enough for the Council's pleasure."

The Black Pearl's head rose from the coils of her body, blinking double eyelids, the fleshy frilled protrusions around her eyes and along her jaw glistening wetly in the morning sun. She seemed confused, but no longer wildly thrashing.

"I won't...I can't hurt you." Was I saying it to the Black Pearl or Ken?

Ken squeezed my wrist. "Your heart is strong enough for this, Koi. I can do this. You can do this."

"I'll never forgive you if you die."

"Yukiko won't let that happen." Ken's voice was firm, but a fierce tic pulsed in his jaw. He'd gone feral Kitsune again, all sharp planes and bloodless lips pressed together in a grim line of terrible resolve. And the sight of him, even bruised and bloodied, still had the power to make my chest ache with an urge to feel those lips on my own, to breathe in his Old Spice and for a short space, not be alone with my fear of becoming a monster.

Morbanoid Koi understood why Ken risked his life. It was atonement. It made sense in a way I hadn't understood until Ullikemi's fierce desire for the sun, Mangasar Hayk's evil, and Tojo's ruthlessness. Something had to be done and I was the one with the power to do that something.

"Into the breach," I said, and stepped through crushed cat tails with Yukiko and Ken sidling after me. The water was a chill shock that grew colder by degrees. It didn't matter, I had to push forward over shifting river rocks and ankle-grabbing slimy river plants. Yukiko kept that cold gaze fastened on the Black Pearl, but I didn't dare pay attention to her for too long. Instead I concentrated on trying to catch hold of a nearby floating coil.

"Watch out!" Kwaskwi called from above. The Black Pearl's tail swiped toward us in a rolling wave of brackish water. Ken waded in front of me with surprising speed, using his arms to deflect the impact. With a sharp cry of pain he teetered and began to tip over in slow motion, eyes closed tightly in a face gone as pale as Yukiko's.

I grabbed his arm just as Yukiko caught the slim end of the Black Pearl's gray-tipped tail and slapped it around my bare wrist. A fleeting impression of a hand formed of ice pressing my neck and wet sandpaper on my wrist touched me before the world swiveled in on itself like a movie camera shutter.

A dream. No, two dreams—Yukiko and the Black Pearl—jostled

for dominance in a nausea-producing psychedelic dance of gray, white and black, fading finally into blessed darkness.

A white web of cracks split the bottom left corner and spread in diagonal bursts with a heart-stopping wave of needling cold and the sting of ozone. A precarious urgency gripped me, like standing on tip-toes, reaching for the last clean *shoyu* dish from the high shelf at Marinopolis. Then the darkness shattered, spinning away in shards.

I swam in my river. The metallic, decayed flesh tang of the water, the tiny shapes of darting fish, and the warm sunlight meant home and contentment. The powerful flex of my tail sent me streaming through the water, my length undulating in rhythmic harmony with the current. Warmth on my back made me fairly vibrate with happiness, a song that spiraled out from me in all directions, communicated up and down the river in a joyful prayer to *Abka Hehe*. She would surely send her spotted *kesike* servants to sing feline yowls with me.

What then is that oddly elongated shadow disturbing the bang huahua yu *ahead of my path?*

Just ahead, around the bend, the river entered a narrow valley where the sturgeon glided like torpid ghosts, an easy meal for an agile river dragon, but that shadow was no sturgeon.

Another thought appeared startling in its simple clarity: *It is Koi who knows this. I am Koi.*

I paused, muscles spasming up and down my undulating spine, gliding blind as double eyelids shut in surprise. *I am Muduri Nitchuyhe and you are Baku!*

I reared out of the water only to crash down again in an explosion of frothing water; a choking cloud of plant slime and pebbles and mud.

Time froze. Silt particles suspended in the water were eerily distinct, as was the surprised eye of a brown-silver fish caught mid-flight from my snout.

And then the world spun 360 degrees, vertigo morphing to top-of-a-rollercoaster breathlessness, before morphing again to sour nausea.

Then cold. Glaring, caustic, bone-eating, gorgeous cold. The white perfection of snow-covered land in an unbroken expanse with room enough to breathe and to grow. Teasing wind drove the far-off mournful cry of wolves to my ears, but they were only a minor irritation in the glory of the sunlit morning. I pressed bare soles into packed snow, hardening foot prints into ice, and opened my arms to the whistling wind teasing snarls into my long white hair.

Yukiko's fragment? How did I—?

A flame burst into life within, the crawling heat making me wrinkle my nose in distaste. Acting on instinct, I flung myself to the ground, inhaling sweet snow as a great weight shook loose with a yank that tore through each individual cell in my body. Gasping on my back, I stared up at an endless watery blue sky. I flipped over, only to have the sky blocked by a face so pale it was easily lost in the lazy swirl of delicate wind-driven flakes.

Yukiko stood over me. Not the Yukiko I'd met, but a primal Yukiko that must have inspired all the deadliest snow maiden stories. Unbound, streaming white hair tangled into knots over her exposed, creamy flesh. Her cheeks shone with a faint fever blush and her eyes, the gelid blue of glaciers, were devoid of fleshly aberrations like emotion.

I'm in your dream.

She nodded. I remembered the ice cold hand at my neck just before the dreams. I sat up, distracted by the peculiar homeliness of my own hands. Koi's hands, bitten cuticles and healing scratches from the airport attack so long ago. Eons ago.

You grabbed me in the river to give me your dream? Why?

I stood, shivering in the wind despite the steady, warming flame of my Baku self burning within my belly. A wrinkle marred the pale porcelain of her brow. Her eyes narrowed, piercing through flimsy conjecture.

I remembered Ullikemi's final dream—the great snake and I in a primeval forest of Ken's dreaming. In it, I'd had a presence distinct from the dreamer for the first time. Like now. Only this was Yukiko's primal dream. I had a sense of being Yukiko, like coming in from winter sledding flushed, cheeks wind-burned and still tingling hours afterwards, but also of myself. *Is this what it's like to be invited in? Can I exist as myself, Koi Pierce?*

She gave an impatient nod. Amazing she could convey that mix of disdain and eagerness with such tiny nuanced changes in the muscles of her face. She was giving me her most primal, kernel-self dream. The only reason for pulling me into her dream other than trying to stop me, would be to try to help.

Someone's going to have to die, Ken had said in the truck.

Yukiko was powerful and had accumulated eons of dreaming. It was like offering the Baku hunger a seven layer Opera Cake while Ken was a mere shortbread cookie. The Baku in me hungered for Yukiko, but I held back.

This isn't the plan. But even as the thoughts flickered between us, frigid resolve strengthened the piercing challenge of Yukiko's regard. She knew what I'd left unspoken. This way Ken didn't get the absolution he craved: risking his life. Anger percolated through the corralled hunger.

Who are you to take that away from him?

Yukiko flung her arms wide and the teasing wind swept forward, gentle no longer, gusting strong enough to feel like a punch to the guts, bending me double. The flame of myself deep inside flickered, shrunk to a pinprick. Her bloodless lips curled back in a grimace, revealing pointed canines. With hair streaming like a living, growing ice cloud, she was the very embodiment of winter itself. Some primitive part of my hindbrain recognized a pitiless predator. Fear washed over me.

The air crackled. My eyelids were frozen open, the inside of my nose scraped raw with killing frost. It hurt to breathe.

So stop breathing. This is a dream. Fear had woken the survivalist part of me and rekindled a wisp of the little Baku flame. I lusted for the rich bounty of Yukiko's dream in the same way I'd hungered for Dzunukwa. *A dream. And I am a dream eater. So burn, little flame, burn.*

The flame, all that was Koi and Baku, flared with a searing pain across my middle. Still I held it in check. *This wasn't the plan.*

Yukiko's eyes narrowed to slits of glacial ice, the mortal elemental enemy of fire. She spread her arms again wide and made a harsh whistling noise between clenched teeth. The wind gusted again, knocking me to my knees in the packed snow. I closed my eyes and grit my teeth against the cutting edge of the cold.

If I die here, will my real body die too?

Images flashed. Mom's devastatingly thin face smiling up at me from the worn vinyl of the infusion chair, Marlin clinking her soy mocha against my regular latte at Stumptown with a familiar, endearing impatience, Mt. Hood rising up out of rainclouds over the glass and metal panels of the PCC Sylvania Bookstore like a benediction.

I don't want to die. I don't want to hurt Yukiko, but I am not running away from this. I am Baku. She is in my realm.

I pried open my eyelids and pushed myself up to a standing kneel. Yukiko gave me a slow, fierce flash of her teeth, ending in a sneer just as another impossibly strong gust of wind knocked me flat on my back.

Okay, then. Monster it is.

CHAPTER NINETEEN

The floodgates and the fiery hunger burst loose. Baku hunger consumed the wind to feed my Koi-self flame. I shrugged off the prison of Yukiko's cold. Her eyes widened and an expression disturbingly similar to relief blossomed across her face. Energy, sweet and pure as the driven snow, poured into me.

My flame burned on.

Yukiko's expression screwed into a tight rictus of pain, her hands clawing at her throat like she was choking as energy continued streaming into me, fueling the fire. It burned hotter, gleefully siphoning Yukiko's dream into a heady fizzing that curled warm and heavy into my belly, spreading through arteries with every exultant beat of my heart.

And still the power rushed into me as Yukiko sank to her knees in rapidly melting snow. It channeled up through my spine to the base of my skull where it throbbed, pressure building like a strained balloon. It was so much, so much.

Want more.

Need more.

And I didn't care that Yukiko's hands dropped and fluttered, weak and useless things, at her sides.

She was so old, so drenched in accumulated dream-self. How many centuries? Like Thunderbird and Ullikemi and the Black Pearl herself. The only other times I'd eaten dreams like this I'd drowned in sensation, unable to pull away from the influx of power until Ken had given me the strange haven of his primeval forest dream as a safety valve through which to focus the more powerful ancient dreams. In Ken's dream, I was always standing under the draping filigree boughs of giant cryptomeria cypress, a glowing angelic figure utterly foreign from my own self-image. And yet each time, that image pulled me back to my Koi-self.

I am holding Ken's arm.

Somewhere underneath Yukiko's frozen plains and the Black Pearl's sun-kissed river was Ken and his forest, if I could dig down to find it.

Pain grew, spreading twisting buds all over my head and shoulders, unfurling petals of molten metal to press against my brain. Still, Yukiko's dream burned on, perma-ice consumed by Baku hunger and transformed into a gushing fountain of heat.

No. Enough.

But there was no cessation in the dream. Yukiko *wanted* me here, she'd invited me into the deep center of herself. And she goaded me into eating this dream with abandon, taking us dangerously close to the point where I'd take it all. Putting herself in danger for the Black Pearl? To protect Ken? Or out of disdain for Ken's *Hafu* status and the paltry bit of power his dream could give me? We'd switched places in the dreamscape, Yukiko sprawled back on the snow, somehow turning paler while I loomed over her like some mad elemental. The gushing fountain slowed to a trickle. Still Yukiko didn't fight or protest.

You're dying.

The snow was melting, and with it the hot edge of my anger.

Time sped up, like watching time-lapse footage on the Nature Channel. In no time at all the white expanse transmuted into mud. Slender, green shoots poked up, unfurling into tundra grass. Yukiko was a splatter of white stillness in the ocean of gently waving grass.

What have I done?

Pain spiked through my temples, each breath dragged through cages of iron. I was filled to the bursting and all that power needed to go somewhere or I would explode into fragments like a dream grenade.

The Black Pearl. A voice like a weak sigh at the outermost borders of my consciousness. Yukiko. *Free her.*

I stepped back from her body, horror twisting tendrils all along the spikes of pain. She *wanted* to die, to give her life's energy to set the Black Pearl free forever from decades of Baku-induced dreaming. I was the gun in the hand of the suicide.

I shook my head in denial, gasping with the agony of that movement. I couldn't handle eating the Black Pearl's dream on top of hers without a focus or release.

I tried calling up the verdant scent of ferns and the cool mist of the forest. But that connection faltered against a wall of unease and confusion where there used to be the peaceful haven of Ken's forest dream. He'd given my name to the Council, kept back his true age, his parentage, and he'd fooled me into thinking he was the Council's slave. I no longer trusted that this was Ken's core dream of himself. What if the primal forest was just another layer of Kitsune illusion? Pain equal to the pounding in my temples arced across my chest like a Tesla Coil. I couldn't think straight.

Ken's dream wouldn't work. The Black Pearl was the only being here I could really trust. I'd focus on her.

I began to hum, a vibration low in the back of my throat, and, instead of forest, reached for sun-kissed waters and the blessing of the Black Pearl's praise song for her divine benefactor.

My grassy plain blurred, the colors dripping down around like melting Jell-O in the summer heat. Too late I reached out for Yukiko, but she was gone in an instant, her pale form blotted out by muddy browns and greens that swirled in chaotic patterns like four-year-old Marlin with tempera paints and a Spirograph. Abruptly, the bottom dropped out of my stomach.

When the world settled into itself, I stood on the banks of the Heilong Jiang, staring at the Black Pearl as she stretched out full-length in her beloved river resonating with whalesong at a harmonic fifth below mine. *Oh. I am still me even here in her dream.*

Burning down through Yukiko's dream back to the Black Pearl's had released a scant bit of the building energy, but it was only enough room for a few breaths. I patted down the familiar curves of my own body with trembling hands still chilled by Yukiko's snow.

Abka Hehe? The Black Pearl raised her head to face me, river water streaming from the fleshy frills around her eyes. The humming prayer stopped. *No. You are Baku.* A weary sadness tinged the words, evoking years and years of loneliness in her sunless cavern prison. The absence of anger and the abrupt cessation of whalesong etched a hollow depth to the Black Pearl's grief.

One tormenter is not enough?

The outline of a man shimmered into existence next to me. He wore the blue uniform of the Japanese Occupation, younger and less hunched then when I knew him. My heart leapt. *Dad?* But there was no answer, and the ghostly apparition did not solidify further—a fading ghost memory.

Disappointment crumbled the bones holding me upright and I sagged to my knees. Of course Dad wasn't here. Just as this wasn't the Aisaka but the Black Pearl's dream memory of the Heilong Jiang. Dad had said once, in a lucid period before the dementia became really bad, *we are all alone in death and dreaming.* I was on my own figuring this out.

The Black Pearl's head twisted back and forth in agitation, the movement displacing so much water that my knees were soaked. I thought how Ullikemi had opened gaping jaws and swallowed my head whole in that last dream as I released him, shuddering at the memory of dank snake-breath and darkness.

Surely it didn't have to be that way every time. Maybe I just had to be touching the Black Pearl in this dream as I was in real life. I scrambled forward on hands and knees into the river. *Let me help you.*

Full of lies! Enemy! The Black Pearl's tail lashed out of the water. I ducked, getting a face full of the rotting leaf matter that floated on top. The massive tail skimmed over my head and came down with a solid thwack on top of Dad's ghost. It winked out with a little sucking noise.

I opened my arms in supplication. *I am Koi AweoAweo Pierce Herai*, I said, giving the Black Pearl my name in desperation. *I am not my father. I am American. I just met the Council two days ago.*

You expect me to trust when the enemy skulks in your shadow?

What?

There was another outline of a man, not a shimmering ghost this time, but an oozing inky darkness submerged on the near side of the river. Overshadowed by a hanging willow branch, it had been easily missed, but it began to swim closer. Now that I saw it, I couldn't tear my eyes away, mesmerized by the dark swirls and ripples that hinted at the shape of human limbs. Power leaked from my eyes and ears like snow-colored blood, carried by strangely direct eddies toward the shadow.

Eagerness, anger, and a colossal certainty emanated from it, re-orienting the dream world so that the shadow was the center of everything.

I didn't bring that here.

The Black Pearl submerged her head, bunching muscles all along her spine.

No! Stay, please. I lurched deeper into the river, hands reaching for the iridescent glinting black scales of her disappearing mid-section.

A tingling electricity swept through the water from the shadow, fizzing like stinging acid around my submerged knees. A heaviness, a sense of something massive gathered like a thunderstorm, and then the river ahead of the fleeing Black Pearl swelled up, parting as if Moses stood there with his staff at the Red Sea. An impossible wall of water rose up in front of the dragon. A suddenly dry gulf a quarter mile wide. The Black Pearl came to a sudden, bunching stop at the churning edge where water met air.

The dark shadow rose from the river-bottom. As it breached, the shadow turned to swarthy flesh. A bald head, narrow, glinting eyes, and a mouth set in a toothless smile. Kawano, impossibly present in the dreaming.

A sharp crack split the sky, and then my right arm blazed with pain.

The river, the Black Pearl, everything juddered in jerky stop-motion, and then *skipped*, like a movie projector glitch. The world spun around in a drunken kaleidoscope, and then I was again on my knees in a river, with the sour watermelon rind smell of the Aisaka soaking my pants and the Black Pearl's tail wrapped heavily around my wrist.

Tojo held my other arm, blazing with pain, in a punishing two-handed grip.

CHAPTER TWENTY

"You didn't need to break her arm," said Ken's voice from somewhere behind me. *Be worried*, Survivor Koi whispered, but I couldn't pay attention. I was too busy enduring jagged shards of fire shooting from my forearm, my skin crawling with shock and denial, lungs crumpled like used tissues.

Tojo released my arm. "Pain is the only reliable way to get a dream-eating Baku's attention." I cradled my arm to my chest, blinded with tears, gasping when fresh jolts of fire traveled up my shoulder and licked at my heart with the slightest movement.

I'd been burned, almost lost a finger to Dad's sharpest sushi knife, stung by bees, felt the agony of Dzunukwa's icy hunger, and sliced with Mangasar Hayk's sacrificial dagger. All of what I'd called pain before paled in comparison. *This* was pain: shooting agony, unbelieving, breathless shock. It *hurt*.

A man was angrily monologuing in harsh, archaic inflections I didn't have the energy to translate, and people splashed in and out of the river. It wasn't until someone grabbed me around the waist, jostling my arm again, that some barely coherent part of me processed I was being hauled backwards out of the water away from the Black Pearl.

Tojo grunted in my ear as he dragged me onto the slick riverbank where Ken stood, arms tied behind his back, held by Princess Stewardess. A grim-looking Pon-suma in plaid pajamas faced off with Kwaskwi, weirdly motionless under a huge fine-weave mesh.

So he can't fly away. Not good. And also, fuck, my arm hurts.

"You'll handle the Black Pearl?" said Tojo over my head. He was talking to someone still in the river.

"At least see to her pain," said Ken.

"It would be the diplomatic thing," added Kwaskwi.

"You violated oaths. You were caught. Diplomacy doesn't apply." Tojo spat on the ground. "And the Bringer is ours to deal with."

"We may need her coherent," said the man in the river. Kawano. I squinted into the dazzling sunlight still reflecting off the water. Just like in the dream, Kawano stood waist-deep and naked in the river, bald head glistening wet, skin below his neck leathery with a greenish tinge. What had Ben called him? *A dried up old Kappa.* Not so dry now. The river was his domain and somehow his Kappa magic had let him invade the river even in the Black Pearl's dream.

"Where is Yukiko-san?" Tojo gripped my sodden shirt collar and jerked me up to standing. A nauseating feeling of things shifting in my arm that were meant to be solid made me close my lips tightly. *Mothertrucker.* He gave me a little shake.

"I don't know," I gasped. "I don't know!"

Pon-suma pointed a finger at the ground in front of Kwaskwi. "You stay here," he said. Under the net, Kwaskwi gave a pouty wink and clasped his hands behind his back. Opening the little black doctor bag he had tucked under his arm, Pon-suma approached and bowed to Tojo stiffly. "If I may."

Tojo looked down his arched nose at him in a way that said he didn't trust Pon-suma further than he could throw him, but he released my collar. What was Pon-suma doing here? Where were Ben and the others?

And where was Yukiko?

Pon-suma drew out the huge syringe he'd used what felt like a million years ago on Dad. *Japan is supposed to be the country of cuteness and miniaturization. Why are the syringes all horse-sized?*

He plunged the syringe into a sealed glass vial and drew up the plunger. At least the drug wasn't glowing absinthe green this time. I flinched at his careful touch, pushing up my sleeve. Tojo gave a disapproving scoff. At the first prick of the needle, a warm relief flowed up my veins, loosening muscles stiff from terror, melting the iron cage around my lungs. I gave Pon-suma a loopy smile.

Ken settled back on his heels, relaxing as if some dire struggle had concluded. He was so dramatic. I was fine. Everything was fine! I *loved* Pon-suma's syringe.

"Now," said the old grouch in the river, "where is Yukiko-sama? The Black Pearl will not stay quiet long."

I giggled. "Don't come any closer," I warned him. *Whoops, I think that was English. Does Kawano speak English?* Kawano was dangerously close to revealing if he was naked below the waist.

Tojo's panties were in a bunch and he made as if to grab my collar again. Someone growled, a quiet sound speaking of anger about to boil over and a willingness to shed blood. It was that nice young man that Kwaskwi was trying to hook up with. I blinked rapidly, peering at him. His long hair was smooth and the morning sun picked out gold highlights in the dyed orange. I suppose if the stretchy, swimmer-muscled look floated your boat, he was nice enough. He didn't look nice now, though. He looked snarly. It wasn't really safe to snarl at Tojo.

"Nice boy," I said. "Good boy."

One of the Council black suits appeared suddenly, out of breath. "Tojo-sama," he said. His hair was moussed up into those touchable spikes Ken used to do back in Portland. I sighed. Things were so much easier in Portland. Now everyone was mean. Even Ken! I was supposed to worry about Ken for some reason, but I couldn't quite remember what it was. I was too busy appreciating Ken's nicely defined shoulders. Even more fun to look at than Pon-suma.

"Your knees are wet," I told the black suit in English. My brain was too fuzzy to bother with Japanese. Tojo gave one of those too-pompous-to-live nods. Black Suit swallowed audibly. *Uh-oh, someone's in trouble.*

"We found Yukiko-sama."

Kawano bristled, anger making his body into one slimy-looking bald human. "Like a banana slug," I said. No one else laughed.

Ken shot me a worried glance. *'Pretty boys shouldn't be worry worts,"* I told him. Tojo spun away to follow Black Suit down the riverbank toward a patch of trampled cattails.

"If Yukiko is harmed, Bringer, there will be no path to forgiveness for you."

"It's not *his* fault," I explained carefully to Kawano. My lips felt oddly heavy, and although I was trying to use my most solemn and formal Japanese inflection, my voice came out high-pitched like a Powerpuff Girl. "She *wanted* to die."

Kawano raised an arm, hand outstretched toward me. *He has seriously froggy-looking hands. Why did I never notice before?* "You lie." He lunged. I shut my eyes tightly. *Don't need to see the banana slug naughty bits!*

After a moment where everyone angrily yelled and basically had bi-lingual hissy fits, I realized no one had choked or punched me. I cautiously opened one eye. Princess Stewardess was standing in front of me. "Sir," she said. And then more urgently, "Sir! The Black Pearl!"

"Snakey-wakey," I explained helpfully and Kawano turned to look upriver. The Black Pearl's head reared up out of the water, lashing back and forth like she was gripped in a violent dream. Kawano barked commands to several more black suits milling around. *Talk about anger management issues.* He slipped under water again with nary a ripple. So creeptastic. I shivered. The water around the Black Pearl began churning like piranha had suddenly invaded the Aisaka.

"How long will she be like this?" I heard Ken ask.

"It should wear off in an hour. And then she'll be in more pain. She needs to see Midori," Pon-suma answered. Silly boys. *The Black Pearl isn't in pain, she just doesn't want to go with Banana Slug.*

"Okay Herai-san, time for a ride in the Council limo." Princess Stewardess had me by the elbow.

"Not my name," I told her primly.

"Yes," said Princess Stewardess. "I know your name. Don't tempt me to use it."

"If you even—"

"Shut up," she overtalked Ken. "You can come willingly and protect your little girlfriend here or I can have Tojo bring you later."

Ken's truck was getting carefully backed down the river bank, herded by black suits. All of them had the same spiky haircut. *Do they get a group discount on the mousse?*

"Hey!" Kwaskwi called out. "Dangerous foreigner over here. Don't I get a ride in the limo, too?" He leered at Pon-suma. "With a personal guard, of course."

Kwaskwi was so funny. And he wasn't as big a pouty-face as Ken. Pon-suma should definitely get himself a slice of that. *Relationship goalz. I ship them so hard.*

Princess Stewardess frowned. "Kawano-sama does not wish to involve you in the internal discipline of Council matters." Pon-suma tugged the net off of Kwaskwi.

"No doubt," said Kwaskwi. "So I'm free to go?"

Princess Stewardess nodded. The next instant Kwaskwi vanished, replaced by a large blue jay that streaked out from under the mesh just before it fully crumpled to the ground. I clapped my hands with glee. "That is lit!" The jay flew straight up to the sky, circled once with an angry squawk, and then dive bombed down again, landing on Pon-suma's shoulder with a little flourish of wings almost like a bow.

Pon-suma looked at the jay, rolled his eyes, and then returned to worried readiness.

Shouts from black suits at the river edge caught everyone's attention. The churning water was pushing the Black Pearl back to where a herd of black suits stood with nets and poles, knee-deep in the river.

Princess Stewardess' grip on my arm was annoying, but she wouldn't let go. "I wanna see," I said, tugging, and then repeated in Japanese "*Mitte mittai desu.*" She just pulled me further toward the gravel parking lot. She finally stopped at a truly blinged out, over-sized limo. Is that where all the black suits came from? I pictured them all squeezing out of it like clowns from a Volkswagen Bug at the circus. My giggle earned me a variety of disapproving and worried looks.

A black suit with flat, salt-and-pepper hair popped out of the driver's door, rushed around to the passenger's side and opened the door. I patted his head as Princess Stewardess slid me inside the dark interior. "You need more mousse."

He blinked in surprise. No one appreciated my helpful comments today. Or maybe he thought I meant the animal moose. I had used English. I giggled again.

Princess Stewardess gracefully settled next to me in the way-back bench on leather seats covered in pristine, white ginormous doilies. Ken, a bit pouty-faced, awkwardly ducked into the limo—it must be hard to be smooth with hands tied behind your back. Pouty-face tried to sit next to Pon-suma on the opposite bench, but I reached out with my good arm and pulled him down next to me.

I cocked my head to the side and studied those big, dark mocha-roast eyes, the thick lashes, the sharp cheekbones. Even Marlin called him a hottie, but there was something I was forgetting. Something he'd done I should be mad about...

My broken arm twinged. I wish he'd look at me like Kwaskwi

looked at Pon-suma sometimes. Okay, not like a hungry blue jay eyeing a worm the way Kwaskwi was now, but more like delighted I was alive. *And lose the angry caterpillar brows.*

"Where will they take the Black Pearl?" said Ken.

"Back to the cave," said Princess Stewardess. "But we are to await Kawano-sama at the museum with the rest of The Eight Span Mirror."

"Ooh! Can we stop for coffee at that amazing test tube place?"

"Did you have to give her such a high dose?"

Pon-suma shrugged. He settled against the bench looking squarely at Princes Stewardess in that implacable way that said he was not giving ground. The jay squawked. Pon-suma leaned over and opened the window enough that a bird could squeeze through, but the jay just pecked him behind the ear in a chastising way and turned a beady black eye on Princess Stewardess.

"And Ben, Murase-san and the others?" Ken asked after glancing at the closed, solid plastic privacy screen between us and the black suit driver. The limo was in motion, but it was so smooth I could hardly tell. Did Dad used to ride in blinged-out limos before he chucked it all to work long hours at his PDX sushi restaurant? Eating dreams for the Council couldn't really be that bad.

"They are not implicated in your plot, for now. Kawano-sama detected no lie when they confessed ignorance of what you had done."

"Hey!" I said, suddenly struck by Pon-suma's role as Kwaskwi's keeper, "how come Pon-suma isn't tied up? He kidnapped me and Dad."

"As I said," Princess Stewardess said with a moue of distaste, "None of The Eight Span Mirror is under suspicion here."

"But he's so nice. He would *totally* let Ken go in a hot second if it would help us."

The jay chortled.

"She's useless at keeping secrets," said Princess Stewardess at the same time as Ken held out a supplicating palm and protested, "She's on drugs."

"We cannot talk openly unless you can guarantee her loose tongue won't reveal me to the Council. In English or Japanese."

I blinked. "Ooh, you guys are sneaky," I said. "Is there anyone who's actually on the Council's side?"

"Take us to the museum," said Ken. "But then we'll need this car to get everyone to the cave before Kawano-sama gets there with the Black Pearl."

The banked fire in my arm had slowly been gaining heat. It flared up. Little shooting pains spread up my arm, not cringe-worthy yet, but I could tell a pain inferno was just waiting to pounce. Migraine spikes formed in my temples. Whatever Pon-suma had shot me up with, it had dampened both pain and the bursting balloon feeling from eating Yukiko's dream, but the dampening was wearing off.

Yukiko.

I flashed to her lying, a splotch of white in the green, green grass and knew with heart-certainty she was dead. And her sacrifice was for what? Kawano had stopped us. The Black Pearl had been so close to escape. Whatever Kappa control he had over water had seeped into the Black Pearl's dream. We'd failed. And it was on me. My head suddenly felt filled with lead. It lowered to Ken's shoulder. He stared down at me, surprised.

Ken put his arm around me, but even this soft touch jarred my arm. The pain made me bite the inside of my cheek. I sat up, leaning away from him.

"What happened out there?" he said softly. "What did Yukiko-sama do in her dream?"

"Yukiko's dead," I whispered in English, and then repeated more loudly. "*Yukiko-sama ga inaku narimashita.*" At Ken's sharp intake of breath I squeezed my eyes shut tight, but it was too late. Hot tears spilled out, dribbling down my nose.

"Inconceivable," said Princess Stewardess, like a Japanese Vizzini from the *Princess Bride* movie.

"She wanted to set the Black Pearl free," said Ken. His words were colorless, devoid of feeling, and by their very stiffness indicated surging anger. *Oh god, what have I done?*

"I ate her dream. I killed her."

Ken brought narrow eyes to bear directly on me, pupils dark like they sucked in every bit of light so they reflected back nothing but void. Something crumpled inside my chest. I choked back a sob. At the small sound, he cupped my cheek, holding me still as he bent forward to touch his forehead to mine. "No," he breathed. "No, Koi. This is not your fault."

More tears fell, caused by the broken bone in my arm or the broken place in my heart, I couldn't tell. I let all my limbs go loose and shifted sideways, protecting my arm, so that my face found the comfort of the crease between Ken's neck and shoulder. Breathing in sweat and a faint trace of Old Spice for an instant of escape, denial, of what the world held for me.

I explained in quiet English how Yukiko inserted her primal-self dream between me and Ken in the river, how she goaded me into eating it until the Baku hunger took over, and then Kawano's shadow rose up to block the Black Pearl before I could focus Yukiko's gift of power into releasing the Black Pearl from the prison of her unending dream. I left out how I'd rejected Ken's dream as a focus for Yukiko's awesome power, and how that failure felt like hot welts laid across my heart.

And then I let the tears come; great, gasping sobs that made my arm ring with pain. Ken held me tight the entire time, his slow, conscious breathing finally penetrating through the grief fugue by the osmosis of our body-to-body contact.

"Yukiko-sama chose this as her ending," said Ken in English.

Princess Stewardess gave a disparaging cluck of her teeth. "Yukiko-sama, gone? At the hands of this…this *American*?" She made my nationality sound like it ranked lower than pond scum. "No, I refuse to believe it. She is strong, almost an ancient one. She would not waste her life so unwisely."

I wanted to punch Princess Stewardess, and I wanted her to be right. Oh, how tempting to hope that I was mistaken. That Yukiko was alive. But the Baku heart of me was sure.

"Not a waste," said Ken, firmly. "A long life lived as she willed and ended for a great purpose by her own decision."

Pon-suma glanced up under lowered eyelids framed with that fringe of eyelashes as lush as falsies. "Koi-chan still holds Yukiko-sama's power."

CHAPTER TWENTY-ONE

"I will take you to the museum," said Princess Stewardess. "You will have to deal with the Council guards keeping watch on the Fujiwaras."

"Ben and I can handle the guards," said Ken.

The blue jay squawked, fluffed out its feathers and made a bobbing motion with its beak. Putting my hands to my temples, I pressed thumbs into the indentations above the jawline. It didn't help the increasing pain. If I could just *think*. "You and Ben against everyone?"

"I am the Bringer," said Ken with a shrug. I glanced at Pon-suma, looking for back up on how stupid that sounded but instead he gave a little nod, as if Ken's assumption he could take on a whole bevy of Council guards was unquestionable. Tojo had overpowered Ben so quickly—was Ken's reputation really that deadly even though he was *Hafu*? And injured? When he went all feral-Kitsune, I assumed it was illusion making him fierce, but was that version of Ken his true face? *What the hell do I mean by a true face anyway?* It wasn't like the Baku part of me was any truer than the student/sister/painful introvert Koi

I'd lived for twenty-three years. Maybe trying to pare Ken down to a single truth was just an excuse to stop making the mental effort to understand all his parts.

I'd missed part of the conversation. Princess Stewardess was saying "...even with Herai-sama, how can you be sure Kawano-sama won't stop you again once the Black Pearl gets to the river?"

"I miscalculated," said Ken. He put a hand on my knee and squeezed almost painfully tight. "The river is the Black Pearl's element, and I thought that would balance Kawano-sama's power."

What he didn't say was that if I hadn't been such a wish-washy, whiny Baku about trusting Ken's dream enough to make it my focus for all Yukiko's power, I would have released the Black Pearl before Kawano got there.

"Your mistake was attempting this without The Eight Span Mirror," said Pon-suma gravely.

Ken bowed his head, closing his eyes. "Yes," he said simply, accepting judgment. Admitting his responsibility without descending into a maelstrom of unhealthy self-recriminations.

A soft bell chimed. Princess Stewardess gave us a stern warning look and pressed a button on the armrest. A panel in the divider slid down, revealing our burly driver's thick neck.

"We are close to arrival, Gozen-san," said the driver formally. Something oily and slick twisted in my stomach. A sharp throb in my head answered. The car glided to a stop.

I grit my teeth. "Let me out," I said.

Ken gave me an earnest look. "Koi, listen—"

"Seriously, let me out!"

I pulled the door latch frantically. It clicked, useless. I pounded my fist on the window and the door swung open to reveal a stern face, not the driver's but somehow familiar in an unpleasant way. I leaned over and threw up all over the expensive-looking, shiny leather shoes belonging to the legs blocking my way.

A string of yakuza curses in male Japanese stung the air as wings clipped me on top of my head. The jay winged away, a bright blue dart in the fluffy cloud-littered sky. There was a grunt of dismay and I looked up, already turning red with embarrassment and wiping my mouth with the windbreaker's smelly sleeve.

Recognition slid into place along with a nauseating, acidic smell. Red Shirt from the airport. He kicked off his ruined shoes, gripped me above the elbow and hauled me roughly out. Fresh pain shot up my arm. I couldn't breathe for a long moment.

Red Shirt lunged back into the limo. There was a scuffle. What was happening? Inside the car the thrashing of limbs stopped. Pon-suma got out first, Red Shirt pricking him in the back of his neck with a wicked-looking bowie knife so hard that the shrine boy's pajama top had a spreading dark stain.

Princess Stewardess emerged next and smiled. "Nice work," she said. "And the Council guards?"

"They know nothing," said Red Shirt. "We will make short work of them."

Red Shirt was working for Princess Stewardess all along?

Pon-suma straightened, uncaring of the knife. "Gozen Tomoe-san," he said formally to Princess Stewardess. "I abjure thee."

Princess Stewardess was Tomoe Gozen? Like the historical onna-bugeisha? From that Jessica Amanda Salmonson YA fantasy series? No way. I had to focus. Something was going down here. Tomoe was breaking away from The Eight Span Mirror and making her own political move.

"It's too late to convince me Murase-san and his détente with Tojo will change anything. It's time for The Eight Span Mirror to stop sitting on its ass," said Tomoe.

"He's not trying to change your mind," said Ken's voice. He scooched himself onto the edge of the seat, revealing arms bound behind him in a way that wrenched his shoulders painfully. "And I abjure thee as well."

Pon-suma smiled, showing unnervingly long canines. "Just getting prepared."

Tomoe gave another exasperated cluck, but her glance lingered too long on the shrine boy as if unwilling to turn her back on him. "Don't be stupid," she told Ken and then turned on Red Shirt. "Make sure the Bringer takes care of all the guards."

"Hai!" He all but clicked his heels before handing over a set of keys to Tomoe and then prodding Pon-suma under the archway. Burly Driver jerked Ken out of the limo and pushed him along behind. I made to follow after, but Tomoe stepped in front of me.

"No, not you, Baku," she said. "You and your father are needed elsewhere."

As soon as this was over, I was going to sit down with Dad, Marlin, and Ken to discuss consent, free will, and how to pound the idea through pompous Kind craniums that kidnapping was *not* the answer to every little problem.

"Take me to Dad," I said. It hadn't escaped my notice that my brain was lumping Ken in with "family" when postulating about the future. So I probably should have been concerned about where Red Shirt was taking him, but I was just too exhausted. And sick. *And aren't Tomoe and Ken supposed to be on the same god damn side?*

"The limo is too flashy to fly under Tojo's radar. We'll have to take Murase's K-car."

"Where?" I said, swallowing stinging bile. I called up every ounce of sarcasm I possessed. "No, wait, let me guess. The tomb of Jesus?"

The blue jay swooped overhead, circled us three times, and then alit on the metal chain-top of the rain catcher decorating the front left of the archway's gutter. The long chain tinkled as it chittered. He turned a beady eye on us.

"Apparently, she's got her own plan that doesn't involve Murase or Ken," I addressed the bird—*Kwaskwi? Or one of his minions?*—not feeling a tiny ounce foolish, no siree.

My molars ground together at the thought of this bird actually being able to turn human. Dragons and dream-eating I could handle.

But this, this was weird shit. It was anti laws of mass conservation and crazy in some indefinable way that made hysterical giggles lurk in the back of my throat. "She's got Dad stashed at the Jesus mounds." I turned to Tomoe Gozen, who had, according to Dad's TVJapan samurai dramas, fought with a katana in the Genpei wars during the late twelfth century and carried her defeated master's head into the ocean to drown herself so it wouldn't be defiled. Seriously bad-ass. Still, she was messing with the wrong Baku.

"And you think, what? That me and Dad will somehow convince Tojo and Kawano to suddenly include you in the Council?"

The jay chortled, and Tomoe's face turned a bright pink. She gripped my collar at the throat, jostling my arm in a way that made stars of bright pain explode across my vision. "We have bigger plans than just joining the Council. We are not limited by the Bringer's narrow focus."

Her breath was sour, but it was hard to care when ten foot ice spikes were being driven slowly, inch by inch, into my temples from the pressure of Yukiko's life energy. I was going to upchuck all over Tomoe if she didn't let me go.

I needed to release this power. If my arm hadn't been broken and useless, I would have punched her. The fierce desire to connect my knuckles to her face must have leaked through because she pushed me away, and then adjusted her chiffon blouse and pencil skirt. "Let's go, Koi-chan." Her acid tone made it clear invoking my nickname was not a signal of affection.

Feeling's mutual, bitch.

Ignoring the mad cawing of the jay, I gritted my teeth and followed her to the small car Murase had used to take me to get coffee a million years ago. Man, I could have used some of Enoshima's magic brew right now but I needed to make sure Dad was okay. Hopefully he could tell me what to do to keep my head from exploding.

Anger-charged silence filled the car the entire ride to the Tomb of

Jesus. Even crunching over the driveway gravel sent flights of fiery pain up my arm. Was waiting this long to get it set going to make things worse? Should I have insisted she bring Midori along?

"Get out." Tomoe stood in front of my door. I gave her the look Marlin had perfected when we were teens sharing one bathroom and I was blocking the mirror. With a mad huff of air, she opened the car door. "You want to see your father, right? Get out."

I got out of the car without hurling this time. Tomoe gestured me away from the car, and then spent a few seconds muttering and waving her arms in the air like a crazy woman. Between one blink and the next, the car disappeared and in its place sat a small dumpster. I reached out to the rusted metal and felt the cold glass of the K-car window. Freaky on so many levels.

Tomoe had little patience with my open-mouthed staring and soon we were trudging down the path toward the mounds and crosses without any sign of the jay or anyone. We had even arrived before Kawano and Tojo. Tomoe looked pleased.

"Dad!" He was standing in front of the smaller mound reading the black-painted characters on the wooden sign. At my shout, he walked toward us and put an arm around my shoulders, hugging me close while I gasped in pain. *People need to seriously stop touching me.*

Dad released me quickly. "Koi-chan?"

"Alive and relatively unharmed as discussed," said Tomoe.

He was lucid, so I cut to the chase. "Yukiko tried to help release the Black Pearl by forcing me to eat her primal-self dream." My voice broke. "I didn't know how to stop. I think I went too far, I think she might be dead."

Dad bowed his head, closing his eyes. "The Bringer's feckless actions have upset many plans," he said quietly. He ran trembling hands through his hair, making gray tufts stand up like a bristle brush. "You were not supposed to bear the weight of Yukiko-sama's sacrifice."

"You knew she was going to do that?"

Dad nodded.

"She can't be dead," said Tomoe at the same time as I exclaimed, "Wait, you knew about Yukiko betraying the Council?"

"Many years have we walked this earth together," intoned my Dad in the sing-song words of a Buddhist funeral rite. "And many years shall I mourn her loss."

Tomoe swiped through the texts on her phone. "They're almost here. Time to present a united front as we discussed." She grabbed my shoulder, and I hissed with pain. "Tojo-san broke her arm. You deviate from the plan and it will slow down the process of Midori-san seeing to her care."

Dad straightened. Stiff spine, military erectness of his head and neck, and *awareness* crystalized from within the frail dementia patient he'd become.

Mom's master's thesis had been on the polarizing scales of the open ocean dwelling big-eyed scad who could all but disappear by reflecting the sun's rays, but when passing into shadow emerged solid, heavy, and unmistakably vibrantly alive. The quiet dignity Dad carried in the set of his shoulders, the strong *presence*, as if his spirit saturated each cell in his body like a shining force—this was Dad emerging in the shadows borne of years of pain. The Black Pearl's pain.

I'd been grieving Dad for years. My heart clenched seeing him now, here in this impossible situation. I had the barest glimmer of an understanding of the years of experience he must have lived.

"My head's going to explode," I blurted.

Tomoe scoffed.

Dad cupped his hands in front of his belly and spoke in formal intonation. "Are you able to bear the weight of Yukiko-sama's dreaming for a while longer?"

Could I?

"Yes," I said, as much to fool myself as to please Dad, so achingly familiar and whole from my earliest childhood memories. He should have been this version when Mom was in hospice, or to explain I wasn't a freak doomed to a hermit's life, or to do something other than the epic failure of protecting me from the Kind by keeping me in the dark.

"I've lived a long life," he said. "Many regrets, but now there's you and Marlin-chan." A lifetime's worth of interpreting stoic old-Japanese-man-speak made the unspoken obvious. He'd do anything to protect us, including help Tomoe with whatever political maneuver she was trying to pull. She must have come to the same conclusion because she turned away, mouth curving into a self-satisfied smile.

"Midori will be here soon," said Dad. "She will tend to your arm."

I cradled my arm closer. Was it a good or bad sign that the pain was lessening to a dull throb? My fingertips tingled with numbness. "What is the deal you made with Tomoe? I thought she was going all rogue vigilante?"

"Many of The Eight Span Mirror are more comfortable with following a middle path over Murase-san's outright rebellion."

Outright rebellion is in the eyes of the beholder. Murase drank tea with Tojo and Kawano and wouldn't say boo. If that was outright rebellion, then Ken stealing the Black Pearl out from under their noses was a heinous death-penalty offense.

"Middle Path?" I raised my eyebrows toward Jesus' mound where Tomoe was sliding open the panel door. Even with conditioned trust in parental authority, topped with a dollop of unease due to my sketchy Kind political knowledge, I wasn't just going to sit back and let Dad direct me. Yukiko's life-power throbbed insistently in my veins like blazing ice, and I had the Black Pearl's fragments reminding me in Technicolor and Dolby Stereo what it felt like to be imprisoned far from home. This was not right. And Dad was going along with it. Went along with it for years.

I couldn't go along with it.

This realization was like swallowing a foul-tasting medicine.

"Tomoe-san has sworn that she will negotiate for the Black Pearl's release within a decade. She will ensure you never touch the dragon again."

"But Yukiko forced her life energy into me! She made me... she made me into a monster." A scream built in the back of my throat. Somewhere lurking underneath the last dregs of Pon-suma's dope in my bloodstream was the full, soul-shredding, unavoidable realization that I was the instrument of Yukiko's death. But for now, the dope held back that waiting ghost.

Tiny muscles around Dad's eyes tightened. Two furrows appeared between his eyebrows, the only indications of how deep a wound I'd inflicted with my words.

"Yes," Dad said. "And we will not waste that sacrifice. But releasing the Black Pearl is *my* task. You were lucky with Ullikemi." He said a phrase in Japanese I'd never heard before. "*Settai jikko seigyo.*" I shook my head, a tear trickling down my right cheek.

"I don't know the English word," Dad said. "It's like...washback? From the energy required to release an ancient one."

"When I set Ullikemi free from his Vishap stone the biofeedback should have, what? Given me a mega hangover?"

"Without me there it would have scrambled your brain," said Dad. A light sheen broke out across his forehead. He rubbed the back of his neck vigorously with one hand. "I will not risk you again to fix mistakes caused by my self-deceptions."

Funny how everyone was willing to sacrifice themselves today; Ken, Yukiko, and now Dad. My stomach clenched. And if my arm wasn't broken and we weren't both liable to give each other nightmare fragments, I would have captured his hands and gripped them to my chest, trying to convey the overwhelming fear and love I felt. "No," I said.

"Too late," said Dad. "They're here." He frowned. "That took longer than I expected." He walked toward Tomoe, who straightened into a sentry's position at the cave entrance, defiant and alert.

Gravel crunching signaled the truck's arrival. A trio of shiny, black sedans trailed behind, stuffed to the brim with Council black suits. The truck revved its engine, monstering clumsily over the concrete parking bumps and crushing manicured grass and daffodils before coming to a stop in front of Jesus' mound.

The passenger door opened and Tojo jumped from the cab, a sodden white bundle draped in his arms. My toes curled into tight knots of denial inside my tennis shoes. My good hand balled into a fist and pressed against my ribcage. Not a bundle. Yukiko.

CHAPTER TWENTY-TWO

Tojo strode over to Dad, dropped Yukiko's body on the grass, and gripped Dad by his collar, forcing him down on his knees so his nose was inches away from her pale, wet skin. "This is what happens when half-breeds interfere with centuries of Council guidance. Are you proud of her? Your little *American?*" Spittle flew from Tojo's mouth but Dad didn't flinch, didn't struggle.

Stiffly, I moved closer. "Let him go." The hot wash of Tojo's anger met a little bit of my own as I pushed at his shoulder, allowing a bit of Yukiko's energy to leak out.

Tojo rocked sideways, letting go of Dad in surprise. Spots of tension flickered along his ruddy cheeks and jaw. "You dare," he roared and lunged. A star of pain burst in my left cheek as his fist connected to my face. My knees crumpled, and I just managed to twist onto my unbroken arm as I landed hard on the grass.

Sour melon-flavored foil taste welled over my tongue. Blood. A small pain lost in the general clamor and jangle of bones shifting and a throbbing ache on my cheek. A hand reached into my sphere of vision. I jerked away, heart pounding, reeling from the physical reality my brain refused to accept; Tojo *hit* me. Survivor Koi piped up. *He breaks your arm and you get salty over a punch?* Tojo was officially the top, and only, name on my hate list. He would never touch me again.

"Herai Koi-san. Please. Stand up." Kawano's calm rumble. I wasn't ready to be reasonable. "We are understandably in shock over The Eight Span Mirror's rash actions, but I don't think we need devolve into squabbling children."

Yeah, tell that to your playground bully. I lurched onto my knees, gritting my teeth at the rush of adrenaline and screaming nerves. Where was Pon-suma with his giant syringe? I squeezed my eyes shut and tried to stand. No, doping wasn't what I needed now. I needed Survivalist Koi with a clear head. A pair of hands gently slipped under my armpits and lifted me from behind. Hopped up on Yukiko's energy, even with layers of clothing between us, my Baku senses identified the steadying absence of fragments that had been my only safe human touch for so many years. Dad.

"You will refrain from touching my daughter," said Dad.

Kawano put a hand on Tojo's chest, effectively stopping him from barreling into us like a two hundred pound bowling ball.

"You need us," I said, baring teeth in a snarl. I wiped at my throbbing mouth and my fingers came away streaked with blood. "But Tojo will have to pound me into a pulp before I'd help you."

"That is unfortunate," said Kawano. Pursing his lips, he cocked his head to the side. "The Black Pearl is extremely restless and you've deprived us of our means of keeping her calm."

The canvas sides of the truck bulged for a moment right on cue, and then metal squealed at an eardrum-bursting pitch as the entire truck shook. Car doors slammed. Black suits jumped out of the sedans, pulled long-handled hooks and nets from trunks and rushed to the truck.

Tojo pivoted and in a flash was in the midst of the black suits, barking orders and ripping off the canvas cover.

"I have a deal for you, Kawano-sama," said Tomoe. She sauntered over to our little tableau as if a giant dragon wasn't about to burst from the truck and flatten us like pancakes.

"It is offensive that you would seek to capitalize on the current upheaval to push forward your agenda," said Kawano, flicking a derisive glance at Tomoe and then maintaining a steady gaze on Dad. *Sexist pig.*

"Herai-san will not help you without my word," Tomoe stated simply. She waved a lazy hand at the mad scramble behind Kawano. The Black Pearl's tail swiped a black suit's midsection, sending him flying. More black suits converged with their hooks, but the Black Pearl's head swung wildly, thumping others left and right. Tojo was turning red with exertion.

Kawano swung back around stiffly. Dad straightened up to his full height. "It's time to bend a little, old friend."

Tomoe must have been encouraged by Kawano's silence, although it felt like a pot about to boil over rather than resignation. "Make me a full Council member, promise that we will bring the Black Pearl's release up for public discussion, and Herai-san will help Tojo return her to the cave."

Kawano folded his arms and rocked back on his heels. "You have a deal."

I blinked. Really? So easily? Just like that Kawano gave up his iron-clad determination to keep the ambient magic leaked by the Black Pearl or whatever it was helping with Kind birth rates?

"That's not enough," Tomoe said. Across the grass, Tojo gave an inarticulate roar as the Black Pearl smashed yet another black suit into the dirt. He made a flying leap onto the Black Pearl's rounded neck, a length of chain stretched long between two fists. "If you want the Black Pearl alive," Tomoe said quickly, "you'll have to—"

Dad fidgeted from foot to foot, raising his hands as if to break in, but Kawano beat him to it. With an unnatural loose-jointed shift, as if he sported way more vertebrae than the average human, Kawano rippled himself in front of Tomoe's nose.

"My word is not enough?" His menacing tone was barely audible under Tojo's shouts as four black suits converged with their hooks on the Black Pearl's lowered head. Mouth open wide in a silent scream, the Black Pearl's giant coils grew slack. Tojo twisted his chain tighter around that enormous neck.

That made two of us Tojo had roughed up. *He'll get his*, I promised the dragon.

I had to give Tomoe props, though, she stood her ground against Kawano despite her face going pallid. "The Eight Span Mirror's entire mission is to include more Kind in decision-making. Shouldn't we include Tojo or other witnesses in any Council decision?"

"More Kind? You mean *Haju*." Kawano's disdain was palpable, like *konbu* broth bitterness on the tongue, but Tomoe didn't avert her gaze. If she had, she might have noticed something small and blue streaking over the Black Pearl's prone body and the black limo pulling into the parking lot. Doors opened and all The Eight Span Mirror Kitsune plus Pon-suma jumped out.

At last the gang's all here. I shifted closer to Dad.

"I love being a witness," said Kwaswki, doing his usual melodramatic entrance thing by stepping out from behind Jesus's cross. He settled on his heels with arms crossed next to Tomoe in blatant mimicry of Kawano. "Sorry I missed most of the fun," he said, flashing me his wonderful big-toothed grin. "I've been rounding up stragglers. What am I witnessing?"

"I made Tomoe-san a full Council member," said Kawano. "She may take Yukiko-sama's place. We will bring up the Black Pearl's release for discussion within two months. I so swear. Now," he told Dad, "put her back before Tojo-san kills her."

"No," I said, swallowing a lump of fear. Dad wasn't in any condition to eat the Black Pearl's dreaming, calm her, and get her into the cave, but they weren't paying attention to me.

"Your unholy bargain with Tomoe-san is unworthy of Herai

Akihito. Unworthy of a soldier." Ken's voice was a hushed rasp.

"I'm not a soldier anymore," Dad answered. "Just a tired, old father. Tomoe-san needs a show of power. She needs to bring the Black Pearl back when Kawano-san couldn't. I need her to protect Koi."

"Tomoe on the Council won't erase my childhood or Tojo's anger; there's no such beast as *safe*," I said.

Dad ignored me, striding across the grass as Kawano and Tomoe sidled closer and looked on in a disturbingly similar way. Self-satisfied twins.

Just as Dad laid a hand on a tail coil, Midori and Pon-suma converged, grabbing my clothed upper arms and pushing me back on a makeshift stretcher held by Ben and Ken.

"No," I repeated. But Midori blocked my view. She prodded my arm with gentle fingers. I hissed. "It's broken," she told Ken.

I couldn't see his expression as he was holding the head-end of the stretcher, but his voice came out tight. "Can you give her something for the pain?"

"Yes, but she's going to need the supplies I keep back at the museum. Here," she said, pressing a chemical cold pack to my cheek. "Okay, on three. Lift her and we'll get her back to the limo."

"Wait," I said. "Is Dad okay?"

Ken lifted his end of the stretcher high enough so I could see. Tomoe and Kawano flanked the open mound entrance to the cave, disturbingly chummy while Council black suits were dragging themselves off the gravel and sitting, dazed in the grass. Tojo stood over Dad, who had one hand on the Black Pearl's neck and a familiar far-off glazed look on his face.

The sun beat down making sweat pool under my arms. The groaning of the black suits faded away as well as the upset breathing of Ken and Ben. The hum of the Black Pearl's whalesong, the joyful adulation and supplication to her god, vibrated up from the ground.

By my blood and my heart I was bound to Dad. And by

dreaming, not to mention my good old-fashioned human sense of decency, I was bound to the Black Pearl. The rest was a distraction. Including Ken's secrets and lack of trust.

I swung my legs over the side of the stretcher to the sound of Midori's gasp. "Help me over to Dad," I said.

"Tojo and Kawano won't let—" Ken sputtered. Ben and Midori both jumped in at the same time.

"—with a broken arm!"

"—not your fault this went sideways."

"Everyone just stop!" I yelled.

Kwaskwi chuckled, rubbing his hands together. "Been waiting for her eruption."

I continued shouting. "We did it The Eight Span Mirror way and that turned out just ducky. I'm not The Eight Span Mirror. I don't care about your traditions and duties and who owes favors to who and all that crap. What I care about is releasing the Black Pearl, getting my Dad, and going home. Now I'm going to him," I said in my best imitation of Marlin's bossy voice. "And you can either help me get there—" I gave Ben and the boys the evil eye, summoning up my own powerful voice that was Koi the Baku. "—or you can get shoved."

Ben and Kwaskwi helped me stand while Midori shook her head in disapproval, rummaging through a black knapsack. That left only one *Hafu* standing there who could stop me. When I'd taken my "bound to" inventory, I'd intentionally skipped over one person who had their pesky dark espresso eyes pretty far embedded in my psyche despite how frustratingly dense he'd been since we set foot in Tokyo.

Make or break time. Ken could either get over his angsty guilt-ridden Bringer self and help me fix this giant mess or he could continue to be egotistical and self-absorbed trying to protect me from big, bad evil stuff. If he continued down this path, keeping his own secrets, shielding me from The Eight Span Mirror, the Japanese Kind, and his own wounded heart, I couldn't bear it. "And you?" I said, knowing if I turned and locked gazes, my resolve would melt. "What are you going to do?"

CHAPTER TWENTY-THREE

"I was going to kiss you," whispered Ken, "but I am afraid you will punch me."

Midori handed Pon-suma two flat sticks. He approached me warily. "This will hurt."

At least someone here isn't pulling punches. Midori came at me from the other side, all business.

"I don't have time for this, I—"

Ken scooted in from the front, cupped my head in his large, strong hands and brought his face close enough that I was in danger of falling into the solid, chocolate warmth of his eyes.

"Koi," he said, mingling the stale coffee and sour milk of our breath. Then he pressed his lips to mine; gentle, insistent. My heart slowed in response to the feather brushes of his mouth, blood sluggish and molten in my veins.

Midori yanked my hand forward, and Pon-suma slapped his sticks along my broken forearm. I jerked away with a cry, pain stopping my lungs from expanding, the world going oddly bright and fuzzy around the edges. I blinked rapidly, biting my lower lip as Pon-suma wrapped my arm tightly with a bandage.

"Bastard," I spat. Yukiko's dream energy throbbed down my arms, fizzing at the tips of my fingers. So tempting to give Ken a shove and send him flying across the grass. "Don't do that."

"Kiss you?" He arched an eyebrow.

"Use my stupid attraction to make me fall in line."

"Is that what you think this is?" Ken's eyes narrowed. He spread his arms wide. "It couldn't possibly be that I am drawn to you when you get all cranky and fiery?"

I glared.

"Kitsune were traditionally matriarchal," observed Kwaskwi with a delighted grin. "Suckers for strong women."

"Look," said Pon-suma with an aggrieved sigh. He pointed to where my Dad was herding the Black Pearl.

A sharp pain bit my shoulder as Midori stuck me with another syringe. Soothing warmth coursed down my arm, allowing my ribcage to unknit itself and the whalesong—the Black Pearl's despairing, weary plea to *Abka Hehe*—along with breath to enter my lungs. Dad closed his eyes and walked toward the mound, the Black Pearl's double eyelids fluttered wildly, but she followed after, the rustle of her passage through the grass oddly loud.

Hold on, Dad, I'm coming for you. For the Black Pearl. Ken limped forward as I moved. I held up my good hand. "You won't stop me."

"Not trying to stop you," said Ken. He raised his arms and then let them fall again. "I was an anchor for you with Ullikemi before, let me be again. I *need* this, Koi. Let me help."

"Fine." We reached the white picket fence surrounding Jesus's mound at the same time as Dad and the Black Pearl.

Tojo had been bent over, resting elbows on his thighs and breathing heavily, his chain abandoned at his feet. Now he zoomed over followed by a bevy of black suits brandishing hooks.

"Can you keep all of them off me? That would be very helpful."

Ken gave a slow smile that didn't reach his eyes. "Ben!"

Ben came to stand at his back while Kwaskwi and Pon-suma both took places on each side. Pon-suma stood eerily still radiating a chill menace. Kwaskwi struck a flagrantly ridiculous karate pose. They formed a wall between Tojo and the Black Pearl.

"This is not the way," Murase called out. He was holding Midori's hand, or maybe she was holding his, keeping him back.

"You can't fight change forever," said Ken. It wasn't clear if he was talking to Murase or Tojo. Maybe both. He'd gone feral Kitsune, cheeks cut from sharp planes, eyes narrow slits of glittering obsidian.

"I will crush you," said Tojo.

"I am the Bringer," said Ken with a low, obnoxious bow. Pon-suma licked his lips.

"You are a halfbreed," said Tojo. "A tool for the Council to use and discard." He lifted his chin. "You can't stand against the Council's might."

Kawano and Tomoe had stopped their mutual congratulation party. "Hey," Tomoe called out. "What's going on now?"

"The Council's might?" scoffed Ken. He flung out an arm to indicate the motionless black suits clumped behind Tojo. "Your *kempeitai* illusion? How many are real? How many Kitsune have you really convinced to follow the Butcher of Nanjing? I'm not afraid of your tricks."

Tojo growled. "I am the Council's might. And I will crush you." He brought a fist up into the air. The black suits blurred, went oddly colorless, and then swirled away like small dust devils to reveal only six actual guys standing behind Tojo looking a bit surprised. They looked at each other and their surprise became worry.

"Those odds are a bit fairer," said Ben. She cracked her knuckles and shook out her arms in a way that made me think of pro wrestlers while Murase and Midori continued to argue. Midori hung onto Murase's arm for dear life.

Ken hopped forward on his bad leg and the nearest black suit flinched away.

"We had a deal," Tomoe was saying to Dad. *Wait, that's my fight.* Time to leave all the rest of this stupid mess to the ones who'd created it.

Dad didn't open his eyes or release his hand from the Black Pearl's slowly undulating coil, but he nodded once, still aware at some level of what was happening in the real world. The Black Pearl moved forward, flattening the fence posts, her whalesong quieting to the barest of murmurs.

I reached for Dad's free, dangling hand. Kawano did that weird rippling thing, but I changed direction mid-grasp as he appeared in front of me, digging my fingers into the bare skin of his neck at the shoulder. His eyes went wide, twisting away before I could do anything but get an impression of the world on fire, my nose full of the charred pigskin smell of human flesh burning, and a great sorrow like a leaden cape across my shoulders.

World War II nightmares. No thank you.

Kawano ripped off his Patagonia jacket and swung it into the air, aiming for my face. I glimpsed Tomoe's wide, startled eyes before it settled over my head.

"Don't choose the losing team," I said to Tomoe. Then I punched blindly straight ahead with my good hand, releasing pent up frustration and fear and Yukiko's dream energy. My hand connected with something solid and meaty—Kawano.

I tugged the windbreaker off my head to find Kawano and Tomoe tangled together wrestling on the ground.

"You can't do this," I said to Dad. "I won't let you make the same mistake again. This is not right." I slipped my fingers through his dangling hand.

The world spun 360 degrees, colors and sensations blurring and then fracturing. My stomach seized. It was like riding a Tilt-a-Whirl hepped up on rocket fuel. The fractured colors fell away to reveal a plain, featureless landscape of gray. Dark blue shadows made long, curved shapes like sandstone contours in Bryce Canyon National

Park. I fell to my knees and vomited, wincing in anticipation of pain from my jarred arm, but those drugs Midori had were good stuff. There was a faraway feeling of small tendon and bone bits shifting inside my arm, but then I was vomiting again and it didn't matter. The puddle of puke threatening to soak my knees was dark blue.

A cool palm drew my hair back from my face. *Dad.* But the man standing beside me was not the father and sushi chef I'd known my whole life. It was the young officer from the Black Pearl's dream-memories, with brutally short dark hair unblemished by gray, smooth skin, and shoulders that filled out the cloth covering them. Instead of an army uniform, Dad wore a summer yukata dyed in traditional indigo starbursts and tall-soled wooden geta on his feet.

"Stand up, we're going to be late."

"Late?" I repeated, wiping my foul-tasting mouth with the sleeve of my own yukata. Stomach momentarily quiescent, I stood up realizing that I wasn't in my own body as I'd thought at first, but some young girl with long black hair brushed into a shining fall down to the backs of my knees. Petite feet and slender hands with dirty, ragged fingernails greeted my downward glance.

"The Black Pearl is coming."

"What? Where?"

Dad tugged my sleeve, urging me forward. I tripped over the unfamiliar square shape of the geta. Dad made an exasperated cluck. "We'll miss it!"

"Miss what?" But he was off again, making for a large blue formation a couple of hundred feet ahead. This was so weird, unlike any dream I'd ever seen before. The landscape looked like a movie green screen before fantastic backgrounds and monsters were projected on it for only the movie audience to see. This young version of Dad wove around blue shadows and nodded at empty space like he was greeting people. I shuffled after as quickly as I could, the clack of my geta oddly hollow.

"Dad, wait!"

Dad stopped and turned around, eyebrows knit together in confusion. "Little Sister, what are you playing at?"

Sister? My mouth opened and then closed again without a sound. *Dad had a sister? Why hadn't he ever told us about her? Marlin would freak.*

I caught up to him. "Where are we going?"

"A bend in the river downhill from Tong Jiang. Does brushing your hair make you mindless? Baba just told you this morning about the Black Pearl. About how the Manchurians witness her yearly return singing for her god. I want to see the spotted *kesike* that come to sing harmony."

I stared blankly at Dad. His sister's memories weren't mine. It was just dawning on me that he talked as if his family lived here in Northern China, although it would have been called Manchukuo by the Japanese settlers. Dad had lived in Manchuria? Before he became an army officer?

Frustrated with my empty stare, Dad grabbed my wrist. "Come on!"

Suddenly the gray and blue shapes flickered. A river bend bounded on both sides by tall grass took their place. I blinked. Upriver, a large black shape was swimming slowly our way, just barely visible under the water. The Black Pearl.

I rubbed my eye with my good hand and the gray landscape superimposed itself on the river like a hazy ghost-image. What was going on? It was like Dad had this all-purpose dreamspace he could fill with any memory or dream he wanted, even the Black Pearl's river?

"Shie-chan, don't ruin this. I'll never take you along on Kind business again."

"I'm not—" but Dad was pulling me along again, sliding down the river embankment, wading through the tall grass. Something in the grass coughed. I stilled. A leopard lifted its head from about thirty feet away and regarded me with a pair of unblinking yellow eyes.

Tingles ran up and down my arms. I felt fear but also awe at the beautiful, sleekly muscled feline. This was the *kesike* Dad wanted to see.

I decided I would be happier seeing it from further away. It coughed again and gave itself an all-over shiver before bounding away upriver.

Dad slowed by the river bank, swaying slightly to a music I couldn't hear as the Black Pearl drew closer and closer. "Yes, that's it, old one," said Dad. He bent to dangle his fingers in the silty water. "A rest. In your favorite place. Come."

Something was odd here. The trees behind Dad shimmered strangely. Between one moment and the next they reverted to blue shadows that formed a mound-shaped blob topped by a cross. Jesus's mound.

"You're hiding the mound with this memory. You're fooling the Black Pearl with this fake dream-memory. You're luring her back to the cave."

"Shie-chan, hush." The Black Pearl was quite close now. A half dozen leopards lined both sides of the river, a chorus of quiet coughs punctuating a low-throated throbbing purr. The Black Pearl's head broke through the surface of the river, rearing up as cascades of water streamed down the fringes under those mesmerizing emerald-and-aquamarine eyes.

And then the Black Pearl's whalesong prayer vibrated up through the soles of the geta into my legs, swirled inside my belly, and lodged itself under my ribs.

"Oh, I didn't realize," I breathed. Tears streamed from my eyes. Dad didn't hush me this time. He just gripped my hand in a painful squeeze causing delicate bones to shift.

I didn't care.

Here in this dream-memory Dad had made, the Black Pearl sang her hymn to *Abka Hehe* out of joy. It made an eerie, breath-stealing harmony with the leopard's droning purr. "She's so beautiful."

But underneath the hymn to life and the cradle of the river, to thanksgiving for the blue sky and the warmth of the sun, lurked an undercurrent of pain. Exquisitely sharp, gorgeously lush, a despairing, seductive loneliness I wanted to fold around myself. I could surrender the long hard work of surviving. A deep-boned ache for the Heilong Jiang shot through the melody. The ache was thick, formed like sedimentary rock, layer by layer all the years of imprisonment in the cold dark earth. This was the Black Pearl's song as my father lured her back to prison.

"What are you doing?" I sobbed, tugging on the collar of Dad's yukata.

Dad turned away from the Black Pearl's looming, swaying head rearing out from the water. "It is Japan's destiny to rule the Pacific Co-Prosperity sphere. Those weak Kind that have wasted their resources on Opium trade, who do not bow to divine will but look to decadent Western nations for leadership don't deserve the guardianship of such a powerful ancient one. They must be taken care of."

Taken care of? My jaw tightened. Dad's words skimmed far too close to Nazi Germany propaganda I'd seen in history books. But this wasn't history. This was Dad tricking the Black Pearl now, in my time.

"You're imprisoning her again." I jerked my wrist out of his grasp. The trees, the sun, the leopards disappeared. Only blue and gray shadows surrounded me again, blurring against the stark indigo of Dad's yukata and the iridescent ebony of the Black Pearl's scales. "What could Tomoe promise you for this?"

Dad's lips twisted into a grimace. "Protection for you."

I scoffed, a leopard cough. *Ken and Kwaskwi aren't strong enough? Is the Council all powerful even in the U.S.?* "How can you trade our safety for the Black Pearl's misery?"

"*Your* safety. Tomoe swore that the Black Pearl will suffer only a short while longer. Just enough time for the Council to accept her and for certain adjustments in leadership to be made. The Eight Span Mirror has been working a long time to get someone on the Council. In return, Tomoe promised you would get to choose where you live, and not bind you to the Council as a servant."

I thought about the kanji for slave tattooed on Ken.

A tic in Dad's jaw flickered madly. "It's what I wanted for you, since the first time I held you in my arms. It's the promise I made to your mother in the hospital." He swallowed and looked over my shoulder into the endless, shadowed gray. "I will make sure you get to choose."

And here we were at the same old impasse. My whole life he'd protected me by keeping me apart from the Kind, ignorant of what I was. How was I supposed to choose when Dad kept making decisions for me? "It's not for you to *make sure* I'm anything. That's my job, now."

"Yes," said Dad. He cupped my cheek, a warm, intimate gesture that brought back the endless blue sky, the lazy river, the amber eyes of leopards in the tall grass. I stilled, shocked. Touch wasn't like him. Wasn't like us.

Inside me, the throbbing energy of Yukiko's dream roared into life. Breath exited my lungs in a whoosh as energy buzzed every cell, every space in my body. Dad's fingers curled into my hair, holding me there.

And the energy flowed out of me into my father. The Baku was sucking Yukiko's dream energy into himself.

CHAPTER TWENTY-FOUR

"No!"

Dad's grip in my hair had to have a real life analog; the sting of hair ripping out at the roots felt too deeply shocking.

"I won't fail you this time, Koi-chan."

Whatever dream he had going on here, this wasn't reality. And I wasn't this Shie sister of his. Tomoe had made a devil's bargain with my father. I wanted no part of it.

Instead of fighting Dad, I took deep breaths. *So this is what it feels like to have a Baku eat your dream.* It wasn't really my dream, but Yukiko's, but still I shuddered at the wrenching feel of her energy leaving my body. It left my belly cold and empty and hollow.

"Don't do this to me, Dad."

Dad's eyes focused. "You don't understand the danger here. I will not lose you. Not like Shie, not like your mother."

The Black Pearl glided to the shore, lowering her head so close that her breath bathed us in salty *konbu* and gym socks. *Funny how much that stinks even in this memory dream. Or maybe this is real? Or both?* Her gorgeous, aching song rushed into fill the space where

Yukiko's energy quickly was depleting.

"No one puts Baby Baku in a corner anymore," I whispered. Dad's strength was focused on keeping me from jerking away. Instead, I tucked my chin and pitched forward. My forehead caught the crown of his nose at a diagonal. There was a sickening crunch as my brain matter gonged like a bell, but Dad's hands fell away.

At last, nothing between me and the mesmerizing aquamarine of the Black Pearl's eyes. Her delicate nostrils flared. The whalesong washed over me, a thousand brilliant, tiny cuts.

"I know how this has to happen," I said quickly. "Just go ahead and do it."

The Black Pearl delicately opened her jaw. The fringed gums fell away, revealing two rows of spaced, sharp teeth like an orca's, and also a pair of thin curving fangs rearing over my head.

"I have Yukiko's dreaming," Dad gasped.

I straightened up, broken arm dangling uselessly, but trying with all my might to embody Mom's calm, the iron-clad surety she had even when jumping head first into the unknown. Even with the chemo and the radiation, Mom had always unhesitatingly acted. "I have to try anyway."

The Black Pearl's jaw opened wider, unhinging like a python's, and then dove swiftly to close fetid dark over my head.

I couldn't help myself. I screamed. *It won't hurt you*, Survivalist Koi said drily. *You survived Ullikemi doing the same thing.*

But that was in a dream. This was for real. Wasn't it? *I can't tell anymore.* And then no part of me could think because a tsunami made of whalesong and river water crashed over me. I was drowning, drowning in sorrow and flooded with putrid, silt-swollen water.

The Black Pearl's dream. Her nightmare.

For a long suspended dreaming moment, I choked as my heart stilled under my breastbone, squeezed in an icy grip. The Black Pearl's dream pummeled me like hurricane waves crashing over Haystack Rock on Cannon Beach. But even in the midst of that unrelenting attack, the flame that was Koi, my Baku kernel-self flickered into life.

With a gasp, the pain broke. My flame burned bright and eager. *I'm getting better at not losing myself.*

The thought was wholly mine—Koi Pierce, the coffee lover, the Portlandian, daughter of a sushi chef, and sister of a fashion diva. Baku.

Ullikemi had been whole enough to rail at me, even bargain, when I set him free back in Portland. But the whalesong was all that was left of the Black Pearl. Sorrow and loneliness had slowly eroded her mind inside the dream prison Dad constructed before he left Japan. Everything we'd done in the last day—taking her to the Aisaka River, my Baku touch forcing her to relive her capture—had only made things worse. This storm nightmare was the tattered shreds of her consciousness. But it was full of the Black Pearl's magic and perfect for feeding a Baku.

Okay, then. Burn, little flame, burn.

I ate her dream.

I ate the pain. I ate the sorrow, and my veins hummed with the Black Pearl's life-energy.

I felt so strong. Yukiko's energy was small fry compared to the ancient, fathomless depths of the Black Pearl's dreaming. Her nightmare fueled my flame, and my body turned the heat into a fizzing, zapping energy that raced loony circuits up and down my limbs. I was powerful. I was inevitable. Tomoe was something I might crush accidentally under a heel and Kawano was an irritating fly to swat away.

No one need suffer anymore. I would bust through all of Tojo's goons with one hand tied behind my back. The Butcher of Nanking would bow before me, before the Black Pearl, and be humbled.

How did Dad stay away all these years? The Black Pearl's dreaming made me as giddy as drinking a triple latte laced with Red Bull while sticking a finger in an electrical socket.

Koi-Chan, that's enough. Dad's voice. He must have managed to touch bare skin on my body in reality. That touch usually was a shockingly rare connection that centered me. An eye in the hurricane of my emotional life.

It barely registered now.

Power lit each cell of my body from within. Glowing hot, the pressure in my skull and under my breastbone almost was more than I could bear. But I was Baku. This is what I was made for.

You go too far.

Anger spiraled in from all sides. *You kept me away from this ecstasy.* I was in full control, despite the pain, and I would make everything right. Just as soon as I ate enough of the Black Pearl's dream.

This is the tipping point. Stop now or you will take too much.

Senile old man. I am all that you are and more. I am Baku and this ancient one is mine. Every muscle in my body seized, the darkness became the iridescent scales of the Black Pearl, and then fractured, spinning around me in a dizzying dance. Still the energy poured into me.

Koi AweoAweo Pierce. See this!

The iridescent scales hardened into a shining, obsidian wall surrounding me. Reflected in the dark mirror was my own face, not Dad's dream of his sister, but a dark mass of hair, the angular Pierce family nose, and the slight epicanthic fold above gently rounded eyes marking my mixed heritage. I tried to gasp and couldn't squeeze breath into my lungs. The pressure built and built and built.

A cluster of agony shards burst like a supernova in the middle of my brain.

What am I doing?

Use the Kitsune's dream as you did with Ullikemi or the ancient one's dreaming will overwhelm you.

Kitsune? Pain's jagged claws speared my brain and stopped all coherent thought. Somehow my little kernel-self, the flame of my Baku power burned on, and it was sucking the very life from the

Black Pearl.

And me. I'm not ready to be a dead monster.

With the last shreds of coherent thought and the dregs of my willpower, I jerked away from the Black Pearl and our connection, tumbling backwards. My ravenous flame flickered, then went still. The energy turned off like a spigot. Strong arms caught me. I opened my eyelids, sticky with tears and dried mucus.

An utter absence of light was all I could discern. Panicking, I struck out wildly, open palm coming up against flesh and bone, bound arm waving in the air. I was blind. This happened before when I ate too much of Ullikemi's dream back in Portland: blowback blindness.

"Koi." A voice, not Dad's. Hands holding my arm against my side. The Kitsune. Ken was the first man who wasn't Dad who could touch me without giving me freaky fragments. He felt safe. I'd trusted he wanted to help me and Dad. That's why his fragment had helped me before.

Now I shied away from Ken's forest of cryptomeria cedars carpeted with primeval ferns as if it were rat poison. No, not Ken's dream. I couldn't. Japan had changed everything. I could no longer immerse myself in that dream with the same naïve trust. I needed something else; something warm and safe I could pull around me like one of Mom's island quilts.

"What's wrong with her?" Ken's voice again.

"She went too far. She has to find a way to focus."

"Use my dream," said Ken, and then warm breath sour with bile bathed my face.

"No," I said, cracking open chapped lips, my voice a faint rasp. Not Ken or Dad. Not a Kind fragment; not something foreign and twisty and false.

The blowback blindness was a small worry. It had healed on its own before. Hands helped me lay back, resting my head on hard thighs. Ken's probably.

Someone made a frustrated hiss. Dad. "The Black Pearl is too weak. Even with Yukiko's power I can't finish this."

"Koi," said Ken, urgently gripping my good hand and squeezing. "Don't give up. You have to take my dream."

Now what flared hot was dream-eating fueled anger. "You don't get to tell me what to do!" I could feel spittle fly from my mouth. "I'm not your tool, and I'm not The Eight Span Mirror's pet."

"I never thought—"

"Shut up! Just shut up!" I jerked my hand out of his grip and pressed a fist into my unseeing left eye. The pressure on the orbital bone did nothing to contain the mother of all migraines splitting my skull in a dozen pieces. This was a train wreck. Following Ken to Japan was supposed to help me figure out who I was, help Dad's Baku-flavored dementia, but it had made me blind, blind as I was now in real life to the daunting truth.

The Kind weren't a magical fix for a lifetime of feeling awkward in my own skin or for Dad's anguish. Eating dreams was reveling in strength I had never known before, but it brought me to the brink of a nightmare chasm where I was a monster, killing Yukiko, hurting the Black Pearl when I meant to set her free.

Pain made it hard to think, but I latched onto the need for a safe fragment, a human fragment without the distracting intensity of Kind dreaming, something I could trust in its simplicity. That felt right, returning to who I was before the Kind. The problem was, no humans, unless you counted Midori who was technically *Hafu*, had touched me in days.

Wait. Me, blind. I'm forgetting something about blindness.

Enoshima-san, the coffee guy with the test tubes. He'd given me a fragment when I picked up my coffee that day. It was just a flash, and most likely weak, but it was human.

"Help me up. Let me touch her," I urged.

"She's dying, Koi-chan," Dad said in a tone as dry as the desert, his version of a sob. "Let her die in peace now."

"Please, *Oto-chan*," I said, using a diminutive form of poppa I hadn't called him in ten years. "Take me to the Black Pearl!"

Muscled forearms pulled me up to a stand. Guided by Ken's hand in the middle of my back, I slide-stepped through the grass until water soaked my toes. Water? We'd left the river. This must be the pond.

"Here," Ken said, and plunged my good hand under water until fingertips brushed the hard surface of one of the Black Pearl's coils.

"Now," I said, elbowing him in the midsection with a short burst of dream-energy and anger, "You get the hell away from me."

CHAPTER TWENTY-FIVE

There was a satisfying thump as if he'd gone tumbling into the wet grass. *If only I could see his face.* But if I was going to use Enoshima's fragment, no Kind could touch me.

"I deserved that," Ken said quietly from somewhere on the ground. "There was my mission, and then there you were, so fiery and strong. I couldn't stay away."

I snorted.

"But somewhere in there I relied too much on your strength and your heart. I... I broke this thing between us." There was rustling. Ken made an angry scoffing sound. "You lost your sight again, didn't you?"

I nodded my head. "Espresso eyes won't work on me this time." There was no time for Ken's Hallmark moment. "This is for the Black Pearl. She's the one who's suffered. It has to end."

More rustling and a sigh. "As you wish."

Pushing Ken's angst aside, I settled back on my heels on the grass and closed my eyelids.

Okay, time to strut your stuff.

I forced my brain to picture an ink-dipped calligraphy brush stroking strong and sure down creamy rice paper in the beginning Kanji characters I learned in Portland Japanese School kindergarten on Saturdays: the open box of *day*, the triple straight lines of *mountain*, the squiggly parallels of *river*. I'd used this mental exercise to stop other people's fragments from entering my consciousness, now I used it to push away Ken's cryptomeria cedars, the Heilong Jiang, and drowning darkness.

Here, little fragment, come to momma. And there it was—the slight tickle of Enoshima's fragment, burrowing down at the bottom of my mind away from the roar of Kind power. More kanji strokes painted with all the concentration I could muster, literally using ink to carve out the boxy kanji character *eye* in the whirling storm of Yukiko, Dad, and the Black Pearl's dreaming.

Here goes nothing.

The coffee man's dream surfaced, rising to unfurl tentative wings into the small bit of calm. The dark of my blindness softened and warmed, a cotton blanket instead of crushing fear. A strange anticipation shivered over all my skin, almost like expecting a blow, the exquisite sensitivity to air, scent, and living presence acquired by someone sightless from birth.

I was blind, but quietly confident in my own space, content with the boundaries of my own flesh. Roasted beans—*coffea arabica* from Brazil—released burnt brown sugar and resin to permeate the space like the benevolent blessing of an angel. Reacting like Pavlov's dog, the beloved smell filled my mouth with saliva, relaxed shoulder blades down my back. The raging force of the Black Pearl's dreaming softened to a dull roar.

My lungs expanded with breath as my hands curled around the warmed ceramic of an oversized mug. Simple. Uncomplicated. Blissful. It felt like home.

Yes, this is the center of who I am. Human.

The smell of burnt bark pleases you? The voice was strangely reedy and thin.

Who?

You have eaten my dreams now several times, Baku. You have my name.

Muduri Nitchuyhe. The Black Pearl.

One such as you, the child of a betrayer, is not worthy of the gift of my name. But Abke Hehe *does not always choose the straightest valley or the clearest water for us to swim in. You are not only Baku. You are...more.*

Marlin would have been proud how I kept from mentally rolling my eyes at this. But the Black Pearl deserved more from me, more from all of us.

I will release you from your prison.

The Council sets me free?

No, not them. It is The Eight Span Mirror, the Hafu who fight for you.

There was a long, whistling sigh. I squeezed the mug between my hands and found that it was no longer ceramic, but the damp end of a snout—the Black Pearl's nose. The Black Pearl's dream, a Kind dream, seeping into Enoshima's dream like lazy whorls of ink expanding into spilled water. Would this work if I didn't keep Enoshima's dream pure?

Cruel to torment me with false hope.

I'm not trying to fool you.

And Kawano-sama? The Eight Span Mirror has never been able to stand against him. He stopped you before.

My first attempt to release the Black Pearl seemed like weeks ago, but perhaps only an hour or two had passed in real time. I remembered the strange shadow in the river and Kawano's seriously froggy hands. *Kappa.* River monster.

Our mistake was trying to set the Black Pearl free in Kawano's territory. No river here in Enoshima's dream. I shivered, willing the smell of coffee to cover the silt-mold river scent threatening to take over.

He won't stop us this time.

It may be too late to release me. I am very tired. I am failing.

Let me try again. Don't you want to go home? Sing with the kesike *and* Abka Hehe?

A long, whistled sigh caressed my face with the scent of moldy socks. Enoshima's dream was dissolving. Hastily I focused on roasted beans and warm darkness.

You will release my spirit, Baku? To soar free of this cruel island?

I want to try. I have to try.

So then.

A sound of running water, a splash, and once again I felt the Black Pearl's mouth close around my head. But this time I held onto the smell of coffee beans and my strong, steady Koi-flame. I took in a breath and released it, along with fear and the ratcheting pain in my head. Enoshima's confidence in his own skin, the sureness with which he navigated the dark kept me standing. This was it. Kawano wouldn't give us another chance.

Burn, then. Burn it all.

With a scream, I pushed out the last remnants of Yukiko's icy power twisting around the thick columns of the Black Pearl's like lightning.

Every cell in my body lit on fire, every muscle spasmed and shook in a frenetic dance of power and life and longing.

I poured all of it into the warm absence-of-light. The river scent faded away, conquered by burning and burning and burning. The Black Pearl screamed, resonating at a painful frequency that tingled in my jaw and pinged my joints as if my skeleton were strung together with sensitive funny bones.

Back to my center, to my purest self.

I wasn't sure if that was my inner voice or that which sang as *Muduri Nitchuyhe*. It didn't matter—everything was burning away in the flame, the moldy sock smell, the river, the last vestiges of Yukiko's ice, Dad's memory of Shie-chan, and finally, finally the swish of river water and creeping damp.

Agony warred with release, the burning wiping everything clean, turning everything to ash, thinning the weighty darkness. How long could I bear this? How long had I borne it? An eternity? A nanosecond?

The Black Pearl's whalesong crested, reached a diamond-hard frequency; yearning, striving to break free. Unease soured my belly. I burned and burned and the Black Pearl was still here, still trapped.

It's not enough. Anguish crashed over me, quenching the supernova. Suddenly flaccid muscles sagged. Something heavy heaved itself in the darkness nearby and then another, smaller presence moved.

A life's beginning or a life's end. That is what it will take to release the Black Pearl.

Dad? Ken was supposed to keep you away!

You can't do this alone, Koi-chan.

Not you.

Dad must have convinced Ken, the jerkface, to let him touch me in reality, although all I could feel was the burning energy, the whalesong, and a fizzing, prickling feeling of horror tracing up and down my limbs. Lightning laced through the air, flashing brilliant ice-white, stinging my dark-adjusted eyes with Yukiko's stolen energy. It revealed a stop-motion image of Dad, squeezed inside the Black Pearl's cavernous mouth with me, reaching out with both hands to grasp a curved fang.

No.

I caught both his hands in mine, and wrenched them down against my chest. *Give it back. Yukiko gave it to me.*

Kawano-san pulled Ken into the pond. There's no more time to argue.

I almost got it. Just one more burst.

My daughter, this is not your battle.

It's mine now. *I will set the Black Pearl free.*

Koi AweoAweo Pierce, go kurosama deshita.

It was the phrase Dad thanked his workers with at the end of each day at the restaurant, the phrase he'd said when I walked off the stage at Southridge High School graduation, and it was what he'd whispered as they lowered mom's coffin into the ground. He was using my full name, and he was saying goodbye.

Lightning flared and did not fade. Dad squeezed my hands, forcing them, still wrapped around his wrists, outward to touch the fleshy walls of the Black Pearl's mouth.

Roasted coffee flooded the air.

This is a human fragment. Good. Remembering you are Kayla Pierce's daughter as well as mine will help. The words came with a mental strength, a solidity I'd never felt before. And then Dad flared to life. Where I was a supernova, Dad was the molten heart of a volcano, thick with a sludgy heat powerful enough to melt the backbone of the Earth. Yukiko's power was subsumed into his like a tectonic plate crushed to lava.

And we burned.

Where I thought nothing was left, Dad's molten power scoured away even the ashes and char until there was only my little flame and his glowing heart in a darkness still touched with Enoshima's roasted beans. The whalesong crested again, an overwhelming cry of agony, and then Dad's heart began to feed from my flame as well.

Dad!

Just a little more. The lava engulfed my flame. I was on the banks of the Heilong Jiang, I was behind the sushi counter at Marinopolis, I was tugging on my mother's kimono sleeve, I was touching my head to tatami mat in front of Kawano's stern frown.

Dad's dreams. Not mine. I am Koi. Koi AweoAweo Pierce and I am also human.

Dad was using up every bit of himself, and taking me along with him. A life's end. But the cowardly part of me cringed away from death. I wasn't ready to die.

With everything that remained of me, I conjured up the warm

darkness and the fragrant aroma of caramel roasting Arabica and wrenched myself out of Dad's glowing, hungry power.

Hands, I have hands. With this realization came the sensation of one hand plunged into water and the ability to pull it back.

The world spun 360 degrees, and when it righted itself I clenched my eyes shut against the bright, blurred sun of reality and vomited up bile. Tears streamed from my eyes, and my questing hand found the kneeling form of Dad beside me, one hand outstretched. He moaned. Someone behind me grabbed me by the armpits and pulled me up roughly.

"Get her away from them." Tojo.

"Too late," I said, my voice hoarse and cracking.

Tojo spun away, yelling in harsh male Japanese to someone. Kawano. Trying to stop us again.

Not this time, you slimy eel.

I reached for Dad. He was spasming, muscles clenching up and down his back. Suddenly the whalesong tore itself free of Baku dreaming-space and subliminal vibration, morphing into an audible, keening wail. Tojo rushed back, leaning in so close his cigarette and whiskey stench fouled my air. He put rough hands around my neck. "Make that stop."

Something rank and dripping joined him. Kawano. Where was Ken?

"I know you can hear me, Herai Akihito. Stop now, or Tojo will strangle the life from your daughter."

"Threatening the life of young Kind now?" Murase was here, somewhere off to the left.

"Tojo's always been a death Bringer," said Kwaskwi. "Now he can officially step into the vacant position."

"Kawano," I croaked. "Take a flying leap." I pushed a fist in the direction of his voice, willing there to be some Baku-fueled strength remaining, but my hand met his chest with a meaty, ineffectual thwack. I had completely burned out trying to free the Black Pearl.

"You will stop your father from making this terrible mistake."

I gave a sobbing laugh. Cracking open an eyelid won me only the blurry brightness of blowback blindness. I still couldn't see. All the new layers of Baku powers, the Japanese connection to my father, the romantic self I'd been finding with Ken, all fell away.

It was just me, pared down to Koi again with nothing but my wits. "Bite me."

"You will obey the Council!"

I was so mad I could only yell in English. "Don't you get it? No, I won't!"

Dad cried out. I let my knees sag, suddenly dropping all my weight, but the trick that worked in all the movies failed—whoever held me tightened arms like steel bands around my middle. "Dad!"

The whalesong suddenly stopped like a speaker with the electricity cut. The participants in our little rumble paused between one breath and the next—the turgid, pregnant hush before a hurricane. Around my middle the steel band became rubber. I leaned forward until my hand grazed the stubbly side of Dad's lax face. "Dad?" But there was nothing. No molten volcano of Baku hunger, no gray room of empty dreamscape.

I reached for my own Koi-flame and recoiled from the aching void I found instead.

Something burst. A wind smelling of konbu and socks buffeted my face, whipped through my tangled hair. A sense of joy and release so intense it curled my toes.

And then the wind and the joy rose above my head and blew away.

It was done. He'd done it. We'd done it. *Not with a bang, but a sigh.*

Farewell.

We had done it. Dad, me, and the sacrifice of Yukiko's life energy. The Black Pearl was gone. I could feel it. Maybe her body still lay in the grass, but the whalesong lived, flying away on the wind. The overwhelming absence of her ached like a tender spot in the gums after a pulled tooth.

Men were arguing in harsh voices and hands pulled me away from Dad again. I turned my sightless eyes in their direction. It was over, and all they could do was jabber on like angry monkeys.

"She's gone, dumbasses. There's nothing you can do now."

A hard, open-palm slap rocked me backward. Stinging heat blossomed on my cheek. Kwaskwi and Murase protested over each other in jumbled shouts. I probed my cheek with hesitant fingertips and tried not to laugh. It was such a small pain, nothing compared to the agony of trying to set the Black Pearl free.

"Desist," Kawano snapped.

"She will learn to obey the Council," said Tojo.

"The Black Pearl is gone," said Murase flatly. "We all have some learning to do."

"Herai-san, you have doomed us to slow extinction," said Kawano. "Our learning will be all about loss, now."

Tojo growled. "Imprison them in the Black Pearl's cave. Let the Baku take her place. That will show everyone the Council remains strong."

"That's not gonna happen," said Kwaskwi.

"Pardon me," said Murase. "First you will let Midori tend to Herai-san. Then you will let us all go."

"You dare!" Tojo again in all his huffy glory.

Kawano spoke a sharp rebuke. There was an awkward silence. I could make out the angry breathing of Tojo and Kawano next to me. "Tojo-san may not realize yet what this new dynamic may require." Kawano's voice was so god-damned reasonable. It made my teeth hurt.

Suddenly a soft hand touched my elbow. "Here, this is Herai-san," said Midori. She guided my hand downward onto a soggy shirt-covered chest. "Can you feel anything?"

I shook my head. "Nothing but his heartbeat. Is he okay?"

"His eyes are closed and he looks pale. But he's breathing."

Tojo, Kawano and Murase argued behind us. I tuned it out, trying to gather the courage for my next question. "Where is Ken? Ben?"

Midori hissed. "Kawano-san put them in the pond."

My heart stopped. My stomach felt like boiled lead. I bit my lower lip hard, a small pain to hold back unimaginable loss. *No, no, no, no.*

I felt a cool cloth on my feverish cheek. "Oh, I am so sorry. They're alive, Koi-chan. It's a Kappa thing. They are underwater but breathing."

With painful, slow thuds my heart started beating again. Anger rose on the tide of pain. I stood up. "*Enough.* Enough!"

Silence.

"The Black Pearl is gone. Yukiko is gone. I don't know when Dad will wake up." I reached my hands out blindly into the air where I thought Kawano was standing, curling my fingers like claws. "But I am here. And I am a Baku. It looks to me like the power balance has tipped my way. The Eight Span Mirror's way." I took a gamble. "Right, Tomoe?"

A chorus of soft *hai's* told me Tomoe and Murase were riding the wave of my bravado.

Kwaskwi cleared his throat. "I have the Shishin on speed dial. What do you think will happen to you, weakened by the loss of the Black Pearl and Yukiko-sama, if the Siwash Tyee of Portland and the most powerful Kind alive in the U.S. see you attacking Herai-san this way? Attacking his precious daughter?"

Who the hell knew what a Shishin was. It sounded like a Chinese name. It didn't matter. Tojo and Kawano's in-fighting only made it clear how thin a thread the Council hung on now that the Black Pearl was free. If they didn't want other Pacific Kind rattling their cages, neither of them could afford to lose any more face.

CHAPTER TWENTY-SIX

At the end of my first encounter with a dragon back at Ankeny Square in Portland, I'd missed the after-party by passing out. No such luck this time.

The aftermath of giant dragon confrontations sucked. It was tedious, chaotic, everything felt pointless and nobody brought me lattes or chocolate.

Midori had Dad carried to a limo with the help of Kwaskwi and a black suit, where she tucked me in alongside, reassuring me he was resting in good enough shape. Then she described Kawano releasing Ben and Ken, shivering and pale, from their watery prison as Tojo gathered up the remains of his men.

"Ben and Ken are squeezing into Murase's K-car with Pon-suma," said Midori.

I straightened up. She was narrating. "You know I'm blind."

"Well, yes."

"I thought I was hiding it."

"Not so much. Is it permanent? Or will your sight return?"

"It came back last time." I rubbed my fist into my eye sockets and held up my bandaged arm. "How long will this take to heal?"

"Saaaaa….." *Stupid, infuriating Japanese stalling syllable.* She put two tablets into my palm and held a bottle to my lips. I obediently sipped. Water cooled my scratchy throat. I considered my pride and the crazy shit that just went down.

"Did Ken even check to see if I was okay?"

The smell of Axe Body Spray told me Kwaskwi was close. He placed a finger on my chest, over my heart.

"What are you doing?" said Midori.

"I swear I will keep faith with you, little carp," said Kwaskwi, uncharacteristically solemn. "But I must leave."

"Wait? Why are you leaving?" Panicking, I reached in his general direction with my good arm. He was my last, real connection to Portland, to home.

He took a deep breath through his nose. "Someone has been attacking the Kind in Portland. They have grown bold since I arrived in Tokyo. Elise just texted me; Dzunukwa was attacked."

I pictured the ice hag with her hippie skirt inlaid with polished teeth, catching the light like mirrors. She'd tried to hurt me, but she was one of Kwaskwi's people. He protected his own. The determination in his voice showed me here was the powerful protector I'd only seen back in Portland, willing to do violence in loyalty to his people. Kwaskwi tapped my chest. "I call in the debt you owe me. I charge you to return to Portland within two weeks."

"You may not be able to make such promises. There's so much here still to do," said Midori.

"I promise," I said simply. There was a pause; I was probably missing some gesture on his part. I sensed Kwaskwi moving away. "We Americans have to stick together. We will make sure the Portland Kind are safe," I said loudly.

"Remember who you are, little carp. Remember who you are bound to," the call came in reply.

Kwaskwi counted me as Portland Kind, as one of *his*. That felt right, I realized. Something in my chest that had chafed now settled into a warm, solid place.

From a short distance away, Kwaskwi spoke again. "Will you come, too?" His voice trembled in a way so uncharacteristic of my friend that my stomach plummeted. Whatever had happened to Dzunukwa, it was hitting Kwaskwi hard.

"Who's he talking to?"

"Pon-suma," Midori whispered back.

There was another long silence, Midori gasped.

"What?" I said. "What's he doing?"

There was a muffled moan and then the sound of two people breathing raggedly.

"Ah," said Midori.

"Are they...kissing?"

"Hmmm," Midori said. "Quite."

"Yes," said Pon-suma suddenly and distinctly.

"Kwaskwi disappeared behind the cross. Now a blue jay is streaking up to the sky heading east toward the ocean," said Midori.

Kwaskwi was gone. My eyes felt scratchy and hot, but I must have scraped the bottom of my tear well; no moisture remained.

Midori huffed. "Kawano-san insists on riding with your father."

Guess Kawano thinks he's still king of the roost around here. "No way. This limo is reserved for Baku only. Tell him I'm queasy and about to upchuck. Tell him I'm an unreasonable bitch. I don't care. He's not getting in here."

The limo door shut. Midori spoke in a low tone to Kawano outside. Then the driver's door opened and shut. I brushed Dad's arm lightly. Blessed, blessed silence. Alone with Dad. I settled back against the seat.

The limo started and lurched into motion. After a few moments, a mechanical whirr marked the lowering of the limo partition between driver and passengers. Who was driving? Not the original driver who'd been on Tomoe's rebellion team. I couldn't even remember what he looked like. Maybe he got smooshed by the Black Pearl. I decided I didn't care. I was too tired to keep track of everyone.

On the bumpy road back to the museum, my hazy understanding of what had just happened with the Black Pearl rattled round and round my empty-feeling brain like change in a dryer. I tallied up failures; Yukiko, gone. Dad in a blowback coma. Ken's leg wounded. My forearm broken. My relationship with Ken broken. Making a mortal enemy of the Butcher of Nanjing.

On the plus side, the Black Pearl was free, her spirit swimming the Tsugaru Straits back to the Heilong Jiang and home. That felt right—a small warmth in the aching cold void of my middle.

I put a tentative palm on Dad's head, softly stroking his bristly short hair. There was no moaning, no fever. He was breathing. Another thing to be grateful for.

"Is it afternoon? Any chance of dinner?" I said loudly.

"No, Herai-san. It is late evening," said the male voice of the driver. Apparently I knew him after all. It was Kawano.

"God *damn* it."

"Forgive Midori-san. I forced the issue. We need to talk without extraneous influences."

He means without Tojo breathing bloody murder down my neck and Murase being insistent and reasonable and keeping me from big political blunders. Bring it, frog-man.

"Leave me alone. Leave my father alone. We're not part of your Pacific Basin empire or whatever. We'll just quietly go back to Portland and all this will be yours again." I gestured at the empty back seat.

A long-suffering throaty sigh came from the front. The limo turned to the right, and then we were slowly crunching over gravel. "I think I underestimated your ability to influence the Council's goals."

I had nothing but smart aleck replies for that. I stayed silent.

"You assume, of course, that it is because you are *Hafu*." Kawano chuckled in a smarmy, self-deprecating way. "Would you be surprised to hear it was more because of your youth and American-ness? Never did I guess a girl raised in the self-absorbed U.S. would wreak such havoc on the Council."

"You're calling *me* self-absorbed?" The ridiculousness of that accusation still stung. "I didn't imprison a sentient being in a dank cave."

"The loss of Yukiko-sama by itself is no small thing—she was a grand deterrent to factions that would upset the delicate balance of power between Pacific Basin Kind. But you also took away the Bringer."

"He was never yours to begin with." *Or mine.*

The limo stopped abruptly. I had to put out a hand to stop myself from flying off the bench. Suddenly Kawano's river-smell and raspy voice were right next to me. "He is not America's either, *Koi-chan*. Or The Eight Span Mirror's. He's broken, now. Most likely useless to any faction."

Broken, like me? Like Dad? Dad had given everything to release the Black Pearl, only Yukiko's death kept him from the ultimate sacrifice.

"Let me out."

"And then you stole our future." For the first time I heard emotion creep into his voice. Kawano was truly shaken. And creepily close. My arm was throbbing like Midori's magic pills weren't doing their job.

"Your potential future children aren't more important than the Black Pearl's life. Than her misery."

Silence. Only Dad's even breathing was audible. My skin crawled, waiting for what Kawano would say next.

"You and Herai Akihito will stay here, in Japan. You owe it to the Council and to all the Kind of the Pacific Basin."

"I don't owe you anything," I said wearily. "Where were you when I was growing up? Why didn't the Council stop Ullikemi's murdering human servant? Because it was in Portland?"

"We have become insulated in the last couple decades, a

regrettable result of our dwindling numbers. You and Gozen Tomoe-san can change that. With The Eight Span Mirror's cooperation, there are many wounds to heal."

"I just want to go home."

"I can't allow that," he said, sounding infuriatingly regretful. "You are needed here."

Okay, time to pull out the American guns. "I am not staying in Japan," I said slowly and clearly. I tugged out my phone. "Hey, Siri," I said. "Text Kwaskwi. Kawano wants to hold me hostage. If I'm not on an airplane home in two days call the Shishin or whatever. Send."

Kawano sighed. "That was an unfortunate choice. I wonder if you understand what the price will be."

"Look, I can't speak for Dad, maybe he will want to stay. But this is not my home. I have people waiting for me in Portland."

Kawano didn't need to know I only really had Marlin, and no way was I going to explain to frog-man about the sense that I might never figure out how to make the powerful, hungry Baku meld better with morbanoid Koi. In Japan, all they saw was Herai Akihito's Baku daughter. Portland would give me the space I needed to explore stuff without people expecting miracles or breaking my arm.

"Koi AweoAweo Pierce," he said firmly, my true name like a hook catching between the ribs, "you will come back to Tokyo every year, regardless of Herai Akihito's condition. You owe the Kind that much."

I didn't want to fold, but it struck me that spending time with Ben, Pon-suma, and Midori and the rest of The Eight Span Mirror as we figured out what it meant to be *Hafu* without the Council's monopoly on power and hoity-toityness could be helpful. If I could scrape up the money

"Maybe."

"Three times a year."

"One." The limo door opened. I felt cool, evening air on my cheek.

"Everything okay in here?" said Midori's voice.

"Yes," I said quickly before Kawano could change his mind. "Can you help me with Dad?"

Muscled arms smelling strongly of pond scum, not Midori, took Dad from the car. Then Midori helped me out and took my arm. "This way, watch the curb."

"Why are you guiding her like that?" said Kawano behind me.

"She's blind."

I tried to imagine what Kawano would make of that news and then shook my head. It didn't matter. I was on to the next hurdle. Midori led me inside and through the hall to the bathroom.

"Here are towels," she said, putting my hand on a fluffy cotton. "And soap. I couldn't find your luggage. But next to the sink I left a trainer and matching pants. Do you need me to stay and help?"

Oh god, no. "I'll manage," I said. The last thing I wanted was Midori here when I peeled away my stinking and soiled clothes to reveal the impressive palette of bruises I'm sure covered my arms and legs. "But if you have more of those pain killers before you go…"

She clucked her tongue. "Of course."

After swallowing down another round of chalky tablets, I spent a painful, awkward half-hour sponging myself down and confirming all my parts, albeit mangled, still were attached to my body. It was odd being abandoned with my own thoughts after so many days straight with Ken, Dad, and the others. Odd, and uncomfortable, with the added sour tang of guilt over Dad risking himself in the end because I'd failed to release the Black Pearl on my own. *The blowback is taking a really, really long time to heal.*

But then I realized I wasn't alone. Whoever carried Dad was back.

"You just going to stand there like a stalker?" I said in English.

"That wasn't my plan," said Ken. He must have been hesitating in the doorway. "But when it comes to you, none of my plans quite work the way I think they will."

"Maybe you should quit trying to manipulate me and things

would work out better."

"You're not...I wasn't..." Ken's voice came closer. I backed up until cold metal met the skin on my back revealed by my crumpled shirt. "I wasn't trying to, this wasn't about how I see you, about us—"

"You suck at explaining," I said, crossing my forearms over my belly. "Like the worst."

"Ben's the smooth talker, I've always found greater success through action," the jerkface said, then he was near enough to warm my skin through my shirt and little prickles of expectation raced up and down my spine.

So close, the lingering pond on his skin gave a sour tang to the air between us, but he didn't close the distance. Whether hesitant or teasing, I couldn't know without seeing his dark eyes. I dug my ragged fingernails into my palms to keep them from running along his chest, his shoulders, his back to confirm he was there, he was alive, and not drowned as I'd feared. Even the traitorous muscles in my throat began twitching at the caress of his breath along my jaw, making me lean in, making me want to fold myself like a painted silk furoshiki cloth around the treasure of my bruised heart and give myself to him.

God damn it. He is doing it again. This was the same bathroom seduction nonsense he used in my own home after the Ullikemi showdown, when he convinced me the best way forward was to bring Dad to Japan. Now he was pulling the same shit again. Why? To make me stay? What could he still want from me? The Black Pearl was gone, the injustice righted. The Council was finished. Why was he still here with his stupid warmth and quiet *wanting*?

No no no no no. I pushed past him and fled out the door. Trailing a hand along the wall, I stumbled down the hall toward the clatter of plates and glasses and the cinnamon-garlic smell of Japanese curry. Just as I felt my way to the entrance of the tatami room, a shrill alarm split the air—every phone in the building ringing all at once.

CHAPTER TWENTY-SEVEN

I jumped out of my skin. "Koi-chan," said Midori, tugging me over the tatami to a *zabuton* cushion. "Here, sit."

"It's Kwaskwi," said Ben.

"Mine, too," said Pon-suma and Murase simultaneously. Limping footsteps entered the room behind me. *Ken.* I wished I could see what was going on in the room as the phones were silenced, but it was a relief not to know what expression was in the dark eyes haunting me.

"Ms. Pierce," said Kawano, "you are a wanted woman." He was still here? And he wasn't calling me Herai-san anymore, a concession? It was disconcerting not knowing who was in the room.

Midori touched the back of my hand. "Let me have your phone." It was still ringing inside my pocket. I pressed my thumbprint over the home button and handed it over. Midori clucked her tongue.

"What's going on?"

"Kwaskwi's been trying to get a hold of you," she said. "There are twenty messages and calls from him, and about a hundred from Marlin."

Midori sucked in a startled breath. Ben swore.

"What? What is it?"

No one answered. The tense silence was probably full of meaningful looks and gestures I couldn't see. It drove me crazy. "Someone tell me what's going on."

I expected Midori, but it was Pon-suma who spoke up, laying out devastating facts in his sparse way. "Kwaskwi needs you on a plane to Portland. The attacks on Kind in Portland escalated. Dzunukwa was murdered. Some blame your public altercation with Ullikemi. Attention turns to your sister."

Marlin. In danger. I blindly reached for my phone, pulling it from Midori's limp hand. "Siri, call Marlin." The phone rang and rang. No answer.

"It's probably four a.m. in Portland," said Midori.

"Siri, redial," I shook my head. "She always answers on the second round of ringing. She's an insanely light sleeper."

"Kwaskwi is calling in a favor owed," said Ben. "This must be serious."

"Take me to the airport."

"Breathe, Koi-chan," said Murase. "We will get you home, but we need to buy tickets and arrange for your father's travel. No airline will accept him in a coma without a doctor's permission."

"We can buy tickets at the airport." I missed Kwaskwi fiercely. He would have gotten things moving.

"At least have some katsu curry and let me make some calls," said Midori, tugging on my hand again.

"There is nothing in this world more precious to me than my sister. How far is it to Narita from here? Let's get driving."

"We can get a connecting flight from Iwate-Hanamaki airport in the morning," said Pon-suma.

"We?"

"I'm coming," said Pon-suma, and I imagined the epic kiss Kwaskwi must have laid on the shrine boy and wondered if Horkew Kamuy blushed.

"So there's time for dinner," Midori said. I let her pull me onto a *zabuton*, my knees weak and watery. Dad made *katsu* curry for Marlin's birthday every year, the thin, layered pork cutlets drenched in hot-sweet curry her favorite meal. My eyes felt hot. Not Marlin, not my bossy, artsy sister. I couldn't bear anything happening to her.

I sat numbly, taking small bites of curry and rice from a bowl I held up close to my mouth so I wouldn't spill as much. Midori, Murase, and Pon-suma made calls and talked.

The curry coated my stomach in an uneasy layer of grease. After a few bites, I set the spoon down on the table with a click. Sitting *seiza* was giving me an arthritic ache in my knees. I shifted my hips side-saddle. Midori closed my fingers around a glass and I drank it dutifully, not even tasting the toasted-earth *mugi* tea. After an eternity, Pon-suma came and knelt next to me. "There's a six a.m. flight from Iwate-Hanamaki to Haneda airport. We can take the first flight to Portland that morning. I will buy three tickets?"

"Thank you, yes." I tried a small smile, but the corners of my mouth felt oddly frozen.

"Four tickets, please," said Ken. He was keeping so quiet, like he wanted me to forget he was there, lurking.

"No," I said.

"You need a Kitsune to get your father on the plane without medical permission."

"Tomoe can put on her stewardess disguise again," I said.

"Gozen-san and Tojo-san have already left on Council business back to Tokyo," said Kawano.

"Murase? Ben?" It was a lot to ask when they were obviously needed here to help with The Eight Span Mirror and the fallout from the Black Pearl's release. I was desperate. Ego on my side and arrogance on Ken's had built this wall, brick by brick, between us. Now it separated me from trusting him completely. His image evoked a prickly numbness like an unused limb falling asleep.

There was another tense silence.

"The Bringer's presence in Portland again so soon may be taken by some as an aggressive Council act," Murase observed.

"I'm not the Bringer," said Ken harshly. "That life is over."

"Yes," agreed Kawano archly, "you are released from fealty to the Council."

"And Tojo-san? Will he allow my retirement?"

"Yes," said Kawano, quick and firm. "The new reality of the Council is being explained to him right now." I wondered if that explaining was with words or fists. Kawano had accepted defeat in a seamless way that helped me see how he might have weathered centuries of life and survived the atomic devastation of World War II to craft the Council into a position of international power. Tojo was not, I suspected, as able to roll with the punches.

"Buy four tickets, Pon-suma," said Ken.

"Look, Portland is my home. You have made it clear that your priorities lie with your family here. You can't just leap right back into—"

"Koi! I don't want to stay in Japan," Ken said in English, emotion thickening his voice. "All reasons for being the Bringer are gone. There's nothing here as precious to me as—" He swallowed audibly. "Look, I messed up in many ways. Please don't make me stay away from Portland. Kwaskwi's my friend, too, and this might be a chance." Midori made a hum of distress. "A chance to make my life into something else."

The master manipulator, experienced Kitsune image I'd imposed over Ken since we landed in Narita airport crumbled into pieces, sending cracks shooting through the brick wall between us.

This pleading was of someone as lost, as unsure as I. Someone whose place in the world had been completely upended. If Portland could give me the space to figure out how to be Baku and human Koi at the same time, who was I to keep Ken from having the same chance to figure himself out? He was broken, yes, but his brokenness only made him more real, more true to me.

It was so clear to me now, the joy of running in a shadowed, green primeval forest—honest, true, pure—that was Ken's primal self. It wasn't a sham or Kitsune illusion. I needed to trust my instincts. Even Morbanoid Koi urged me to believe his sincerity, to give into what drew me to him when I first met him on the street in front of Marlin's apartment, the sense that here was a person who saw me, who wanted to see me, and wasn't afraid of the Baku inside.

Survivalist Koi pointed out having him in Portland might ultimately help Marlin.

"Okay, Pon-suma. Four tickets."

I retreated into myself as Midori helped me finish off the curry, cutting the katsu into bite size pieces. The others kept up a conversation on logistics of our trip, and Murase and Kawano got into a heated debate about how the Council should spin the news of the Black Pearl's release.

Midori fussed with my arm splint bandage, rewrapping it too tightly, and insisted on brushing the worst snarls out of my hair. She pulled it back into a low ponytail, and her cool, dry palms on my hair made me think of Mom and how Marlin had done the same for her so many times in the hospital because I'd been terrified of accidentally touching her. My eyes were cried out though, the dryness extending down my throat and into my lungs.

Then, Midori was helping me stand. She led me to one corner of the room and heaped up more *zabuton* into a semblance of a pallet. "Your father is here beside you," she said. "No change. His pulse is steady, his color good, but still unconscious."

I felt for his arm with hesitant fingers. Dad lay on his side. I felt for my phone, cradling it between my cheek and the *zabuton*. "Siri, text Marlin. I'm coming. I'm coming as fast as I can. Send." Dad's rhythmic breathing swept me into an exhausted, restless sleep.

CHAPTER TWENTY-EIGHT

Pon-suma woke me at some ungodly hour of the morning. There was a flurry of hasty packing and irritated confabs. Meanwhile I confirmed that I was still blind, and the flame-kernel inside me was entirely dead, aching, and cold. Then Pon-suma trundled me and Dad into the back of the van he'd used to kidnap us ages ago. The front passenger door opened and shut and Pon-suma grunted.

"I'll get you there," said Ben, and then the van's engines started.

"Don't use this arm until you see a doctor in Portland," said Midori. "You need a cast." She must have been standing outside the open doors of the van. I nodded in her direction.

"And *you*," she said next, "try to keep off that leg for at least one day."

"Yes, ma'am," said Ken. His voice, suddenly emanating from the front corner of the van when I'd no idea he was even there set my heart racing. Great. Relationship goalz. Locked in a van for hours with my comatose father and a broken Kitsune. This is not what I would have chosen for my last day in Japan. I hadn't walked the scramble crosswalks in Shinjuku, or ambled the gravel path under towering cypress to Meiji Shrine, or sat at a mom-and-pop stall at Tsukiji fishmarket at six a.m. eating insanely fresh sea urchin and salmon roe rice bowl.

Instead, I ate evil and released the dragon. No sushi for me this time. Just a tender spot where I thought I'd been carefully building friendship and intimacy. My chest hurt like my ribs were trying to knit together over a tenderized heart. I sucked in a constricted breath and was mortified to hear it leaving in a shudder.

"Here." I held out my phone in the direction of Ken's voice. "Has Marlin replied?" Let him think my emotional breakdown was entirely for Marlin. Which it was. Entirely.

The van doors slammed and Ben revved the engine. "No," said Ken, "I'm sorry. No texts. No voicemails. And I've tried calling Kwaskwi three or four times."

"Okay," I said.

"I won't tell you it will be okay," said Ken.

"I wouldn't have believed you if you had."

"Will you believe anything I say now?" Ken touched my good wrist with a gently insistent grip that would not allow me to jerk away. A porcelain mug was placed in my hand, warm on the bottom from the hot liquid bathing my face with notes of burnt sugar steam.

"Oh my god," I said, and took a sip. It was the bitter richness of Enoshima's coffee. "How did you do this?"

"Kitsune magic," said Ken. We turned a corner roughly, and he steadied the coffee by cupping my hand with both of his.

The bottom dropped out of my stomach. The fresh scent of ferns, and the cool mist of a forest caressed my face. Inside me, a little flame leapt to a weakly flickering, pale yellow life. I was still blind, even in this fragment. Ken's fragment. But I was also still Baku, it seemed. So I would heal, after all. And maybe Ken would have something to do with that.

Too soon, the sensations faded away.

"Probably not," I said. He kept his hands on mine. I waited, frozen, but for the taste and warmth of black gold slowly melting the stiff cage around my heart.

Ken sighed, and his hands dropped away. "Not Kitsune magic?"

"Not believe anything you say," I said. "But that doesn't mean you can't prove yourself with actions."

"You'll give me another chance?" Somehow I was a hundred percent sure there was a crooked grin and an arched eyebrow on his face.

"For coffee this good, you can even sit next to me on the plane."

From the front of the van came Pon-suma's low chuckle, and then we were driving toward the south. Toward an airplane that would take me back to Portland—and home.

ABOUT THE AUTHOR

K. Bird Lincoln is an ESL professional and writer living on the windswept Minnesota Prairie with family and a huge addiction to frou-frou coffee. Also dark chocolate—without which, the world is a howling void. Originally from Cleveland, she has spent more years living on the edges of the Pacific Ocean than in the Midwest. Her speculative short stories are published in various online & paper publications such as *Strange Horizons*. Her medieval Japanese fantasy series, *Tiger Lily*, is available from Amazon. World Weaver Press released *Dream Eater*, the first novel in an exciting, multi-cultural Urban Fantasy trilogy set in Portland and Japan, in 2017. She also writes tasty speculative fiction reviews on Amazon and Goodreads. Check her out on Facebook, join her newsletter for chocolate and free stories, or stalk her online at kblincoln.com

Thank you for reading!

We hope you'll leave an honest review at Amazon, Goodreads, or wherever you discuss books online.

Leaving a review means a lot for the author and editors who worked so hard to create this book.

Please sign up for our newsletter for news about upcoming titles, submission opportunities, special discounts, & more.

WorldWeaverPress.com/newsletter-signup

THE LAST DREAM OF HER MORTAL SOUL

K BIRD LINCOLN

PORTLAND HAFU, BOOK THREE

Even a dream eater can't escape the final sleep...

Kwaskwi calls Koi home to help solve the murder of Dzunukwa, whose body is found in the witch's hut in Forest Park with a haunting, strange quotation about dreams and death that seems to be calling out a Baku. Can KoI, saddled by a broken and lost Ken, help Kwaskwi figure out who is targeting Kind in Portland before others from her new-found family die?

***

Coming Spring 2019!

World Weaver Press

Publishing fantasy, paranormal, and science fiction.
We believe in great storytelling.

www.WorldWeaverPress.com